Olivia, Finding Her Way

An Olivia Series Novel

TESSA PALMERI

ISBN: 0996800611
ISBN-13: 978-0-9968006-1-7

DEDICATION

To my husband and children and sister.

ACKNOWLEDGMENTS

Thanks go to my fabulous husband for his patience and for believing I can do whatever I put my mind to. I'm also thankful to Cate Courtright for her professional help and to my many supportive friends who have been so encouraging. I can't name all of you here, but I'm especially grateful to Kara, Loren, and my sister. Last but not least, thank you God, not only for my life experiences—good and bad—but for being there with me through them all.

CONTENTS

1   I'm Outta Here!   1

2   Dying to Change   8

3   Scavenger Hunt   16

4   Secret Stash   23

5   Sunflower House   30

6   Laundry Date   37

7   Cameron's Birthday   45

8   Turning Point   51

9   Maladjustment   58

10 Family Weekend   67

11 Give Me A Break   77

12 Who Wants Pie?   84

13 Foiled   93

14 Not. Gonna. Happen.   101

15 Roommate From Hell   107

16 Can I Drive?   112

17 Surrender   116

18 F.R.O.G.   122

19 Goody Two Shoes   129

20 Intervention   133

21 Fancy Meeting You Here   141

22 Have Mercy   146

23 Wild Horses   152

24 That Wasn't Mickey Mouse   157

25	Bear Trap	165
26	From Santa	171
27	Wrap It Up	177
28	Surprising Announcement	186
29	Happy New Year!	195
30	Meeting Monique	201
31	Room Rules	207
32	Self-Defense	212
33	Mine	217
34	Thunderbird	222
35	Focus Group	228
36	Gloria	235
37	Spring Break	245
38	It's About Time	255
39	Sleepover	264
40	Eavesdropping	270
41	Job Offer	278
42	Begrudging Brandy	283
43	Got Any Bread?	290
44	Grand Opening	295
45	Welcome Home ...?	304

CH. 1 ~ I'M OUTTA HERE!

Peering through my bedroom window, the sight of Cameron's blue truck coming up the driveway made me giddier than I already was. I did a happy dance and grabbed the last of my things before flying down the stairs and out the front door to greet him.

Moving day had finally arrived. My boyfriend, Cameron McClain, and I were leaving the small town of Leeville, Texas and were headed for New Haven University. The bed of his truck was loaded with suitcases, a few boxes, and his guitar case. He pulled up next to my car and bounded up the front porch, every bit as excited as I was.

"This is it, Olivia, the day we've been waiting for," he said, beaming his gorgeous smile at me. My feet left the ground a couple of inches as he spun me around, making my long, brown hair fan out around us.

"Is it really happening? Pinch me to make sure I'm not dreaming," I said. He distracted me with a kiss as he squeezed my butt. "Cameron!"

"Well, you asked for it." Yes, I had. And my mom and sister, Emma, had seen him do it. I was too happy to be embarrassed. They had come outside to see us off. Emma smiled, but my mom looked away.

My dad wasn't there because he'd left for work already.

We'd said our goodbyes the night before. It had been a nice father-daughter moment. At least, at first it had been. Then he ruined it with a crappy comment about my plans of pursuing a liberal arts degree.

I hadn't decided on a major yet, but I was leaning toward something in social and behavioral sciences. Since none of that was math-related, he didn't approve. He was an engineer, along with other things such as opinionated, judgmental, and critical. He looked down his nose at the whole idea of a liberal arts education.

"Bye, Emma. I'll miss you." I hugged her, feeling a tug at my heart for how *much* I was going to miss her, especially because we'd gotten closer over the summer. She had turned fourteen a few weeks ago. It was unfair that, just as she was reaching an age at which she was more fun to hang out with, I was leaving. That morning, she wasn't exactly pouting, but she wasn't her usual feisty, talkative self, either. She'd recently expressed her dread at becoming the only child left at home.

"I'll miss you, too," she murmured and wiped a tear from her eye. Her long, dirty-blonde hair fell forward, covering her face, and she said, "You didn't see that."

"See what?" I gave her shoulder a gentle shove and turned to my mom. She and I weren't close. I didn't have the same emotions about telling her goodbye that I had with Emma.

"I'll see you later, Mom," I said, and we hugged briefly.

"Be careful on the road," she instructed and looked at Cameron. "Watch out for each other, okay?" She seemed uncomfortable, which was how I felt, too.

"We will, Mrs. Miller," Cameron assured her and got into his truck.

"And, um, call home if you need anything. Don't be a stranger," she added with a self-conscious laugh.

"I won't," I said, getting behind the wheel of my car. Cameron started up his engine, pulled through the circular driveway, and I followed him. Driving away, I waved at my mom and sister, relieved to be done with that moment of awkwardness. I couldn't wait to get away from home. Well, away from my parents anyway.

While sitting at a traffic light, the last one before leaving my hometown, the tassel that was hanging on my rearview mirror caught my eye. It was from my high school graduation cap. The morning sun glinted off of the shiny, gold-colored charm with the number 1991 on it. I decided it was time to take if off and stashed it in the glove compartment. That chapter of my life was closed.

Cameron and I stayed together on the highway for the first two hours, but I lost sight of him when we still had thirty minutes to go. I was hungry and wanted to get out and stretch, so I stopped at Suzy's Southern Cooking. I was betting that Cameron would think to stop there too, and I was right. A few minutes later, he pulled into the parking lot.

"How did you know I'd stop here?" I asked.

"I had a feeling." There was a sparkle in his expressive brown eyes.

We shared a knowing look, and a rush of the warm fuzzies made me throw my arms around his neck and kiss him. That parking lot was where we'd been standing the first time we told each other "I love you."

Pretending to be nervous, the way he'd been that day, he stammered, "Um, Olivia, there's something I've been thinking about ... that I want to say—"

"Wait. Let me guess," I interrupted, "you've decided to become a bull rider?"

He chuckled. "No, that's not it—"

"You're actually a wizard, and you've cast a spell on me?"

"Nope." He laughed harder.

"Oh, I know, I know. You're really a prince from some tiny, remote island, and you're ready to claim me as your princess?" We laughed together.

He cradled my face in his hands, and the silliness

subsided. "No, nothing like that. I love you, Olivia."

"I love you too, Cameron." I settled into his embrace and savored the moment.

From the doorway of the restaurant, we heard a sweet southern voice ask, "Are y'all coming in, or what?" A waitress was standing there, watching us with a smile. We laughed and headed for the door, hand in hand.

* * * * * *

I pulled up in front of Bellamy Hall, my new home for the next nine months, and the long-awaited adventure began. Everything happened in a whirlwind; checking in, finding the right dorm room, and hauling stuff into the building amidst hundreds of other people trying to do the same thing.

The students, parents, and younger siblings who'd tagged along were being directed and helped by dozens of campus staff and student volunteers. You could tell who they were by the blue and black NHU T-shirts they were wearing, emblazoned with the Hawks mascot. The air was thick with anticipation and expectancy. My mind had to work overtime to make order out of the barely controlled chaos.

Standing in the check-in line, I overheard a heated conversation between a mother and daughter. The girl must have criticized her mom for saying something that embarrassed her, and the mom hissed, "Well, maybe you should have written out a script for me, so I'd know what's okay to say and what's not."

Ouch! Thank God my parents hadn't shown any interest in coming with me today.

I was assigned to room 107 on the west side, the women's wing, and Cameron was on the east side, in room 328. He helped me unload my car first. In making trips back and forth from my room, I saw several girls checking him out. It made me pause and take a closer look at him, as though I were seeing him for the first time.

I knew he was good-looking, of course. I just hadn't taken recent stock of how much hotter he'd gotten since we'd met, much less how other girls would see him. He had a great tan and had bulked up from lifting weights and playing basketball over the summer. His biceps were bulging against the sleeves of his T-shirt, and the muscles on his chest and back were nicely sculpted. The length of his brown hair was just right—not too long, but not too short—and stylishly cut. When he smiled, which he was doing a lot, it showed off his straight, white teeth and adorable dimples.

A flutter of panic threatened to turn me into one of those clingy, possessive girlfriends who has to make sure all the other girls know her guy is taken. I fought the urge to make a public display of affection to mark my territory.

I stayed with Cameron's truck, and he made his first trip up to his room. He returned, and his roommate, whom we'd never met, was with him. His name was Gary. He was wearing a Donkey Kong T-shirt and athletic shorts. He was nice, but I picked up on his shyness right away, because making eye contact didn't come easy for him.

Having unloaded everything, Cameron and I moved our vehicles to the parking lot and walked back toward the building together. "So," he said, stopping to face me and took my hand.

"So," I copied him. We exchanged awkward smiles. It was a defining moment for us. Would we try to hang out together *all* the time, or would we be comfortable going our separate ways? We both started talking at the same time and laughed.

What the heck was our problem?

Actually, I knew what mine was. And maybe it was his too. Having indefinite plans made me nervous. Would we meet up later at a certain time and place? What were each of our expectations for how much time we'd spend together? It wasn't something we'd ever talked about.

"How about we go unpack and then meet at the dining

hall at about twelve thirty?" I suggested.

"That's a good idea." He nodded, relaxing some.

I kissed him and said, "See you later."

Great. Now I'm analyzing every move, looking for hidden meaning. For example, what did it mean that I kissed him first? Would he have kissed me goodbye if I hadn't done it? These concerns were unfamiliar to me. We'd enjoyed a strong, eight-month relationship, but in new surroundings, around new people, I didn't know how to act.

Anxious to get settled in, I put all my clothes away, set up my TV and VCR, and then carefully removed a framed photo collage that I'd folded up in my sheets. It had been a going-away gift from my friend Kate, an aspiring photographer. The pictures of myself with Cameron and our friends held great memories. I was so glad Cameron was there with me at NHU, but I would miss my friends.

By the time I'd put everything away and made my bed, my roommate still hadn't shown up. I was anxious to meet the person I'd be sharing the room with. There was a sign on the door that read, "Welcome, Olivia Miller and Ruth Ann Schubert". The name Ruth Ann sounded old-fashioned, and I had to resist forming any ideas of how she would look or what she would be like.

I called home, letting them know I'd gotten there safe and then stretched out on my bed to look through the welcome week folder I'd been given at check-in. The schedule was packed. There was no shortage of things to do. Dozens of clubs and organizations were offering free food throughout the week as a hook to get students to come by their information booths.

A "Dorm Living Tips and Guidelines" flyer advised on common sense stuff; wear flip-flops in the communal showers, keep noise and music levels down in respect for your neighbors, always lock your door, etc. Microwaves and mini fridges were allowed, but I didn't have either.

Maybe Ruth Ann would bring one, or the other, or both. It would be weird not having access to a kitchen. It would also be different having to go down the hall for the bathroom and shower, but dorm life was part of the college package that I'd been looking forward to.

I had finally arrived and was starting this new chapter in my life. My naiveté did a good job of convincing me I was ready, but I had no idea what was in store for me.

CH. 2 ~ DYING TO CHANGE

Cameron was waiting for me in front of the dining hall, and he said, "We'll have to find somewhere else to eat." A sign on the door told us that it wouldn't be open until later in the week.

A guy who was passing by asked, "Are you wondering where to get lunch?" He was wearing one of the volunteer T-shirts.

"Yeah. Do you know if anything is open at the Haven yet?" Cameron asked.

"Not today. Some places will be tomorrow, but I could show you where to get free pizza right now, if you want."

"Sure. That sounds great," Cameron replied.

"Yeah, thank you," I said.

"All right. Follow me. By the way, I'm Luke."

We introduced ourselves, and he said, "Welcome to NHU. I work in the New Student Development Center. That's where the pizza is." He led us to a building where about twenty students had gathered around a table with several pizzas.

"Great timing. You guys help yourselves," Luke said. "It was nice to meet you."

"Thanks, man. You too," Cameron said.

We were waiting for our turn to get pizza and drinks. I

was relieved that the earlier awkwardness between us seemed to have resolved itself. A guy came up and clapped Cameron on the back. *This must be his best friend, Scott.*

"Hey, Cam. What's going on? Getting some free food?" he asked.

"Yeah, hey, Scott. I'd like you to meet Olivia."

"Ah, the famous Olivia from Leeville. It's good to finally meet you," Scott said with an easy grin and put his hand out for me to shake. He was taller and stockier than Cameron but looked how I'd imagined he would, even down to the Wrangler jeans and cowboy boots.

"Hi, Scott. It's good to meet you too."

Watching the two friends catch up on each other's latest news made me envious that Cameron already had a connection with someone on campus besides me. Having grown up in New Haven, he and Scott had been friends since childhood. I'd met Cameron when he'd moved to Leeville in the middle of our senior year. His dad had gotten a job transfer, and since his parents were splitting up—and his mom's new boyfriend was a total jerk—Cameron chose to move with his dad. I was so glad he had!

We joined some other students at a table. They talked. I listened and people watched. This new social setting held some fascination for me, but at the same time, it was nerve-wracking. I felt a nagging, internal pressure to appear more confident than I was about assimilating into my new environment. Did anyone else feel this way? Or was it just me?

I'd lived in a small town and been around the same people my whole life. In fact, our graduating class of 1991 only had about a hundred students in it. In contrast, NHU's undergraduate enrollment was four thousand, and there were at least a thousand freshmen among them. My emotions alternated between excitement and anxiety.

Another student in a welcome week T-shirt announced that he'd be starting a campus tour in a few minutes. Cameron and I had done that back in June during a visit for advising, but this guy, whose name was Nathan, said, "You may have already been on a tour, but if it wasn't one of *my* tours, you haven't seen or heard everything you need to." *Props for this guy's confidence!*

So, we joined the tour and found that Nathan was right. There were some places we hadn't been to yet, like the computer labs, career center, and bookstore. Plus, he gave us insider tips on things to check out and things to avoid around campus.

Near the end of the tour, Cameron started holding my hand as we walked around. His touch was comforting, and I hadn't realized how much I needed it for reassurance.

"You have an admirer," he whispered in my ear. I assumed he was talking about himself and told him thank you. "No, I meant the tour guide. He's hitting on you. But don't get me wrong, *I'm* admiring you, too," he added and kissed me on the cheek.

Very interesting. Nathan and I had been chatting, joking back and forth. It hadn't occurred to me that he was flirting, except maybe one time because he'd winked in my general direction. I'd chalked it up to him squinting from the sunlight. I wasn't sure I agreed with Cameron, though I did get some satisfaction out of the fact that he had started holding my hand to let Nathan know we were together.

"What has he done that makes you think he's hitting on me?" I asked Cameron.

"He commented on your bracelet earlier, and then asked you about the charms on it. Classic flirting. When a guy does that, he's letting you know he's looking closely at you."

"Huh." I looked at my bracelet and thought, *he might be right.* By asking me about it, Nathan had drawn me into a more personal conversation. It was a silver charm bracelet that I'd gotten from my grandparents. I didn't wear it often, partly because it didn't have many charms on it, but also because I didn't usually wear much jewelry besides earrings. The newest charm on it was a graduation cap from my sister, Emma. She'd been hanging out in my room when I was packing and had talked me into bringing it with me. Then, I'd put it on that morning as a way of showing her I'd be thinking of her while I was gone.

* * * * * *

Returning to my room, I found that my roommate had arrived. She and her parents had finished bringing her stuff into the room. I guessed they were her parents, anyway. They looked older, but not old enough to be her grandparents.

"Well, hello, there," the woman greeted me in a formal, genteel manner. "Ruth Ann, this must be your roommate," she said to the girl. Her tone made me think of a kindergarten teacher.

I introduced myself, and we all shook hands. Ruth Ann was about the same height as me with shoulder length, mousy brown hair. She was homely looking, but that may have been due to the clothes she was wearing; a blouse, buttoned all the way up, a long, plain skirt, and Mary Jane shoes with ankle socks. Her expression and mannerisms were polite but reserved.

"Well, dear, I suppose we'll be leaving now," Mrs. Schubert said and patted Ruth Ann's shoulder. I detected a slight change in Ruth Ann's demeanor—maybe a hint of liveliness—at the mention of them leaving.

"Yes, Mother. I think I've got everything I need. Father, thank you for helping me carry all my things in." She spoke in such a prim and proper way that I couldn't help wondering if she was trying to be funny. She walked stiffly to the door to see them out. They went through the motions of hugging goodbye, and I thought about how similar it was to my experience that morning with my own mother.

"Finally!" Ruth Ann exclaimed once they were gone. "I thought they'd never leave." She burst into a fit of laughter that took me by surprise. I started laughing, too. At least maybe she would have more personality than the Stepford child she was just acting like.

She unzipped and flung open the suitcase on top of her bed. As she dug around in it, I tried to make small talk with her. She said she was from a small town about five hours west of New Haven and, like me, was undecided on her major.

"Found it!" she announced and held up a box of Clairol hair color. "Have you ever colored hair before?"

"No ... have you?" I asked. What an odd thing to do when you haven't even unpacked yet.

"Nope. I was never allowed to, but it's the first step to the new me." She grabbed a towel, headed for the door, and looked over her shoulder with a mischievous smile. "You wanna come?"

"I guess so." I didn't have any other plans until dinnertime, so what the heck?

Off we went, getting to know each other over a bathroom sink with a bottle of red hair dye. As I was helping her, I got a drop of dye on her shirt by accident. I apologized, but she brushed me off, saying it didn't matter.

"Don't worry about it," she said. "I'm never going to wear it again."

"Oh ... okay."

"I'm so sick of my clothes. My mom is such an Emily Post wannabe, and this is her idea of what a proper young lady should look like. But I'm done with all of that. Coming here gives me the chance to become a different person, live in the real world, you know?" She looked at herself in the mirror and started laughing. The red color had come out much brighter than I'd expected, but she liked it.

"What do you mean, the 'real world'?" I asked.

"Ugh. I'm a small-town preacher's kid. I may as well have grown up in a convent. Even worse, I was their 'late in life' child. I mean, did you see how old they are? It was like being raised by grandparents or something. And my mom is such a control freak that I had no choice but to fulfill the role of dutiful, doting daughter. Well, those days are over!"

I thought that I'd led a sheltered life, but compared to her, I'd been a wild child. Church events were the extent of her social life. She wasn't allowed to date or go on sleepovers. As I would witness first-hand over the next several months, she wasn't exaggerating about leaving all that behind and sowing her wild oats.

The version of Ruth Ann that I came to know was a total contradiction to the person she'd been in front of her parents. She wanted to completely change herself, even her name. When we went back to our room, she took the sign with our names off the door, tore out the part that said "Ruth" and put the sign back up.

"There," she said. "Now I'm Ann. Just Ann. Forget you ever heard the name Ruth." She shuddered and tore up the piece of paper with "Ruth" on it.

* * * * * *

Following a barbeque dinner for incoming freshman, each floor had meetings with their resident advisors to go over rules and other stuff. The RA for our floor was a junior named Gina. I got the distinct impression she saw us as a bunch of brats she'd been charged with babysitting.

She began the meeting with, "I'm not your mother or your maid. Therefore, I'm not here to clean up after you or your mistakes. And, I'm not here to be your best friend, either." She went on to talk about things I'd already read in the housing contract, but the basket of condoms she passed around surprised me. Some of the girls grabbed a few of them. Others passed the basket along to the next person, which was what I did, but Ann grabbed a couple.

Gina told us about the rules concerning guys in the west wing. She explained that male visitors were allowed but had to be escorted in and out through the security desk where we would also need to sign them in and out.

She droned on, and I tuned her out, looking around at the other girls I would be living in close quarters with for the next nine months. Some looked nervous and hung on Gina's every word as if there was going to be a test, but some looked bored.

There were girls who I could easily tell what sort of clique they'd been a part of in high school. I shouldn't have been stereotyping people. Besides, for all I knew, the other girls were there to reinvent themselves, like Ann was. *It'll be hard to get to know people if everyone is on a mission of personal transformation like she is.*

Back in our room, Ann discovered that I'd brought some movies with me. She'd never seen any of them.

"We didn't even have a VCR in our house, and I wasn't allowed to go to movies unless they were animated," she complained.

"Oh, my gosh! I thought *my* parents were strict. My dad has a 'no rated R' rule, but I at least got to see PG-13."

"You have no idea how strict they were. It's a wonder I'm even allowed to be here!"

"How *did* you talk them into letting you come?"

"Oh, well, that's easy. It was either send me here— which by the way is the closest state university to the pathetic town I'm from—or keep me at home where I'd end up marrying a farmer and bearing his ten children. Thank the Good Lord my parents at least have higher aspirations than that for me." She held up the VHS box for *Sixteen Candles* and asked, "Can we watch this?"

"Sure."

So, my first night at college turned into a 1980s John Hughes chick-flick marathon. Ann was enchanted with the movies. They'd been a staple of my teen years, but she didn't know anything about them; the storylines or who the actors were and what else they'd been in.

As I was drifting off to sleep around three o'clock in the morning, I noticed something odd. Ann hadn't unpacked anything. Her bed wasn't even made. She was just lying on a comforter she'd thrown over it. I thought that was strange. Unpacking and getting settled in was the first thing I'd done upon arrival.

What was she waiting for?

CH. 3 ~ SCAVENGER HUNT

Tuesday's welcome week themes were "Taking Care of Business" and "Student Organization Day". We got our pictures taken for student IDs, found out about campus jobs and tutoring, and got overloaded with brochures and flyers for every sort of club and organization imaginable.

"Have you seen anything you're interested in?" Ann asked me.

"I don't know. It's all too much for me to take in right now. It gives me this feeling I get sometimes at restaurants with complicated menus. Makes me want to not order anything."

"That happens to you, too?" she giggled.

"Yeah, I feel kind of pressured to make a decision right now without understanding what I'm trying to choose from. I need more time to think about this stuff," I explained, and I really did need more time; time away from the masses of people vying for me to sign up for anything and everything!

If I put my name down for something, I'd feel obligated to do it and then feel bad if I didn't follow through. What if I changed my mind? Would it make me look bad?

Ann and I were approached by more than one student inviting us to join churches and Christian organizations. She wasn't necessarily rude to them, but she made it clear she wasn't interested. I was a little ashamed of myself for following her lead on that.

I was raised Baptist. My family was one of those that, if the church doors were open, we were there. I knew my parents expected me to find a church to attend, but I had zero motivation to do so. I wondered what compelled students to go when their parents weren't there to make them.

I saw Cameron off and on that day in passing, but I mostly hung out with Ann. We had fun together. She was unlike anyone I'd ever known, and she kept me guessing at what her next move would be. She was coming out of her shell at warp speed, but I could tell she was still trying to figure out who she was or wanted to be. Or maybe it was that she was trying to figure out who she wanted *other* people to think she was.

That afternoon, the Bellamy Hall RAs assigned us all to random groups for a scavenger hunt. It put me in the first situation in which I had to be sociable on my own. I hadn't had to do that in a long time, and it was unnerving. The others in my group were sort of uncomfortable at first too, but once we formed a plan, it was less awkward.

There was some stuff on the list that required going off campus for, so we split into two groups. A girl named Elaine, who was from the New Haven area and had a car, volunteered to drive. She came across as a serious person; not unfriendly, but quiet and thoughtful.

The two guys with us were Jared and Tom. Tom was a high school football jock. He was nice and wasn't too much of a meathead. Jared had a good sense of humor and gave me the impression he might have been a class clown at his high school.

"So, do you know anything about Tom and Jerry? Are they from around here?" I asked Elaine. We were waiting in the car while the guys went into McDonald's for a Happy Meal toy that was on our list. She looked at me funny and cracked up laughing, making me aware that I'd misspoken and called Jared by the name of the mouse in that classic cartoon. I was embarrassed but then laughed with her.

She said. "I had the same thought earlier. They *are* kind of like those characters."

"Oops. I didn't even mean to say that. I'm glad I didn't do it in front of *them!* How embarrassing."

"That's okay. I needed the laugh. So, thank you!" She sighed and drummed her fingers on the steering wheel.

"Been a rough day?"

"Yeah, you could say that," she replied with an eye roll and brushed her shoulder-length, jet black hair out of her face. "I'm not even supposed to be here—living in the dorm, I mean. I was supposed to live at home and commute, but three weeks ago, my parents decided to sell the house. They packed up and moved out of state," she explained in exasperation. "It was a miracle I even got a room at Bellamy."

"That sucks. They didn't give you any warning?"

"Nope. They told me one day that my mom had taken a job offer in Louisiana, and just like that, they were on their way. While the rest of you guys were spending the summer getting ready for dorm life, I was passing up on all the good sales, thinking I wasn't going to need any of that."

"Well, at least you got a room."

Tom and Jared returned, and Elaine asked, "So, what did you get?"

"A stupid Barbie," Tom grumbled.

"Yeah," Jared said, "the kid in front of us got the last Hot Wheels."

Tom held up the miniaturized doll and complained, "I can't believe I had to buy a kid's meal for *this.*"

"Where is the kids' meal?" I asked, looking around the backseat where they were sitting.

"He ate it already," Jared said.

"Aw, poor Tommy. We'll try to get the Hot Wheels next time, okay?" Elaine consoled him. Jared laughed and got a thump on the head from Tom for it.

We made a couple of other stops; a funeral home where I went in and got a business card, and a Chinese restaurant where Elaine got a takeout menu. Then we met up with the rest of our group at Bellamy and collaborated on finding a few of the remaining items, one of which was a children's picture book.

"Oh! I just remembered, I have *Green Eggs and Ham*," I told them and jumped up to go get it from my room. I heard them asking each other what I was talking about. One of the other girls commented sarcastically that those things weren't on the list. Duh! As if I would have actual green eggs and ham in my room.

I returned with my autographed Dr. Seuss book, and then they understood what I'd meant. I smirked at the girl who had made the comment. Her name was Brandy. From what I'd already seen and heard, she was a classic know-it-all.

She kept talking about what a "great asset" she was to the team because she knew the campus so well. She'd moved in a week early to participate in a leadership development program. *And in the famous words of Dana Carvey's Saturday Night Live Church Lady character, "Well, isn't that special?"*

Elaine gave her a golf clap and said, "Bravo." I stifled a laugh. She reminded me of my best friend, Lyla, in Leeville.

Our team didn't win anything in the scavenger hunt, but at least it had been kind of fun. Feeling sapped from the social interaction and from having stayed up so late the night before, I headed back to my room. That's when I saw that Brandy, the know-it-all, had the room across the hall and one door down from mine. She was an uppity snob. I planned to steer clear of her, but I would find that, no matter how much I tried to do that, she had a way of insinuating herself into *my* business.

There was a note from Cameron on my door that said, "Ice cream?" He was asking if I'd be at the ice cream social later that night. *Yes!* I had hardly seen him at all that day and was missing him like crazy.

* * * * * *

I dozed off and was awakened by Ann. She had her back to me and was rummaging around in a box under her bed.

"What's up?" I asked her. She spun around with her hand over her heart. I'd startled her, and her face was pale against the alarming, artificial color of her hair.

"Oh, my God! You scared the crap out of me! I thought you were asleep. Did I wake you?"

"Yeah, but that's okay. What time is it?"

"About a quarter to seven."

I yawned and said, "I wonder what we're supposed to do for dinner."

"I don't know. A couple girls from my scavenger hunt group invited me to go to a club, or a bar, or something. Do you want to come?"

"I'll pass. I'm going to the ice cream social."

"I'm skipping that. It sounds lame but suit yourself. See you later."

I got up and ate a granola bar to hold me over until I could forage for my next meal. I decided it was time to brave taking a shower in the communal bathroom. Being a modest person, I wasn't crazy about having such limited privacy.

While I was in one of the shower stalls, a couple of girls came into the bathroom, talking and giggling. I couldn't see them, and they couldn't see me, but my face turned red at the conversation I overheard. *Yikes!* I wasn't used to being around people who used such offensive language and talked so openly about sex, especially casual sex. I didn't like it, and it made me feel small and naive.

You need to snap out of it, Olivia. This is the "real world", after all. You're not in Leeville anymore.

* * * * * *

The ice cream social was in one of the big lounges at the Student Haven. People stood around in clusters talking together. I didn't know any of them, and Cameron wasn't there yet. I hated being by myself with nobody to talk to and felt like a fish out of water. Getting in line for some ice cream, I kept an eye on the door for Cameron to arrive.

"Hey, there. Olivia, right?" someone asked. I looked around and saw Nathan, the tour guide, approaching me.

"Yeah," I confirmed. "How's it going?"

Well, I had just been wishing for someone to talk to, right? Too bad it was someone Cameron thought was hitting on me the day before.

"Good. Have you been getting settled in all right?"

"Pretty much."

"So, tell me again where you and your boyfriend are from."

"I'm from a small town north of Aberdeen called Leeville. Cameron sort of is too, but he's originally from around here. How about you?"

"I'm from all over the place. Military brat—" he was saying when a hyper, petite girl came up and jumped on him, piggy-back style. "What the hell?" he laughed.

"Hi, big brother!" the girl exclaimed and giggled.

"Amy, what are trying to do, break my back?" Nathan said, laughing. He eased her down to her feet. "Olivia, this is my sister, Amy. She's a freshman, too."

She dragged Nathan off to join her in a different line with her friends. And then I was alone again. I got ice cream and sat down at a table by myself, feeling even more self-conscious and lonely.

There were two girls at the table next to mine, but they hadn't offered for me to sit with them, and I wasn't confident enough to ask. They looked like snobs, anyway. I missed the ease of having my close friends around.

Cameron and Scott walked in, and I heard one of the girls say to the other, "Oooh, dibs on the guy in the black shirt." Scott was wearing blue, so the girl was talking about Cameron. *Is that jealousy stabbing me in the heart? Or fear?* No time for introspection, I needed to act.

I called out to Cameron, and they headed in my

direction. Cameron slid into a chair and put his arm around me. I leaned over and kissed him with such intensity that he looked at me in surprise. He liked it though and kissed me back.

The girls at the other table were smug. Their flirty smiles were gone. I was conflicted about what I'd done, but hadn't he done something similar the day before?

CH. 4 ~ SECRET STASH

Cameron and I spent the next afternoon together, just the two of us. It was heavenly. With him by my side, I got more comfortable about being on campus. We strolled around, holding hands and looking at the booths that were set up for "Celebrate Diversity Day". There was even an ethnic food fest. I wasn't adventurous about trying much, but it was still interesting.

"Let's look at this, Olivia," Cameron said as we approached one booth in particular.

"Okay. What is it?"

He handed me one of the brochures from the table and said, "Study abroad. Wouldn't that be cool?" There was a slideshow playing on a portable media center advertising the program.

"Yeah," I agreed, but I wasn't sure how I felt about it. I'd never been "abroad", and the idea of it intimidated me. Not to mention the old tapes playing in my head of every crummy thing I'd heard my dad say about foreigners and foreign places. I hated those tapes. I thought I'd left them behind, but when you've had certain attitudes forced upon you, it's hard to get rid of them.

I'd recently come to understand how many limitations I'd been living with because of my dad's opinions and critical influence on me. Having been told my whole life what was "right" and acceptable—according to him—had made me fearful of new things and reluctant to face challenges.

"You okay?" Cameron asked. I'd been blankly staring at the slideshow screen, not paying attention to what he was saying.

"What?" I refocused and gave him an apologetic smile.

"I think I lost you for a couple of minutes there."

I shook my head, clearing away my morose thoughts. A look of understanding crossed his face, and he asked, "Your dad?"

He read my mind. *It's cool how he "gets" me.*

I nodded. "Yeah, sorry. What were you saying?"

He led me away from the table, and we sat down on a nearby bench. "It's okay. He's not here, you know. Try to get him out of your head," he encouraged me.

"I know. Thank you. So, is study abroad something you want to do?" I asked and made myself lighten up.

"Maybe. I don't know. It would depend on where and whether or not it had anything to do with computer science, I guess."

I nodded in agreement, remembering that he, like all my other friends, knew what he was interested in. I was still clueless. Granted, I had at least narrowed my major down to something in social and behavioral sciences because of a scholarship I'd gotten. But until I'd taken some classes in those subjects, I had no idea what I was interested in or good at.

"Oh, hey, guess what. There's an open mic night at Diversions tonight," Cameron said.

"What's that?"

"It's where whoever wants to sing or perform something, can go up and do it."

"Oh, I know what open mic night is, but where did you say it's going to be?"

"Diversions. It's a campus nightclub. I went to see my

friend Pete perform there a couple of times. It's pretty cool."

"That sounds fun. I didn't even know NHU had a nightclub. Do you want to go?"

"Yeah. In fact, I'm signed up to do a song," he said with a grin.

"Then I'll be there! What are you going to play?"

"I haven't decided yet. It'll be a surprise. Maybe even to myself," he chuckled.

* * * * * *

At the club, it was last minute, right before he went on stage, that Cameron decided on a song. He performed Stevie Ray Vaughan's "Pride and Joy". He did a great job on it. He was so talented, and I got that old familiar rush of excitement and pride as I watched him on stage.

His song was different from everyone else's musical performance. That was by design. Since he went near the end, he'd had a chance to gauge the crowd and see their response to the other performers. Then, when he gave the audience something unexpected, he got the best applause.

He stashed his guitar in a safe place and came to the table where I was with Scott, Gary, Ann, and a few other people. We all gave Cameron an extra round of applause.

"Great performance, man," Scott congratulated him.

"Thanks. That was such a rush!"

"You were awesome," I told him and squeezed his knee under the table. He reached down and intertwined his fingers with mine, making my skin tingle with the electrifying sensation of his touch.

I loved him so much and wished I could have him all to myself right then. He must have been thinking the same thing and asked me to dance. The DJ had started playing music, and a few other people were already on the dance floor.

During a slow song, Cameron held me close and whispered in my ear, "You are so gorgeous. Guys have been checking you out all night, and it's killing me." I was flattered but shook my head in disbelief. The look of longing on his face gave me butterflies in my stomach.

Hmmm ... Is he doubting our recent declaration of purity? A couple of nights before we left for college, things had gotten more intense between us than they ever had. Even then, it was mostly PG. Amazingly enough, we were both virgins and were on the same page about keeping it that way "for now", and we'd agreed to try to not cross "the line". However, what exactly "for now" meant was undefined.

"Well, you have nothing to worry about," I assured him.

"I know. I love you," he said and kissed me.

"I love you, too. I've been seeing girls looking at you too, you know. You're smokin' hot."

"Thank you, but yours are the only eyes I want on me," he whispered near my ear. His lips grazed my neck, sending a shiver through me.

* * * * * *

"Survival Skills Day" introduced students to health services, campus police and security, and drug and alcohol awareness. Alcohol was permitted on campus, but of course, underage drinking was prohibited. Then, that night, the west wing RAs had a "pajama party" for the girls in Bellamy Hall. I was glad it wasn't Gina running the show. It was another floor's RA named Lauren. She was the type of RA I wished I'd gotten because she didn't treat us like complete pains in her butt.

There were ice breaker activities, music, food, and drinks. It turned out that the "pajama party" was also an opportunity for the freshman girls to get the rundown on campus policies about sexual harassment. There were open discussions about date rape, or acquaintance rape.

A couple of RAs did some corny improv routines of possible situations a girl might find herself in and what to do about them. I sure didn't expect to ever be in any situations where that would be an issue for me.

That night, Ann revealed that she'd brought her mom's secret "hooch" stash with her. She had several bottles of liquor packed with towels in a box under her bed. There was rum, gin, vermouth, whiskey and vodka.

I was shocked and asked her, "Won't your mom know you took these?"

"Who cares?! If she says anything about it, she'll have to admit that she's a closet drinker." She was giggling hysterically.

"So, your dad doesn't know about this?"

She fell on her bed in laughter. "Are you kidding? The good Reverend Schubert? He has no idea!" She was having such a good time I couldn't help laughing with her.

"Have you ever even drank before?" I asked.

"No! Have you?"

"Some ... but other than vodka with orange juice, I haven't had much hard liquor."

"Will you try something with me?"

Having heard the campus rules earlier that day, I was hesitant but figured what the heck? We were in our own room, and it wasn't like we were going to have a wild party. Ann only wanted a taste of something. We decided on the gin.

She poured some in little bathroom cups the size of shot glasses, raised hers, and said, "Here goes." We drank at the same time and both started gagging and spitting. It was awful!

"Oh, my gosh, Ann! Are you sure your mom didn't put something else in that bottle? It tastes like old lady perfume must taste!"

She wiped her mouth and burst into laughter again. "Then the joke would be on me, wouldn't it?"

"I don't see how anyone could drink that. Maybe you're supposed to mix it with something."

"We need some advice. I wish I could ask my mom," she said which led to another fit of giggling.

Deciding against trying anything else that night, she put it all back under her bed. Then, we stayed up late again and watched *Pretty in Pink* and *Ferris Bueller's Day Off.*

It was the fourth night in our room, and she still hadn't "moved in". She'd hung up a few clothes, and her toiletries and cosmetics were sitting out, but she hadn't made her bed, and there was nothing on her desk besides her purse and room key. She was acting like someone living out of a suitcase in a hotel room instead of a dorm.

* * * * * *

Things got crazy Friday night. All that stuff we were told about underage drinking proved meaningless for the girls on our floor. There was a big party, and it was obvious that Gina's hands-off attitude was for real. I wasn't sure where the beer came from, but there was a lot of it.

Mine and Ann's room became popular because she went public with her smuggled alcohol. I wasn't all that comfortable with the idea of the stuff being served right out of our room. She wanted to share though, so who was I to stop her? The party consisted of mostly girls, but a few guys were hanging around, too.

I called Cameron to see if he wanted to come down, but he didn't answer. Then I remembered that he and Scott were having a guy's night with some of their friends from high school. It had made me jealous for his time, but whatever. I knew I should learn to share him since, after all, we were in his hometown.

The vending machine in the lounge was raided for snacks and sodas. I tried some Jack Daniels with Coke, like I'd seen Cameron drink on graduation night. It helped me loosen up enough to join in the fun when the guys brought out some Nerf blaster guns. Ann and I paired up, and we were ruthless in our attacks on the others. It was such a riot! I hadn't laughed so hard in a long time.

The only one not having fun was Brandy, the know-it-all from the scavenger hunt. She didn't approve and made sure to let us know.

"You people are being so loud. It's like you don't even realize you're breaking the rules. Or maybe it's just that you don't care," she said from her doorway with her arms crossed and a scowl on her face.

"Oh, get a life, Brandy," another girl called out over the music. That girl was her roommate, Bridget. She complained about having gotten stuck with a colossal stick in the mud.

"That's okay, you're welcome in our room anytime," another girl offered.

"Cheers!" Bridget exclaimed and raised her red Solo cup.

That night, I drank more than I had since my wine cooler days as a freshman in high school. I didn't get sick, but I came close. Ann, on the other hand, got sick as a dog. I had warned her, and so had a couple of the other girls, but hey, I guess you have to learn from experience, right? She ended up spending the night on the bathroom floor, hugging a toilet. At least she didn't throw up in our room.

CH. 5 ~ SUNFLOWER HOUSE

The annoying sound of the phone ringing the next morning woke me up way earlier than I would have liked. It was Cameron.

"Hey, could you come meet me at the main door?" he asked.

"Ohhh," I moaned, holding my head. "What time is it?"

"About nine thirty. Are you okay?"

"Yeah. I'll be there in a few minutes." I hung up and rolled out of bed.

Ugh, the place was a mess. Ann had managed to find her way back to the room and was passed out on the floor by the door. I pulled on some jeans and a T-shirt and grabbed a hair scrunchy to pull my hair back. Knowing my breath must be horrible, I shoved a piece of gum in my mouth and stepped around Ann to get out the door.

"Good morning?" Cameron questioned. I collapsed on the sofa where he'd been waiting near the security desk.

"Not so much," I replied, wincing.

"Uh, oh. Do I detect a hangover?"

"Maybe a little. Turns out I'm living on a party floor, and my roommate was the generous supplier of the hard stuff."

He looked at me in disbelief and mild amusement.

"Ann?"

I nodded my head. Regretting that, I gently laid it against his shoulder. "I know, right? She's full of surprises."

"Well, I was going to ask if you wanted to come with me and a few other people to go hiking, but—"

"Hiking? Where?"

"A place called Comanche Park out by the lake."

"Oh ... um."

I wanted to say yes, mostly so I could spend time with him, but I knew I would be miserable. Not to mention, I'd never owned a pair of hiking boots in my life. I looked at him sadly and asked, "Would it be terrible if I said no?"

He was disappointed, but said he understood if I didn't feel like going. I promised him I'd get a pair of hiking boots and go with him the next time.

I went back to bed and woke up later to find Ann watching *Better Off Dead.* She was bleary eyed but recovering.

"This is my favorite. Can we start it over?" I asked.

"Sure, but let's get something to eat first. My belly button's about to contact my spine."

* * * * * *

"You're looking at it upside down," Cameron teased me.

"Thank you, Captain Obvious. I know it's upside down. It helps me understand the route I want to take if the direction I'm going is *forward* on the map. You know, I'm *walking* forward, so I'm moving forward on the map, too."

"That's one of the craziest things I've ever heard," he chuckled.

I smacked him on the shoulder with the campus map and said, "In case you hadn't already figured this out about me, I'm directionally challenged. I get lost all the time, and I'm kind of freaking out about finding my way around this place."

It was Sunday afternoon, and we were going around campus following our schedules to get a feel for where our classes were and how long it would take to get from place to place. I was envious of his natural sense of direction.

"How is it that you so easily know where to go and how to get there?"

"Highly developed spatial reasoning skills," he said which got him another smack with the map. "And I *have* been here a few times, remember," he added.

"Yeah, but I think even if I went through this twenty times, I'd still feel lost. And it's so hot!" I complained.

We were approaching a park bench that was under a big oak tree. I sat down on it, flipped my head forward, gathered my long hair up, and tied it in a knot at the back of my head. August in Texas was hot as hell. I was sweating through my T-shirt, and the heat was giving me a headache. Yet, somehow my sexy, hot boyfriend looked annoyingly cool and calm.

"You're getting yourself all stressed out." He sat down with me and put his hand on the back of my neck. He started massaging, and I turned my back to him so he could do my shoulders and upper back.

"Oh, thank you. That feels amazing." A delicious breeze picked up and cooled me down a little.

"Better?" he asked, his mouth near my ear. Despite the hundred-degree heat, I got goose bumps.

"Yes. Your hands are magic."

His lips pressed against the back of my neck, and he said, "Hmmm. Salty." I turned toward him, and he kissed my lips.

I smiled dreamily at him, and he asked, "So, do you feel like a college student yet? Are you ready?"

"I think so. You?" I replied.

"Pretty much. It'll sink in once I'm sitting in class, I guess. I keep thinking I should have already bought books, but everyone says go to class first."

"That's what I've heard too. I bet the line at the bookstore will be a mile long."

We were quiet for a moment, and he strummed an

imaginary guitar on his kneecap the way he sometimes did absent-mindedly. I wondered what he was thinking.

I'd heard that some other girls had gone hiking with him and Scott. Did I have anything to worry about? Had there been any "bonding" moments between fellow hikers? Was I being paranoid?

"You look so serious," I said and touched his cheek.

"Will you come with me to my mom's tonight?"

I was surprised. "Um ... is Jerry—"

"No, Jerry's gone on a long haul," he assured me. I'd had an unpleasant experience with his mom's boyfriend and hoped to never see that man again. He'd grabbed my butt and then made some inappropriate comments about me to Cameron.

"Oh, okay. Yeah. Are we going for dinner?"

He nodded. "I'm cooking."

* * * * * *

Spending time with Cameron and his mom, sans Jerry, was so much better than the first time I'd been to her house. She and I were both relieved to have the opportunity for a second first impression. I got to see the rest of the house and some childhood portraits of Cameron that were hanging in a hallway. He'd been such a cute little boy!

"How's the sunflower house doing?" I asked, remembering that Mrs. McClain had an amazing garden in her backyard.

"Oh, it's incredible," she said, beaming with pride. "Cameron, why don't you take Olivia out there? I'll finish cleaning up these dishes."

It was getting dark, but that added to the romance of the garden. We walked through the vine tunnel along the stone path that ended near the box-shaped lines of sunflowers. The flowers were tall—as tall as us. He led me into the "house" that they formed and took me into his arms. It was almost magical, being enclosed by the walls of the tall flower stalks.

"I hope being here hasn't brought back bad memories

for you," he said. I shushed him with my finger over his lips and then kissed him.

For the first time in several days, I got the familiar safety and comfort that only he could give me. We laid down on the warm grass and talked—and made out—in the moonlight for over an hour. My anxieties from the first week of being away from home washed away, if only for a while, and we enjoyed each other in that beautiful seclusion.

Later that night, still feeling good from the special time with Cameron, I went ahead and wrote some letters to my friends back home, Lyla and Kate. I also wrote to my family and Mrs. K. She was my mentor and former boss at the Cambridge Community Center, aka the CCC. None of the letters were long. I just wanted to say hi, things are going fine, here's my address, that sort of thing.

* * * * * *

Classes started the next morning, and I officially became a college student. I looked around at the other twenty-five or so students in my first class, Freshman Seminar. At first, I didn't see anyone I knew from the dorm, but then I saw Elaine's jet-black hair. She was looking around and spotted me. I smiled at her, and she waved me over to sit with her.

The instructor, Professor Graves, gave us his first piece of advice for academic success. "For each class on your schedule, you should expect to spend approximately two to three hours of study time for each hour spent in class."

In other words, since I had an eighteen-hour load, I could expect to spend at least thirty-six hours on homework and study time outside of class. Add the eighteen classroom hours back into that, and that equaled more than a full-time job! What was I thinking, signing up for so many classes?

I made bug eyes at Elaine and held out my schedule for her to see. Her eyes bugged out too, and we stifled our giggles as Professor Graves continued in a monotonous tone.

"This class is designed to help incoming freshman. It will be taught by a team of faculty and assistants with the goal of providing you with college survival skills. Grades will be based on attendance and class participation, plus some short writing assignments."

That last part was met with a few disgruntled sounds from the class which he heard and added, "Not to worry. It's an easy A as long as you show up." I sure hoped that was true.

* * * * * *

That first week was frustrating and exhausting, to say the least. I struggled with remembering the best routes between classes. By the end of the week, I still had to carry around a map.

My time was spent reading syllabi, learning about different instructors' expectations, gauging the best time to shower without having to wait in line, and figuring out the best places to eat on campus. Oh, and buying textbooks, of course. That was fun, despite the long lines and too many bodies stuffed into the store at one time.

I loved books, even textbooks. Within hours of leaving the bookstore, I had devoured the first several chapters of my Intro to Sociology book. The next time class met, the professor—a middle-aged, professional looking woman— asked who had completed the reading homework. I was the only one who answered. I didn't want to already be thought of as the teacher's pet, but I couldn't deny the satisfaction of the professor's approving nod in my direction.

Getting together with Cameron was hit or miss. There was still an occasional strangeness between us about how much time we should, or shouldn't, spend together. I got the feeling that we were both unsure what the other wanted or expected, but neither of us was willing to be the one to bring it up. For all I knew, it was my imagination.

CH. 6 ~ LAUNDRY DATE

"It's so cute the way your lips move when you're reading silently to yourself," Cameron said. He'd walked over to where I was sitting on one of the couches in the Student Haven's game room. I'd been working on a reading assignment for my Social Problems class while he and Scott played pool.

"I'm so glad I can amuse you," I said, embarrassed of my annoying habit.

"Hey, don't be mad," he chided. "You want to go grab something to eat when Scott and I are done here?"

"Just you and me?" I asked quietly.

"Sure, if that's what you want."

"That's what I want," I replied with a smile. It wasn't that I didn't like Scott, I just wanted some time alone with Cameron.

They finished their game, and we told Scott goodbye and went to the food court. It wasn't crowded, and I was glad we found a table to ourselves.

"You want to try a bite?" he offered, holding out his sandwich. I wrinkled my nose, and he chuckled. "I just figured I'd offer."

"Sorry, honey, you've gotten me to try a lot of new things, but tuna and mayo—that's never going to happen.

35

So, how are your classes going? Do you like your professors?"

"Yes! It's awesome, Olivia. There's a Computer Science club that Gary and I joined, and one of our professors is the faculty advisor for it. We'll be working on a project for a contest." He told me about a lot of stuff I didn't understand, but it was cool to see how excited he was. I wished there was something that I was that passionate about.

He asked, "How about you? What do you think of your classes?"

"French and College Algebra are going to be continuations from high school. Which is good, because I need a couple of easy ones. I think I signed up for too much. Intro to Sociology and Social Problems are the most interesting. I like those professors best, anyway."

"Yeah, having a good professor can make all the difference."

"Tell me about it. My psychology professor is a different story. She's made comments that are ... almost anti-Christian. Maybe I'm being too sensitive."

"I've got one like that, too. Try not to let it bother you."

"I'm just not used to such open disdain, you know. Oh, and there's this guy in that class who wears a jacket that's like a hooded sweatshirt. He sits there zipping it up and down repeatedly," I said and laughed. "Nobody else seems to notice. Sometimes it sounds like he's keeping the beat to a song that only he is hearing."

"That would drive me crazy," he cringed. He couldn't stand repetitive noises like that. "There's this girl in one of my classes who smacks her gum all the time. It doesn't bother anyone else. Only me."

"You could wear a jacket and zip it and unzip it over and over again and see if it bugs *her*," I suggested, and we laughed. "Have you had the experience of being put in your place by upper classmen yet?"

"No, I don't think so. What do you mean?"

"You know, those students who've been here for a year

or more. They like to remind freshmen that we aren't at the top of the food chain anymore like when we were seniors in high school. There are several girls in my Social Problems class who are sophomores, and they're determined to make me feel stupid during discussions because I'm so young and inconsequential."

"Oh. That sucks. It's not as though they're so much farther ahead. I don't know if this is true or not, but I've heard that in Greek, sophomore means 'wise fool'."

"Sounds about right. I hope I don't act that way next year."

"I don't see you ever being like that. Technically, if you go by number of hours, you and I will be sophomores after this semester," he pointed out.

"That's true." We'd both gotten credit for AP classes and summer courses at Cambridge Junior College, otherwise known as CJC, near Leeville.

"Are you homesick yet?" he asked.

"I don't know. I don't miss *home* necessarily, but I already feel out of touch with Lyla and Kate. I miss them."

"Have you written to them yet?"

"Yeah. How about you?"

"No. That might be weird if I wrote to Kate and Lyla," he joked.

"Very funny. I meant, have you been homesick?"

"Nah. Nothing like when I moved away from here in the first place."

"Oh, yeah. I forget sometimes you're from around here to begin with."

My growing sense of being an outsider made me envious of him for belonging somewhere. It was silly to begrudge him, and I tried to shake off the feeling as soon as I became aware that I was having it.

* * * * * *

Over the next couple weeks, I tried to settle into a routine. It was more difficult than I expected, which disappointed me and led to lots of insecure moments.

Sometimes I embarrassed the hell out of myself. Like, one morning, I had to rush to class because I'd overslept. I was so focused on getting into the classroom and taking my seat, that it took almost a full minute for me to figure out that I wasn't even in the right classroom. The professor and several students gave me funny looks. I stood up and went right back out of the room and heard a couple of people snickering.

Finding the nearest bathroom, I cried like a schoolgirl. I got so mad at myself. I was sure that I was the only person who had ever done something so stupid. It took me a while to get a grip. I eventually went to class, late of course, but at least I walked into the right room. To avoid ever doing that again, I got into the habit of double checking my printed schedule with the numbers above the classroom doors.

I had to get used to professors who didn't have any concern for their students. Sure, in high school there had been a few of those, but I guess they were held to a higher standard of courtesy. Not so much in college.

Professors could say whatever they wanted to whomever, no matter how rude or inappropriate. And some of them got a power trip from being in the position to influence us. It gave me some idea of what my dad had meant when he warned me that my liberal arts teachers would fill my head with "garbage".

College algebra sucked because the professor was a jerk. He was a strange, short little bald man who wore bow ties. He had on a different one every time I saw him. That's not what made him a jerk though. His response to me asking for help with something in class earned him that designation.

"I cannot stop my lecture to backtrack for you, miss. It would hold up the rest of the class. If you can't keep up, I suggest you come to my office hours," he said, completely humiliating me. If that wasn't bad enough, he added, "Or there's always the option for you to switch to a pre-algebra class."

I wasn't about to do that. I'd done fine in algebra in high school and resented him for suggesting that I needed a remedial class. He didn't even know me! My feelings were hurt, and I didn't hide it well. A guy named Michael who sat behind me offered to help me after class. I was grateful, and it made me feel less lonely. That was something I was feeling more and more often.

Why did I feel so lonely when I was constantly around so many people? Maybe it was that I was mostly surrounded by strangers. I'd lived in Leeville my whole life and had known a lot of the same people since childhood.

How could you tell if someone was being genuine? There were a couple of girls in one of my classes who I'd chatted with a few times. They were nice, but they never asked me anything about myself or invited me to do anything with them. I started to get the feeling they were only tolerating small talk with me. So, I backed off and didn't talk to them anymore. They weren't interested in getting to know me.

Going through the motions of small talk and that awkward getting-to-know-you dance was exhausting. Sometimes, I invested the time and energy, and it turned out that people brushed me off. Maybe there was something about me they decided wasn't worth their time. Either that, or I decided there was something I couldn't stand about them. Some of my dad's critical nature had rubbed off on me after all.

More often, I found myself looking for opportunities to be alone, away from all the noise and people, so I could rest my mind from the social expectations. I wanted to feel like I could be myself, but I started to forget what that was like and doubted that people would accept me for who I was. Whatever caused people to gravitate toward others to seek friendship wasn't happening for me.

Ann, on the other hand, was turning into a social butterfly. She liked to party, and I got pulled into it some, along with a few other girls on our floor. Nothing meaningful in terms of possible friendships resulted from it though. That crowd was kind of superficial and shallow.

From hanging out with them, I got into bad habits of staying up way too late and drinking more often than I should. Tiny, quiet warning bells sometimes sounded in the back of my mind, but I was good at ignoring them. What was wrong with having some fun?

* * * * * *

One Saturday afternoon, I needed to make myself scarce because Ann had a guy in our room. We hadn't previously discussed how we'd work around such things, but I figured it was a good time for catching up on laundry. There was only one machine in the west wing laundry room that wasn't being used. Since I had three loads I wanted to do all at once, I decided to check the laundry room in the guys' wing. There I found plenty of machines not being used. That was a guys' dorm for you.

I got the machines going and called Cameron's room from the security desk. He had told me that he and Gary would be working on a project, but I wondered if he'd want to take a break and join me.

"You want to keep me company in the laundry room?" I asked.

"Hey, yeah. I'll bring my laundry down too. Other than taking it to my mom's one time, I haven't done it since I got here," he chuckled. "You want to have a laundry date?"

"I'd love to. I've got my Walkman. Bring your portable speakers and some music, and we'll raid the vending machines."

And so, Cameron and I had our first laundry date. He cracked me up with his admission that he didn't know how to wash his clothes.

"Are you for real? Wait, so does that mean your dad did your laundry?"

"Well ... no," he replied in mild embarrassment. "We had a maid."

"You did? I didn't know that."

"Yeah. The Snyder Architecture corporate office offered it as a job perk for my dad, and who were we to turn it down?"

"Okay. I can't believe I'm teaching my boyfriend how to do laundry, but here goes," I said and showed him what to do. It was strange at first, but we were both in a good mood, and it became comical. I learned that he wore boxer briefs which made me blush and think about things I shouldn't.

He gave me a boost to sit on top of the machine. With him standing in front of me, I wrapped my legs around his. The warmth from his hands spreading out across my back sent tingles all through me.

We were listening to a tape he'd made for me from the new Buddy Guy album. Even though we were in a roomful of washing machines and dryers, with the pervasive smell of detergent and fabric softener, something about it was romantic. I kissed him and got all hot and bothered, thinking about him in his underwear. And *out* of them, for that matter!

We had the room to ourselves and made out for a few minutes until a guy came in to move his clothes from a washer to a dryer. He looked at us funny. As he was leaving, he smiled and nodded at Cameron. We laughed, and Cameron said, "That guy's on my floor. He's jealous."

"Whatever," I said, rolling my eyes.

"Don't 'whatever' me. You've probably had guys hitting on you all the time around here."

"I'm flattered that you think that, but you're delusional."

"I bet it's happening, and you don't notice it. That's one of the things I love about you. You're beautiful and amazing and don't even know it."

We got chips, Reese's peanut butter cups, and sodas from the vending machines and hung out, waiting for our clothes to wash and dry. He asked me how my classes were going.

"I guess they're going okay. I like my sociology classes."

"And what, exactly, are those about?" he asked.

"The study of human beings in society."

"That's kind of broad. What do you mean?"

I happened to have brought my textbook with me so I could do some reading, and I used it to help explain. "It's the study of why people behave the way they do as a result of the social situations they're in. And the study of social groups and organizations—the formation of them, what keeps them in place. There's the study of society in regard to all kinds of things, like family, race, gender, class, religion, politics, even age."

"It sounds like you're pretty into it," he commented.

"Yeah, I like reading about it. And the lectures are good. I'm struggling with how to make a connection to a possible career though."

"Don't stress about that already. You're just starting to learn about the things that interest you."

"I know," I said and kept to myself that I'd started to feel—again—like I had no real direction or goal to work toward.

CH. 7 ~ CAMERON'S BIRTHDAY

Ann's transformation of herself continued. It was in a way that made her very different from me. I had a feeling that she was already in the habit of skipping classes, and I didn't ever see her study or do homework. Also, her wardrobe steadily changed. She had a few pairs of jeans that she'd put holes in and spent lots of time trying to make look authentically grunge. Her makeup consisted mostly of dark eyeliner, and lots of it. Then, a single ear piercing turned into double, and triple, and quadruple in one ear.

Guys living the grunge lifestyle began coming and going with her from our room. Whether they were boyfriends, dates, or friends, I was never sure. I had asked her about the guy who had been in our room with her the day Cameron and I had our laundry date. She claimed they were just hanging out because his roommate had a girl over. It was funny, the ripple effect of roommates getting displaced when other people wanted privacy.

She suggested that if either of us wanted privacy in the room, a hair scrunchy on the outside door handle would be the sign. She put it into practice one Sunday night which happened to be Cameron's birthday. He and I had gone out to eat and then for a stroll around the outdoor mall in New Haven. It had been a pleasant evening, and I was looking forward to us going to my room afterward, but when we got there, a blue scrunchy was on the door handle.

"Aw, man, that sucks," I said.

"What?" he asked. I pointed to the scrunchy, and he gave me a knowing look and suggested, "Let's go to my room."

"Is Gary there?"

"No, he's at a Nintendo tournament. I can't believe how much that guy plays video games."

In his room, I looked around in mild amusement at the clutter and disarray which was worse each time I saw it. There were clothes and towels draped over chairs and empty soda cans and food containers on the desks. It was hard to tell if Cameron or Gary was the bigger culprit because it all ran together. It was different from my room, or at least *my* side of my room. I was a total neat freak myself.

We hung up the Fabulous Thunderbirds poster I'd given him for his birthday. "Are you sure you like it?" I asked. I had never been good at gift giving and had agonized over what to get him.

"It's awesome. I love it. Thank you."

"You're happy, welcome birthday," I said, nervously jumbling my words. I giggled, and he smiled at my blunder, putting his arm around me. The music he'd put on was the Journey album we'd listened to on Valentine's Day. *Hmmm, he's feeling romantic.*

He raised my hand to his mouth and brushed the back of it with his gorgeous, full, kissable lips. I leaned toward him, putting my face between his neck and shoulder. Inhaling deeply of his intoxicating scent, I then exhaled slowly against his neck. I knew that was one of his biggest turn-ons. It made him shudder and tighten his arms around me.

Maybe it was the music, or the fact that we were alone in a bedroom for the first time in a long while—or maybe it was both—but suddenly, I felt vulnerable. The emotional difficulties and struggles I'd been pushing aside and ignoring during those first few weeks of college made me feel like I wanted him more than ever. I needed comfort, and I wanted it to come from him.

Enjoying what a good kisser he was, I savored his mouth on mine. Everything about him was so familiar, so safe. He gave me such a sense of well-being. I focused on the way his hands warmed my skin. His long, perfect fingers gently curled around the side of my neck, his thumb caressing my cheek.

He brushed my hair behind my shoulder so he could kiss my neck, and I closed my eyes. The slow deliberateness of his affections was tantalizing. His tender touches and kisses made me want more.

The song "Open Arms" started playing, and he eased me down to lie on my back. Lying next to me on his side, propped up on his elbow, he looked at me intently. His eyes, the color of creamy milk chocolate, settled on my lips, and he leaned over to kiss me.

I let him take the lead for a minute and relished the sensation of his tongue teasing my lips open. He sucked on my bottom lip, and then our tongues mingled, making me breathless. The feel of his lean, hard muscles as I rubbed his shoulders and back made desire spread through me, leaving a trail of aching warmth down the center of my body.

He'd pushed the bottom of my shirt up and surprised me by moving his head down to kiss my bare stomach. I let out a quiet moan and ran my fingers through his hair as his lips made their way around my belly button and up to my ribs.

"That feels so good, Cameron," I whispered. He brought his mouth back to mine and maneuvered his hips so that I could feel his arousal pressing along my thigh. I gasped and turned my body to face him.

"Can you feel what you do to me?" he whispered.

"Yes." I draped my leg over him, attempting to pull him

on top of me. He resisted and gently pushed me onto my back, reminding me of that "line" we didn't want to cross. Where exactly was that line, anyway? I was frustrated and disappointed. To my absolute horror, I felt like I might cry and hid my face against his chest.

"Oh, no. What's wrong?" he asked.

"I'm confused," I managed to say. It was crazy and embarrassing that I was so emotional.

"I think I'm confused too. I'm sorry. I shouldn't have let this happen. Especially since it was my idea to avoid this kind of thing."

"Are you having second thoughts?"

"About what?"

"About ... you know ... the stuff we talked about the day after I spent the night at your house," I stammered.

"I don't think so. I mean, *no*. I'm not."

"You have a funny way of showing it," I said, but not in a rude way. I didn't want to make him feel guilty, but I did wonder what he was thinking.

"I know, but it's hard," he said, and we both laughed at the double entendre. "Damn," he muttered and sat up. "It's not right that I want you so bad and can't do anything about it."

I didn't trust myself to say anything, because what I was thinking was, *why can't we do something about it without having sex?*

He laid down again, leaving a few inches of empty space between us, and traced his finger along the side of my face. "You're just so ... innocent, and I don't want to spoil that."

"But you're innocent, too, right? What would be wrong with us ... losing some of that innocence together?"

Did I just say that? Wasn't the guy supposed to be the one saying that kind of thing to the girl? I couldn't help it though. I wanted him.

"You have no idea how much I'd like to try that ... but I'd hate myself if we did. I know it would change things. I've seen how some of the guys around here are fooling around with girls and what it's like for them afterward—all awkward and weird, and they start avoiding each other. It makes me glad we decided against it ahead of time."

"Yeah," I agreed, but I was tempted to argue our case; that we were in love and had been together for nine months already. Didn't that make us different from those other people? But I knew he was right and conceded, "I've been noticing some of that, too. Fooling around complicates things, doesn't it?"

"Seems like it. Do *you* still think we're doing the right thing?" he asked. Was he looking for affirmation from me? I knew he wanted what was best for both of us, and I loved him for that.

I nodded and said, "Yes ... for now. Don't you?" Those two little words "for now" hung there again like they had on graduation night.

"Yes," he agreed.

"I love you."

"I love you, too. More than ever."

* * * * * *

Upon returning to my room, I was glad that the scrunchy was gone from the door handle and that Ann wasn't there. I got ready for bed and tried to read but couldn't shake an unsettled feeling I had. I wondered if it was homesickness. It was unbelievable to me that I would miss home after being so ready to get out of there.

The next day, I got a card from my best friend Lyla that cheered me up some. The fact that it was one of her leftover Thank You cards from graduation made me laugh, and there was a paw print from her dog, Versace, that she'd somehow inked inside of it.

She'd also written a letter that told me a funny story from home. Her mom had put an old desk that she was getting rid of at the end of their driveway with a "Free" sign on it. We were neighbors, and my sister Emma had seen the desk and asked Lyla if she could have it, which of course was fine.

Emma wanted to paint it a different color, so they carried it over to the garage at my house, and then Lyla took her to buy some paint. I was so glad to hear all that! It warmed my heart that Lyla was taking the time to hang out with Emma.

They got started painting it, and my dad came home and asked what they were doing. Emma was so excited, telling him about how she was painting it purple to match something else in her room. Lyla wrote, "Olivia, you'd be proud of me. When your dad made a crappy comment about us 'going about it all wrong', I kept my mouth shut."

My dad had told them they shouldn't have painted it without stripping and priming the wood first. Yep, that sounded like my perfectionist, opinionated, controlling dad all right. Emma's response was that she wanted to start using the desk right away and didn't want to take the time to do all that other stuff.

Lyla said that my dad brought it up again later, and Emma told him, "Dad, give me a break. I don't care if it doesn't look like a professional did it. It's going in my room, so relax, *nobody* will think you did it."

Bravo, Emma! She was four years younger than me and was learning sooner than I had to not let our dad make her feel like she had to do everything his way.

CH. 8 ~ TURNING POINT

Brandy, the know-it-all party pooper ratted out her own roommate, Bridget, for having alcohol in their room. I happened to be in the hallway to witness the confiscation. There was a university staff member present. He was probably recruited by Brandy because she couldn't get Gina to give her the time of day.

Bridget passed by me and muttered, "You and Ann will be next if Brandy has anything to do with it." *Well, great!* I didn't have any alcohol in the room, but Ann sure did. I had no idea where she got it from, but she had a steady supply line.

I was fretting about that when Cameron broke the news to me that Dr. Seuss died. He'd read it in the newspaper.

"How sad," I said and really *was* sad, even though I didn't know the man. "What did he die of?"

"He had oral cancer for years, so I guess it was that. The autographed book I gave you may be worth something someday."

"I'd never sell it." He'd given it to me on our six-month anniversary. It symbolized an inside joke we shared. I was a picky eater, and we often quoted lines from the book when he got me to try new things.

I was in a funk, and a big red fifty-eight on my algebra exam made it worse. *How the hell did this happen? That's a freaking F! I don't make Fs!* My face burned, and I could feel my blood boiling. There was a tap on my shoulder, so I flipped the test over and turned around. It was Michael, sitting behind me.

I must have glared at him because he reared back and said, "Whoa, sorry. I just wondered how you did, but I think I can guess."

At a glance, I saw that he'd gotten a B. I didn't feel like talking, so I turned back around. I would have to ask someone for help, and I hated that. *I'm such a loser.* Maybe I should have done what Dr. Bow Tie suggested early on and switched to pre-algebra.

Michael called to me as I rushed out after class, "Hey, wait up, Olivia. Wait up. Wow, you walk fast." I stopped and let him catch up, and he asked, "Are you in a hurry?"

"Well, kind of," I said, wanting to get away.

"Look, about your test grade, don't be so hard on yourself. It's not like I'm a math rock star, either. Maybe we could get together and study, you know, help each other out." He'd helped me a few times, but we'd never met outside of class. I wasn't sure that was a good idea.

"Thanks, but I don't know when I'd be able to," I said, trying not to sound rude but wanting to put him off. The last thing I needed was the complication of a study "date" with another guy. He was cute, though.

Wait a minute. Why was I thinking like that? What did his looks have to do with anything? It wasn't like he'd asked me out or something. Wow! I was lousy at math, and a total dork.

Just needing to be alone, I thanked him as nicely as I could and went to my room. Everything was spiraling downward. Things that shouldn't have bothered me so much were overwhelming me. I couldn't breathe or think straight. Was I having a panic attack?

There was a note on my door that a package had been delivered for me, and I went and got it from the front desk. It was a care package from Mrs. K that contained notes from her and a few other people I used to work with at the CCC, including Diana, the person who had taken my job when I left. Her son, Anthony, had colored a picture for me, and there was also a small framed scripture verse that said, "God created you to do amazing things! -Ephesians 2:10".

I'd been repressing and denying it, but the truth was, I was homesick. Plain and simple. I curled up on my bed, holding the framed scripture against my chest and choked back tears. How could God have created me to do amazing things? I couldn't even pass algebra, and I went around lost half the time. How could a lost failure feel like God created them for anything meaningful?

A headache was coming on. I sat up and found some Tylenol. I'd been getting headaches more often, and Tylenol only worked about half the time.

All of a sudden, Ann burst into the room. I turned my back to her and wiped the tears from my face.

"Oh, good you're here!" she exclaimed. She didn't pick up on the fact that I'd been crying and said, "Hey, you want to go to a party with me? It'll be awesome. I heard about it from Greg, the guy I told you about yesterday."

"Um, I don't know," I mumbled but gave merit to the idea that the distraction of a party might be what I needed. Maybe there would be something good to drink.

"Uh, oh. Nooo, Olivia, don't be sad. It's Friday. Let's go let loose!"

I knew I shouldn't sit around feeling sorry for myself, and besides, Cameron and I didn't have any plans. There was something going on with the Comp Sci club that he and Gary and some girl named Emily were going to. I'd heard a lot about this girl Emily. She was like a novelty because there were only a couple of girls in the club. Hmmm, should I be worried about my boyfriend spending time with this other girl who held the same interests in computer stuff that he did? Why was I looking for things to worry about? Didn't I have enough on my mind already?

I sat up and said, "Okay. What time?"

"Yay!" She jumped up and down and clapped.

Come on, Tylenol, do your thing.

"Greg said to get there around eight or nine o'clock, so

let's go shopping first. Do you mind driving?" she asked, which was a pointless question since she didn't have a car.

"I don't mind. What are we shopping for?"

"Fun stuff! I got a check from my parents in the mail today. Come on, let's go spend it!"

She was so happy and excited it was hard not to get caught up in it. I changed into something more party worthy. For me, that was jeans and a nicer shirt, plus I braided my hair. Her outfit, however, was ripped jeans with a plaid flannel shirt over a black tank top, and her hair was a red, flyaway mess. On purpose.

Her mission at the mall included buying a pair of chunky Doc Marten combat boots. They completed her grunge look. Then we went to the Piercing Pagoda for her to get a nose piercing. She tried to talk me into one, too. Instead I agreed to a double ear piercing. It reminded me of how mad my dad had gotten at my sister, Emma, for doing the same thing even though she'd been told not to. I wondered how she was doing and if she was getting along okay without me there to stick up for her.

"Let's get something to eat and go to the music store," Ann said. "There's a new album everyone's talking about. I'm going to be so mad if they don't have it yet."

We ate greasy fried chicken—Ann's idea—and headed to the music store. The whole outing was about what *she* wanted to do. It wasn't that there was anything I wanted to do, but it would have been nice if she'd asked. It was usually like that with her, though. In fact, she had never asked me much about myself at all.

That irritated the crap out of me. I tried to be the kind of person who didn't talk about myself a lot and let other people feel comfortable telling me about themselves. But it had seemed lately that nobody cared about me, or my feelings, or what I wanted.

Ann didn't even notice I'd gotten quiet and was sulking. I thought about telling her my headache had come back and that I wanted to go back to the dorm, but I remembered that all I would do there was feel sorry for myself.

She gave me directions, and it turned out the party was at an apartment off campus. I had a strong suspicion she'd only invited me because she needed a ride to the mall and then to the party.

She introduced me to a few people who were all older than us, and I was told to help myself to beer from the fridge. I wasn't much of a beer drinker but went ahead and looked to see what they had. I was pleasantly surprised to find some Shiner Bock which I knew I liked, thanks to Cameron getting me to try it.

A guy in the kitchen handed me a bottle opener and started chatting with me. His name was Craig. He was a music major in his junior year. He asked me about myself, and I relaxed some, feeling like maybe I wasn't a total loser. The three beers I managed to slam down in a short amount of time helped with the relaxation, too. I wasn't quite sure what my hurry was to get wasted, but it helped numb my bad attitude.

Craig and I joined a few other people outside on the balcony where a heated philosophical discussion was going on. I didn't have anything to offer, so I sat back and watched and listened. The philosophers were a guy and a girl who must have been in the same class together. Their banter seemed harmless, but I sensed it would turn into an argument.

I went inside to use the restroom and then looked for Ann. Not finding her anywhere, I went out on the balcony again to ask Craig if he'd seen her. He wasn't there anymore, but I found him in the kitchen making out with a girl. He had her up on the counter and was standing between her legs with his hands up the back of her shirt. I interrupted and asked if he'd seen Ann.

"No, sorry. She may have gone off somewhere with Greg."

Well, that didn't help me at all. Who was Greg, and where would Ann have gone with him? To another apartment or something? I didn't want to hang out and be an audience for Craig and his make out partner, so I went back out on the balcony.

Predictably, the debate had turned sour, and the tension was thick. I wasn't crazy about sticking around for it, especially because another guy and girl had started making out right next to the others who were arguing.

Where the hell was Ann, and what the hell was I supposed to do? There was no place for me to go. I'd drank too much and knew I shouldn't drive. Even if I were to leave, taking off without Ann would have been wrong.

I walked around the ground level of the apartment block, thinking I might hear other people on another balcony and find Ann or someone who might know where she was. There were a few other parties going on, but nobody was helpful.

At a loss, I called Cameron from a pay phone by the apartment complex office and was so relieved that he answered. At first, he sounded humored by my predicament, but when I told him why I didn't want to drive, he got worried. Then, when I told him I wasn't even on campus, he was irritated. He asked what the name of the complex was and said that he would come get me.

I made one last unsuccessful attempt to find Ann and then left a note on my car, letting her know that Cameron had picked me up. Why was I being so thoughtful of her?

Cameron pulled up in his truck, and I got in, saying, "Thank you. I'm sorry if I woke you up."

"I wasn't sleeping. Scott and I were playing video games with Gary."

"Oh, okay. Sorry anyway."

He was quiet on the drive back to the dorm but finally said, "This isn't like you, Olivia. What's going on?"

"What do you mean? I'm not exactly drunk. At least I knew I shouldn't drive, right?"

"Well that's good to know, but what I meant was, going off to a party with Ann to someplace like that."

"Like what?" I got defensive.

"Forget it. I'm surprised, is all. You should get something straight with Ann. If you're going to go out partying together, you need to be more responsible about letting each other know what your plans are."

As he was parking the truck at Bellamy Hall, I unbuckled and muttered, "Okay, I'll be sure to do that. Thanks for the ride, *Dad.*"

I got out and slammed the door. I heard him call my name, but I didn't turn around. He'd made me feel like my dad did, and I couldn't deal with his disappointment.

In my room, I unraveled into a crying mess. I searched through my tape collection for something melancholy or angst-ridden, and the best I could find was Sinead O'Connor. I shoved my ear buds in and cranked the volume up on my Walkman.

Lying in the dark, I tried to let the music chase the demons out of my head. It worked, and with most of the alcohol burned off, I started thinking more clearly. I was so embarrassed! Cameron had been right, and if he'd sounded judgmental, it was probably my own stupid perception. I thought about calling him. But lying there trying to formulate what I would say, I fell asleep.

I didn't recognize it at the time, but that night was a turning point for me. And not a good one.

CH. 9 ~ MALADJUSTMENT

The next morning, I felt dead inside. Cameron hadn't called to check on me, and I didn't know how I was going to retrieve my car from that apartment complex where I'd left it. In fact, I wasn't even sure how to find my way back to it. I did know one thing: I wasn't going to ask Cameron.

Ann hadn't returned yet. Around one o'clock in the afternoon, I gave up waiting on her. I at least remembered the name of the apartment complex, and the guy at the security desk was able to give me directions to it. The next question was, how would I get there?

Elaine and I had gotten to know each other better in our Freshman Seminar class. I called her, and she said she'd be happy to give me a ride. I was grateful, because if she hadn't been able to, my next option would have been the bus. I'd learned my way around campus enough to get where I needed to go, but I'd never used the bus system. The thought of having to do that made me want to cry, or throw up, or both. I was starting to retreat to an insecure, scared place.

Meeting me in the lobby of Bellamy Hall, Elaine speculated, "So, there must be a story behind this."

"Ugh. My roommate dragged me to a party last night and then disappeared on me. I'd been drinking, so I didn't want to drive and had Cameron pick me up." I was glad Elaine didn't ask why I hadn't gotten Cameron to take me back to my car.

As I was getting into her car, she said, "Oh, sorry. You can move those to wherever," about a stack of magazines on the passenger seat. I picked them up and set them in my lap. The one on top was a People magazine announcing that Patrick Swayze was the sexiest man alive. The other magazines had articles about him too.

"I'm noticing a theme, here," I teased.

"Yeah, he's pretty hot," she said with a nonchalant shrug. "And hopefully my future husband."

We laughed, and I pointed out that, "He's about twenty years older than you, isn't he?"

"So? Love *can* transcend age, you know?"

"Maybe."

I flipped through the pages and scanned an article about Patrick's body and soul. My eyes lingered on a picture of his muscular back and trim waist, and she said, "Get your eyes off him. He's mine."

"All right, all right." I closed the magazine. "Did you see *Point Break?*"

"About five times. Did you?"

"Yeah, but only once." We'd arrived at my car, and as I was getting out, she asked, "So what are you doing for the rest of the day?"

"Not much. Why? What are you doing?"

"A group of us are going to the rec center to shoot some hoops. You want to come?"

I scrunched my face up at the thought of trying to play basketball in front of other people. "Um, I don't know. I'm a spaz with sports." I was not a fan of anything that involved balls bouncing or flying anywhere near my face.

"Okay, well, if you change your mind, we'll be there around four o'clock. Tom and Jared reserved a court for us. Oh, that's right, you know Tom and Jared, or should I say, Tom and Jerry?" she snickered.

"Those guys from the scavenger hunt?"

"Yeah, them and a couple of other people. It's not a real game or anything. Believe me, I'm the worst! It's just for laughs."

"Okay, I'll think about it." I wasn't interested, but I didn't want to be rude.

The note I had left on my car for Ann was still there. She'd tried to write something on it in lipstick. It looked like "Ok".

* * * * * *

There was a note on my door from Cameron asking if I needed a ride to go get my car. I called him and said, "Thanks, but I had a friend take me."

"Oh, okay." I detected a hint of disappointment in his voice. Or maybe it was surprise. "Are you still mad?"

"No," I replied, and I meant it. I'd thought about it all day, and I wasn't mad at *him* so much as I was at myself.

"That's good."

There was an expectant silence that I broke by saying, "I'm sorry ... about calling you 'Dad'."

He chuckled. "Thank you. I couldn't believe you said that."

I laughed, too, glad we could joke about it. "Trust me, you are *nothing* like my dad, but I felt like I was being scolded."

"Well, I'm sorry. I didn't mean to."

"I know. Thank you. And thanks for coming to my rescue. Ann still hasn't shown up, but I'm going to let her know that wasn't cool. What are you doing today?"

"Scott and I are going out to his parents' ranch. They need extra help with something. I think we're going to stay the night out there."

"Okay. Have fun." I tried not to sound disappointed. I considered for a millisecond asking if I could go with them. But how lame was that, inviting myself?

I worked on some homework and toyed with the idea of meeting up with Elaine at the rec center but fell asleep reading my psychology book. I woke up past four and laid there staring at the ceiling with a headache.

Ann finally returned, and I asked, "Where have you been?"

She looked like crap. Her clothes were wrinkled, and she reeked of cigarette smoke. I was betting she had a hangover too, even though it was almost six o'clock in the evening.

"Where?" she asked with a spaced-out look, her eyes barely focusing.

"Yeah. What happened to you last night? You deserted me at that party."

"Oh," she giggled. "I was with Greg."

Suddenly wanting to take my bad feelings about a lot of stuff out on her, I angrily said, "Well, have you ever heard of common courtesy? You could have let the person who drove you there know what your plans were."

"Geez, Olivia, don't you think if I'd known how the night was going to go, I would have told you? When I went looking for you, *you* were the one who had bailed."

I tried to explain to her about how things had happened, with the guy and girl getting into a fight, and everyone else making out, and not knowing where I should go. But she was acting ditzy and was unwilling—or unable—to understand that what she'd done sucked.

* * * * * *

My lonely struggle with algebra continued over the next couple of weeks, and I sunk further into convincing myself that I was an idiot. I'd asked Cameron for help, but he didn't seem to have time for me. He was busy with his own friends, his classes, and the Comp Sci club.

I gave in and asked Michael for help. I made sure to meet with him in a public place, like the library. I didn't want him getting any ideas, or Cameron either. Although I did mention to him that a guy named Michael was helping me. It didn't bother him, so maybe I was worried about nothing.

Things with Ann got worse. Everything about her was bugging me. She acted sketchy, smelled of cigarette smoke all the time, and her side of the room resembled a homeless person's heap. She was dressing full-on grunge and had friends from that crowd meeting up with her in our room. Her parents called for her a few times. Usually, she wasn't there, and I played messenger. If she was there, she begged me to make excuses so she wouldn't have to talk to them.

She'd been borrowing my boom box to listen to this new album by a band called Nirvana and used up the batteries instead of plugging it in. There were a couple of good songs on it, if you were into that sort of thing, but I got tired of hearing it over, and over again.

Gone were my hopes that we'd become good friends. We were very different people, and she didn't give a damn about me. Sometimes she was nice, if there was something she needed or wanted from me. More often than not, she was grouchy and catty, usually from a hangover. It was difficult for me to not be catty back, and I took demented pleasure in making loud noises "by accident".

As a matter of fact, cattiness was going around on our floor. Girls were yelling at each other, slamming doors, and sulking. The "honeymoon" was over. The novelty had worn off, and we were getting sick of each other. Pranks turned from funny to mean. I'd never gotten involved in all of that stuff, so I hoped they'd leave me out the drama.

Because I kept to myself, people mostly left me alone. I wasn't rude, but I measured out kindness carefully to protect my fragile confidence. Other than Cameron and Elaine, I didn't have any friends. I wore my earbud headphones everywhere I went, which helped me avoid having to interact with people. I hated it that I was being like my dad, so quick to judge others. Nonetheless, I slipped into a bad habit of evaluating everyone and everything through a critical lens, exactly like him.

Speaking of parents, my fear of turning into my mom resurfaced. She was overweight and didn't do much to take care of her appearance. I wasn't becoming a total slob, but I had gained some weight from inactivity and eating too much junk food all the time. However, no matter how much I knew I should, I didn't get off my butt and go running or do anything else that resembled exercise.

Sadly, I hadn't embraced the college culture like everyone else had. I didn't care about going to parties or campus sporting events, and I avoided the social opportunities arranged by the administration because they were lame. Were they lame, or was I being critical and looking for excuses?

Cameron's adjustment to college life was going perfectly fine. He had joined a club that he liked and was able to share his interests with other people. His roommate was quiet and reasonable, and his best friend was at the same college with him. His classes were everything he'd expected and hoped for. He knew exactly what he was working toward. I was disgusted at myself for being jealous of him.

He and I ate lunch together a few times a week, studied with each other occasionally, and did our laundry together, but we weren't going out on any real dates anymore. In his presence, I heard myself complaining about stuff more often. I was becoming a whiner. He was patient and made suggestions, but that often made me more irritable. Probably because I was enjoying my pity party and wasn't ready to get over it.

I blamed some of my gloominess on my psychology class. Parts of it were interesting, like developmental psychology, but I made the mistake of reading ahead in the textbook. There was a chapter about abnormal behavior and psychological disorders that clued me into how mentally messed up people can get. I was letting that stuff play with my mind, spent too much time overanalyzing things, and wondered if I had mental problems.

Twice a week, I dreaded walking into that class. It didn't help that the professor cracked jokes about God and belittled Christianity. One day, she was in the middle of a lecture and misspoke, "If God is impotent ... Oh, that's funny. Freudian slip. What I meant to say is, if God is omniscient—" Blah blah blah.

During all of that, Zipper Guy was pulling the zipper up and down on his jacket. Sometimes fast, sometimes slow. I wasn't sure how everyone else was able to concentrate. I myself was on the verge of doing a Linda Blair head spin like in *The Exorcist*. I couldn't wait to be done with that class, but I had two months to go!

My friends and sister sent cards and letters from home which sometimes lifted my spirits, especially the ones from Lyla. She must have had a supply of obscure greeting cards she was trying to use up. One of the cards she sent said, "Happy Retirement", which got a good laugh out of me. Nowhere in her letters did she ever explain her use of random cards for inaccurate occasions. It kept me guessing what she'd send next.

I tried to write back to everyone, but because my moodiness continued—and worsened—my replies became more sporadic and superficial. I was embarrassed that I wasn't "living the dream" at college, and I didn't want my friends and family to know.

Letters from Kate about how well she and Josh were doing at Aberdeen University depressed me. She was loving her photography classes, and he was living it up in an expensive campus apartment, "kicking butt" in his business classes. My jealousy made me feel yucky.

Maybe I should have gone to AU after all. I hadn't wanted to because it would have meant living at home. At least I'd have been around people with whom I didn't have to pretend to be somebody else. But then I wouldn't have been at the same place as Cameron.

Would I have been able to deal with that? Why was I even wondering such a thing? I loved him, and I loved being at the same school as him, but honestly, I was feeling disconnected from him. I knew the problem was me. I was acting and thinking differently.

I'd discovered that he was an avid major league football fan. Our time together began to revolve around the games. One Saturday afternoon, he came to my room to hang out with me. Immediately upon walking in, he turned my TV on to a game. I sat on my bed trying to read, growing increasingly irritable from the noise of the fans cheering, the heavily padded jocks smashing into each other, the refs whistling, and the voices of the announcers.

"Could you turn it down, please?" I asked.

"Yeah, sorry," he said and turned it down some. "This is going to be a good game. You should watch it with me."

I made an excuse of needing to study and tried to tune him and the TV out. He'd tried to teach me the game in hopes that if I understood it, I'd become interested, but I couldn't get into it. That disappointed him more than it seemed like it should. He developed a habit of making passive-aggressive comments that led to me feeling guilty for not wanting to share that interest with him. The more he made those comments, the more I resisted. It was a frustrating struggle that was just one of the reasons there began to be tension between us.

If he wasn't watching football, he was off doing other things that didn't involve me. He'd passed me up socially, and I couldn't do anything about it. I realized too late that I'd missed the window of opportunity for getting involved in clubs and organizations. Everyone else was well established in their social groups. I was on the outside of it all, looking in.

Why was I feeling so insecure? What was wrong with me? I'd reverted to the way I'd been during my senior year of high school, feeling like I wasn't good at anything. I'd been so confident and sure of myself just two months before. What had happened? Had I only fooled myself into thinking I could play this college game? I worried there was something wrong with me.

Clinical depression sometimes shows up for the first time when kids go off to college. At least that's what my psychology professor had said. Was that happening to me? Why couldn't I adjust to being away from home and embrace and enjoy the freedom I had wanted so badly? College was supposed to be about growing up, personal enrichment, enlightenment, and all that great stuff. Where was all that, and why wasn't it happening for me?

CH. 10 ~ FAMILY WEEKEND

My parents called to tell me they were coming for family weekend which had snuck up on me. Honestly, I'd been hoping they wouldn't find out about it, but they got an invitation in the mail directly from the university. Thanks a lot for that, NHU administration.

Cameron's dad also came to campus, arriving in time for the football game. They invited me, but I declined, saying I should stay at Bellamy so my parents would know where to find me.

I straightened up my room. *My* side didn't need much cleaning, but Ann's was a disaster. I sprayed air freshener all over her clothes, which hadn't been washed in weeks, and then shoved them into her closet and under her bed. I had no idea if her parents were coming. I hoped not because she wasn't anywhere around, and I'd get stuck talking to them if they did show up.

My phone rang, and it was Emma. "Olivia! We're here. Can you come to the desk and let us in?" An excitement came over me that I hadn't expected, making me race out the door and down the hall.

"Emma!" I exclaimed and ran to hug her. Then I hugged my mom and asked, "Where's Dad?"

"He's driving around, trying to find a parking place," my

mom said, sounding on edge. To my embarrassment, she'd chosen to slum it that day and was wearing one of her sweat suits that fit way too tightly. At least it wasn't the pinkish-beige one that made me think of a lump of Silly Putty.

"Can I see your dorm room?" Emma asked, bouncing up and down on the balls of her feet.

"Yeah. Should we wait for Dad?"

"You two go on," my mom said. "I'll wait here for him."

"Okay. I'll ask the guy at the security desk to let you through. I'm in room 107."

As we walked away, I asked Emma, "Is she okay?"

"I don't know. Dad's in a mood, though."

"About what?"

She shrugged and replied, "I don't know. I've had my headphones on the whole way here."

"Well, it's so good to see you! I've missed you."

"I've missed you, too."

We went into my room, and she was fascinated with it. She commented on different things, especially how it was so much smaller than she'd expected.

"What's your roommate like? Your first letter said she was cool, but you haven't said much else."

"She was sort of cool at first, but she's kind of ... gone to the dark side."

"What does that mean? Is she a devil worshipper or something?"

"What? No! I just mean she's different than she was at first."

We both fell on the bed laughing. There wasn't even anything that funny, but we were giddy with the excitement of seeing each other. There was a knock on the door, and I let my parents in. My dad gave me a sideways hug, looking irritable but keeping it in check.

"So this is it, huh?" he asked and looked around, uncomfortable and disinterested in being there. He was a tall man, about six foot, two inches. Somehow the room became even smaller with him in it.

"Yep," I replied. "Thanks for coming."

"Sure. How's your car doing?"

"Okay. I haven't driven it much since I've been here."

"It's not good for it to sit too long. Try to drive it around every couple of days."

"Okay."

My mom was looking around and began studying the photo collage that Kate had made for me. *Uh, oh.* That picture of me and Cameron sitting on a *bed* in a *hotel* room on graduation night would be hard for her to miss and even harder for me to explain.

I caused a distraction by asking if they minded meeting up with Cameron and his dad to go eat later. Cameron's dad had suggested it, and since our parents had never met, it seemed like a good time and place.

"That's a good idea," my mom said, thankfully turning away from the picture. "So, his parents are here today?"

"Well, his dad is. I'm not sure about his mom." Even though she lived in the same town, I doubted she'd put in an appearance since Mr. McClain was there.

"Can you show us around campus some?" Emma asked, trying to contain her eagerness.

"Great idea!" I exclaimed in relief and ushered them all out of my room.

I gave them a campus tour, and we ended up at the Haven. Emma was captivated by the whole place. I could tell the wheels were turning in her mind about going to college someday.

"When are we meeting up with Cameron and his dad?" my mom asked.

"Oh, yeah! The game is probably over by now, so we could head that way. It's a great barbeque place. I hope it's not too crowded."

We walked back to Bellamy Hall, loaded into my dad's car, and promptly got stuck in traffic from the football game getting out. I gave my dad directions while trying to carry on a conversation with Emma.

"You had Mrs. Crane for freshman English, right?" she asked me.

"Yeah."

"That's who I have. She remembered you and asked if I was your sister. She says 'um' all the time! I counted one class period, and she did it almost a hundred times."

"I remember that. And *um*, it drove me crazy."

"Oh, I almost forgot," she said and started digging around in her purse. "Lyla asked me to give you this card."

"This ought to be funny. She sends me the strangest cards." I opened it and tried not to laugh too loud at the "Congratulations, Eagle Scout" on the front of it.

"I don't get it," Emma said in confusion, but she laughed with me.

"I don't either!"

I heard my dad clear his throat and sigh. The negative vibes coming off him were strong as we sat in long lines of traffic at every light. I tried not to let it bother me, but I'd always been affected by his moods. About a block away from the restaurant, I suggested he let Emma and me get out to walk the rest of the way.

"We can go see if Cameron and his dad are there yet, and if not, we'll get our name on the list for a table," I said.

"Fine. Go ahead, but where am I supposed to park? This place is a madhouse," he complained. I pointed up the street at the restaurant's designated parking. My mom started to open her door, making him ask, "Where are you going, Sheila?"

She quickly replied, "I'm getting out now, too." I didn't blame her for making an escape.

We entered the restaurant and didn't see Cameron yet, so I gave my name to the hostess. About five minutes later, Cameron walked in, and relief washed over me.

"Wow," he said, grinning at me because I'd hugged him like he'd saved my life. Mr. McClain gave me a fatherly hug, and I introduced him to my mom and Emma.

The hostess called my name and showed us to a table at about the same time that I saw my dad walk in the door. His posture and mannerisms spoke volumes about his mood. I hoped and prayed he wouldn't humiliate me. Eating at a restaurant with him could be problematic under normal circumstances. Add traffic frustrations and sitting at a table with Mr. McClain, whom he'd never met, and it could be disastrous.

There was small talk around the table, and things were going as smooth as I could hope for. That is, until Mr. McClain said, "Olivia, you missed a good game." I cringed, wishing I could have censored any football talk. My dad hated all sports, but especially football.

"Oh, yeah. Did we win?" I asked.

"Yes, but it was close," Cameron said.

"I just don't understand why anyone, much less hundreds of people en masse, would want to waste their time sitting and watching a football game," my dad growled. My mom narrowed her eyes at him.

"You're not a fan?" Mr. McClain asked from across the table.

"Not in the least. I'd rather dig a ditch than go to a football game," my dad said with emphasis.

I didn't see Mr. McClain's or Cameron's reaction to my dad's comment because I couldn't look up from the plate in front of me. I was paralyzed and wanted to disappear. Or better yet, make my dad disappear.

Did he even care that he was insulting something that was meaningful to other people at the table? No, of course not. You see, that was one of the problems with my dad. If he didn't find it important, he didn't think anyone else should either.

"That's interesting," Mr. McClain commented, and in a friendly and curious tone asked, "What type of ditch would you dig? Would it be for anything in particular?"

Emma was taking a drink and almost blew it out of her nose. She tried to recover without laughing. I couldn't help smiling and looked at Mr. McClain with admiration.

My dad didn't answer the question, and he was mostly quiet the rest of the meal. That was fine with me. I hoped he didn't think Mr. McClain was a smartass, but then I didn't much care at that point. In my mind, I was applauding Cameron's dad for his brilliant and quick comeback.

As our families drove away, Cameron looked at me the way someone would look at a sad child. "That bad, huh?" he asked and hugged me. He rubbed my back, and I exhaled a sigh of relief under his comforting touch.

"Yeah. Let's go do something. Let's go running." I needed to move, to burn off the pent-up nervousness.

"Really? Okay," he said, but I was already running, pulling him along by the arm. We ran a couple of laps at a nearby intramural track. For once, I outran him. Not by much, but I gloated.

"Oh, this is killing me, Olivia. We just ate an hour ago."

"Whatever. You know I beat you, and it has nothing to do with barbeque," I said in a sing-song voice, doing a victory dance. He tackled me to the ground while we were still catching our breath.

"I'm sorry your dad is such a difficult person," he said.

"Difficult person? You're too kind."

"You know what my dad said to me before he left?"

"That he never wants to see Dr. Miller again?"

"No. He said, 'Olivia's dad sure is opinionated, but you know what they say about opinions? They're like buttholes. Everybody's got one, some peoples' just stink worse than others.' And he said it with such a straight face!"

I laughed so hard I could barely breathe. Every time I tried to stop and sit up, I couldn't do it. Cameron was laughing too, but he was laughing at me!

"It's so good to see you laugh," he said.

He began kissing me, and when he gathered me into his arms, I couldn't stop the hot tears that came on instantly. He kept kissing me. I sensed a desperation and passion coming from him that I wasn't sure what to do with. I reached up to wipe my face, but he stopped my hand and brushed the tears away with his own fingers.

"I seem to make you cry a lot these days," he said, the sadness in his voice tearing at my heart.

I shook my head. "It's not you. It's a lot of things, but it's not you."

"Talk to me, please. I'm here for you, Olivia. I love you."

I collapsed against him and cried some more. *I bet he's getting tired of this. Why am I such a walking disaster?*

He held me against his chest, and I remained silent, unable to articulate my feelings into words. "Okay, if you won't talk, then I will. You haven't been yourself the last few weeks. I don't know what you're having such a hard time with or how I can help you. Have I done something to upset you?"

I pressed my hand over his heart and straightened myself up. "Don't, please. I can't deal with you thinking any of this is your fault. It's not you. It's me."

"What is it? Why are you unhappy?"

"I don't know."

"Okay, let's try something. Think of three words that describe what you're feeling. You don't have to give details. Just give me three things."

I thought for a moment and said, "Lost." He was quiet and waited. "Disappointed ... Angry." Once I got started, I had more than three things. "Confused ... Stupid ... Lonely." With that last one, I saw his face fall. I'd wounded him and hadn't meant to.

"Lonely?"

"Yes, but not because of you. I miss my friends. I miss Mrs. K. I miss ... familiar things and people. I think I expected that making friends here would be fun and easy, but it hasn't been. I don't even want to try most of the time. I think I did with Ann at first, but you see how that turned out."

"I wish I could make it all better for you."

"But you can't be responsible for my happiness."

"True, but it would still be nice if I could help."

"Thank you. You're too good for me."

"Don't say stuff like that, please. You know what, I'm thinking of one more thing to add to your list. Scared. You seem scared."

I nodded and thought about it. "Yeah, I am scared. I'm scared of feeling ... unimportant and useless. I'm scared of having no direction. What if I can't hack this college thing and stop trying and give up, and then have to go back to my parents' depressing house and face their eternal disappointment?"

"You're doing fine in your classes though, aren't you? I thought you were anyway."

"I guess, except for algebra. But it's not just classes and grades. What if I still can't figure out what I want to do with my life?"

His hands went up in a time-out gesture. "Let's not go down the 'major question' road. *Or* the 'what if' road, for that matter. Instead, tell me three other things, but this time, they have to be positive things. Things that make you happy. What makes you feel content or peaceful ... and safe?"

"When I'm doing something that I know how to do and can do it well. But it's been a long time since I've felt that way about anything."

"Okay, hold the details. What else makes you happy?"

I knew what he was doing. He didn't want me to get bogged down and start complaining or snowballing. "Okay. *You.* You help me feel content and peaceful and safe." I thought hard for a third, but nothing came to mind.

"And? One more."

"I don't know. A big bathtub full of hot water that I can soak in for hours with a good book by candlelight," I laughed, embarrassed that it was the best I could come up with.

"I wish I could make that happen for you, but I don't

know of any bathtubs around here. Oh, I know! How about I ask my mom if you can go to her house and use her bathtub?" We laughed at the idea, but it sounded wonderful to me.

"Your turn," I said. "What makes you unhappy?"

Without skipping a beat, he said, "You being unhappy. And me not being able to do anything about it. And losing you."

Oh, no! My stupid problems were making him worry about losing me. Why couldn't I snap out of this?

I cleared my throat and asked, "And what makes you happy? And don't say me."

"Well, okay, if I can't say that, then, I guess ... playing guitar, and learning about computers and programming. And seeing you laugh."

"I said you couldn't use *me* for one of them."

"Too bad. I made up the game. My rules."

He got to his feet and reached for my hand, helping me up. I hadn't run in weeks, and I could already tell that I was going to be sorry for pushing myself so hard and not stretching afterward. That bathtub idea was sounding better than ever.

Walking back to Bellamy Hall, I told him about a recurring nightmare I'd been having. "In the dream, I'm lost on campus, trying desperately to find my locker." That got a laugh since we didn't even have lockers.

"Maybe it's a high school throwback," he suggested.

"Yeah, but it's literally a nightmare. I rush from place to place, from building to building, getting more lost every minute. I feel like I'm in a fog or a daze or something."

"I'm sorry. Are you still feeling that lost on campus?"

"No, not really, so I don't know why I keep having the dream. The thing is, I have that foggy, dazed feeling even when I'm awake sometimes," I admitted. "And don't blame it on drinking. I've hardly drank at all since that night you had to come pick me up."

"That's good. Do you think you should go to the doctor?

I mean, maybe you've got sinus congestion or pressure or something. Maybe that would also explain the headaches you've been getting."

"Maybe."

Deciding I'd dumped enough on him for one day, I didn't mention the mini panic attacks I'd been having.

CH. 11 ~ GIVE ME A BREAK

I got good at staying busy and keeping myself distracted but doing so made me tired and cranky. I pushed myself hard in my classes, out of fear that if I didn't stay ahead, even the slightest hiccup would set me back. However, it was unsatisfying, unproductive busy work that didn't make me more prepared for class or result in better grades. I was spinning my wheels.

Spending time with Cameron became more of a strain. Besides him getting annoyed by things I was doing—like smacking my gum and micromanaging everything—there was stuff about him that was bugging me, too. I got in the habit of correcting him about stupid, inconsequential details. That made me feel like crap since it meant I was turning into my dad. Cameron started being snarky back. It was unlike us to talk to each other the way we'd started to.

Everything went downhill one day when we were on our way to dinner. He'd been in a good mood and was making playful, teasing comments about my bad mood. It got on my nerves, and I lost my sense of humor. Not that I had much of one to begin with.

I'd had the kind of day where I should have stayed in bed because I was unsuitable for human interaction. If I'd stayed in bed and called the whole day off, then maybe, just maybe, I could have avoided the path of destruction I was headed down. But no, there I was, sitting in Cameron's truck, about to change the course of our relationship.

"Okay, I'm asking you, for the *third* time, Olivia, where do you want to go eat?" he asked, his tone revealing his impatience.

"And for the *third* time, *Cameron,* I don't know," I said, unable to hide my own annoyance. "Would you please decide so we can go and be done with it?"

He took a deep breath, let it out slowly, and said, "I'm going to ignore that you just made it sound like going to eat with me is a chore you need to cross off your To Do list."

"Oh, please. You know that's not what I meant."

"But I'm always the one who decides what we're going to do and where we're going to go. Sometimes I want *you* to pick. What is the deal with your chronic indecisiveness?" His voice was laced with anger.

"Excuse me?" I demanded.

"Why is it so hard for you to make up your mind about something so simple?"

"Oh, I don't know, Cameron!" I shot back at him. "How about because I've never learned to think for myself very well, and when I do make decisions, I usually do it wrong and get criticized for it?" Boy, did that come out of left field. I couldn't believe how stupid that was!

"Really? You're gonna do that right now? I thought you'd left that crap behind. Your dad isn't here, Olivia. This is just you and me," he said and then muttered, "Unless you don't want it to be."

"What?!" That was as stupid as the stuff I'd said. Suddenly, I wanted—no I *needed*—to get away from him. I crossed my arms over my chest, fixed my eyes straight ahead, and said through gritted teeth, "Just take me back to the dorm ... *please.*"

"As you wish," he growled and made an illegal U-turn.

Riding back to campus in silence, I was shaky with

anger, and my heart ached. This was so stupid! Why was I acting like this? I needed to get away from him before I made things worse.

I prepared to make a run for it from the parking lot, but he grabbed my hand and said, "Wait. Please." I waited for him to come around and open the door for me. We walked together into the building, and he asked me to come to his room with him. His tone was softer, so I cooperated and went with him. Thankfully, Gary wasn't there. I sat down on the edge of his bed, and he sat down next to me.

"I'm sorry. I shouldn't have said those things," he said with real sincerity.

His apology relieved some of my anger. I got to my feet and stood in front of him. Resting my hand on his shoulder, I said, "It's okay. I'm sorry, too."

I looked into those expressive, chocolate-colored eyes of his and saw his forgiveness. Cradling his face in my hands, I brought my lips down to his. He responded by putting his arms around me and pulling me down onto the bed with him.

My emotions were all over the place. Now that I didn't want to get away from him so badly, I desperately wanted to get *closer* to him. Passion was unleashed inside of me, and I was all over him. Kissing him frantically, I needed something to help me feel better and wanted so badly for it to be him. He kissed me back with the same intensity, sucking my bottom lip into his mouth until it almost hurt and running his hands along the sides of my breasts.

On my knees, straddling his waist, I laid down on top of him. The shirt I was wearing had a low neckline, and I loved the look on his face as he got that visual. He groaned and kissed the exposed flesh at the top of my breasts.

I lifted up some, hoping he would touch me, but he flipped me over to where he was on top. I whimpered, thinking he was about to put a stop to this, but he didn't. Lowering himself onto me, with his eyes closed, he indulgently rocked his hips against mine. We were both lost in the moment, and I thought, *screw the lines. I'm ready to cross all of them. I'll beg him if he resists.*

He pushed his hand up the front of my shirt. It wasn't slow and sensuous though, the way I'd always fantasized about; it was rushed and insistent. His hand touched my breasts, caressing me over my bra.

I was breathless from his weight on top of me and the urgent, almost rough way he was kissing me, like he was trying to devour me. His fingers slipped inside my bra, making me snap to attention.

"Wait," I pleaded. It was all happening too fast. My head was spinning. I didn't *want* to stop, but we needed to slow down.

He jumped up as if I'd caught fire or something. Standing next to the bed, he ran his fingers through his hair, breathing hard, in and out through his nose.

"I can't keep doing this, Olivia," he said angrily. "You're pushing too much."

"*I* am?!" I asked in indignation. I sat up and pulled my shirt down, feeling a burning shame like never before.

What the hell did he mean? Was he saying I was taking advantage of him? No way!

"Um, I'm pretty sure *I* didn't just put your hand up my shirt. That was all you," I said, my tone dripping in sarcasm that I'd been awful quick in resorting to.

"Yeah, but ... but you got on top of me first."

He was right, but I hadn't *made* him respond the way he did. I replayed how things had gone from innocent kissing to—to I don't know what that was—in mere minutes, and my embarrassment deepened. I'd been using him to help me feel better about myself. Instead I felt worse. Way worse.

"You're right," I conceded. "I'm sorry ... again. I'm sorry for being ... so sorry all the time. I hate myself. I feel so—"

"Oh, Olivia, don't do this right now," he muttered. I looked up and saw on his face how sick and tired he was of me. "Stop complaining about how miserable you are. You don't need to keep telling me about it. Trust me, *I know already!*"

"Well, excuse the hell out of me! I'm so sorry I'm cramping your style." I shot up from the bed and positioned myself closer to the door.

"Would you stop? I don't need your apologies. I need ... I need you to be *you!* My God, I'm not *trying* to be mean, but ... I don't know who you are anymore. I feel like I'm losing you, and ... I think it's because you're losing yourself. You—"

"What is that supposed to mean?"

"You're *so* unhappy, and I'm at the end of my rope trying to help you when all you want to do is feel sorry for yourself."

I couldn't take it anymore and turned to leave, but he reached out to stop me. "*Don't* run away from me ... please."

I looked at him and, in as controlled a voice as I could, said, "I don't know what else to do. You don't want to hear about my problems anymore, so I should go."

"Maybe," he sighed, "... maybe so. Maybe you need a break. Maybe *I* need a break. Maybe we both do, so you can figure out who you are or whatever will make you happy."

My heart stopped. I may have appeared to be all in one piece on the outside, but inside, I was shattered. I broke into a cold sweat and was afraid I was going to throw up.

"Are you serious?" I asked with a shaky voice. What could I say or do that would end this horrific conversation? What could I possibly do to ever get my mind past what he'd just suggested?

He didn't answer but nodded his head, ever so slightly, and I saw tears gathering in his eyes.

"Okay, Cameron," I said, managing to keep my voice even, "if that's what you think will help me." How ridiculous. How was that going to help me?

"I don't know what will help you, but you won't let me, so you have to figure something out. Call Mrs. K. Or Lyla. Or Kate. Somebody. Try to sort out what's making you so miserable," he pleaded.

What came out of my mouth next was evidence of my oncoming mental breakdown. "Is this about that girl in your computer science club?" I was grasping at straws. Was he pushing me away because he wanted to see other people?

"Who?"

"You know who. That girl you're always talking about. What's her name? Emily?" Now that I thought about it, he had been talking about Emily quite a lot. Maybe I was onto something.

"Emily? What are you talking about? That was a giant leap, Olivia! Why did you even say that?"

I glared at him, my mind scrambling for a way to backpedal out of the new can of worms I'd opened.

He got a knowing look on his face and conjectured, "Unless that's what *you're* doing. Is that what *you* want? Maybe you want to go see if that guy Michael can help you figure out what you want. He helps you with your algebra, so maybe he can help you figure out what's wrong with you."

Suddenly, I snapped inside. I couldn't see anything but my own pain and rage.

"Yeah. Thanks, Cameron. That's the best idea you've had all night. Maybe I'll just do that!" I exclaimed and stomped out. He didn't try to stop me this time.

I took off in a blind run all the way out of the building; down the hall, the stairs, through the lobby, outside, and down the street. I ran so hard I thought I was going to have a heart attack. I was running scared. The last time I'd run that hard was the night my dad and I had fought when I was sixteen. The fear and hopelessness were similar.

I got lost. No surprise there. I kept running. People looked at me with mild concern but mostly ignored me. Finally, reason began setting in. I slowed down, stopped in a grassy area, and threw up. Thank God nobody was around to see that happen. My stomach was empty, but I dry heaved until I wanted to die.

I had to figure out where I was. There was a church up ahead, and some people were standing outside of it talking. I looked like something out of a horror movie and would have hated for them to see me. But for a moment, I considered that I might actually need medical attention. Would student health services treat me for stupidity and a broken heart?

I made myself focus on the church and remembered which one it was, calculating that I must have run for over a mile. Struggling to process what had happened between me and Cameron, I painstakingly made my way home. Home. What did that word even mean to me?

I'd made a terrible mistake. No, I'd made *several* terrible mistakes.

CH. 12 ~ WHO WANTS PIE?

Like the total loser that I believed myself to be, I went around sulking for the next few days. I was plagued by headaches and considered going to a doctor. I even had an almost morbid wish that there *was* something wrong with me so I would have a plausible excuse for the way I'd been acting. I imagined walking into a doctor's office and asking for any and all tests to be run to determine what was making me into a monster.

Purposefully taking different routes around campus helped me avoid running into Cameron. He didn't call me, and I didn't call him. I listened to a lot of sad music and didn't do much besides study and sleep.

One day, Ann told me, "I've seen your boyfriend walking with some other girl a couple of times." Her comment was met with dead silence by me, and she asked, "What's going on with you two?"

"Heck if I know," was all I said, but I was dying to ask what the girl looked like and if they'd been holding hands or anything.

"Well, if I were you, I'd be taking issue with the cute blonde. They looked pretty friendly with each other."

Yep, that sounded like Emily from Comp Sci club. Maybe my wild suspicion was proving to be correct. Or maybe my suggestion to Cameron that he might be interested in her actually set it in motion. *Good job, Olivia.* Nothing like shooting yourself in the foot.

"Whatever," I said to Ann, hoping she'd leave me alone about it.

She shrugged and said, "Here, this was in my mailbox," and tossed a card to me.

It was a "Happy Easter" card from Lyla. In October. I was such a mess I couldn't even laugh about it.

* * * * * *

Elaine invited me again to join her and her friends at the rec center.

"Thank you, but this is where—if I could think of one—I'd give you some lame excuse for why I can't go."

"Fine. But if you change your mind, we'll be there tomorrow around four o'clock." Then, she quietly added, "You need to get out and do something. You'll never convince me that hiding out in your room feeling sorry for yourself is doing you any good."

That afternoon, there was a group of people hanging out in the Bellamy lounge. It was mostly girls, and they were having a lot of fun. In the middle of their cluster was none other than Cameron, playing his guitar.

He looked really good and was being so charming, flashing his gorgeous smile. *But I don't get to enjoy that anymore.* I'd lost any claim I ever had to that. My heart sank, and I quickly got out of sight. I didn't want him or anyone else to see me cry.

In desperation to distract myself, I called Elaine and told her I'd be at the rec center the next day. She was glad I'd changed my mind. It was time I became more social. She was right. There was no use sitting around feeling sorry for myself. If Cameron was moving on, then so should I.

Before meeting up with Elaine and her friends at the rec center the next day, I left a note for Cameron at the security desk in the guys' wing. It said, "It sure looks and sounds like you've moved on, so I guess I will too. Enjoy your freedom from me. It's well deserved, and you've earned it. I hope you find someone who makes you happy."

I knew it was snarky and regretted it later, but I thought *something* needed to be said.

* * * * * *

I heard lots of noise, laughter, and cheering coming from one of the courts on the lower level. Looking down from the balcony, I saw Elaine, Tom, and Jared. There was another guy and girl with them who I'd never seen before.

Elaine and the girl were wearing long, baggy basketball shorts and tank tops. They also had on baseball caps that were turned backward. Hearing me laugh at them, Elaine looked up and announced to the others that I had arrived.

"Come on down, Olivia!" Jared called to me.

"Okay, give me a minute," I replied and made my way down the stairs and onto the court. I was nervous and self-conscious but was proud of myself for trying.

The guy I didn't know was big, tall, and muscular, and said, "Hi, I'm Doug."

I introduced myself, and the other girl said, "And I'm Lisa. I'm so glad you decided to come. Now we have six, so we can play three on three."

"Okay," I said, "but fair warning, I'm no good at this. You know those kids in PE class who found any excuse to sit out?" Nods all around. "Well, *I* was one of those kids."

Elaine said, "Me too!" and we went to high-five each other but missed, getting a laugh out of the rest of them.

"That's okay, Olivia," Doug reassured me. "Let's do some drills to get you warmed up, and then we'll pick teams."

"Drills, huh?" Elaine smirked. "You're such a jock, Doug." That comment got a ball bounced her way which she deflected by turning and letting it hit her shoulder.

Jared caught the ball on the rebound and teased, "You're supposed to catch it, Elaine!"

Doug's drills consisted of dribbling, passing, and shooting. All of which required skills I didn't have, but I did the best I could.

Lisa announced, "Okay, no hard feelings, but I suggest that Olivia be on one team and Elaine be on the other."

"Good idea. That way neither team is overloaded with too much *talent*," Elaine said.

"Yeah, go ahead and tell yourself that," Lisa said and laughed. Watching them interact was comical. Lisa's fun-loving, easygoing personality was the opposite of Elaine's serious, sarcastic nature.

"Okay," Elaine said. "and I suggest Lisa and Doug be on a team together. His height is an advantage, but hers is a *dis*advantage."

"Hey, yeah, they'll cancel each other out for the same team," Jared agreed.

They had a good point. For as big and tall as Doug was, Lisa was a tiny waif of a girl. If she turned sideways, you could hardly see her. Just kidding, of course, but she was really thin. And short! She couldn't have been much over four feet. She herself had cracked a joke about having to shop in the children's department for the "gangsta" basketball shorts she was wearing.

"Sounds good, and we'll take Olivia on our team," Doug chimed in. So, it was us against Tom, Jared, and Elaine. Our time on the court could have been a blooper reel of tryout rejects for the Harlem Globetrotters.

Elaine hadn't been kidding about her inability to play basketball, so I didn't feel too bad about my own blundering attempts. I was surprised at how much I enjoyed horsing around with all of them. With more laughing going on than anything else, the guys razzed us for being so bad.

My heart was still broken in pieces, and more than half of myself was missing, but for a few hours, I was able to pretend that I was okay.

* * * * * *

In Freshman Seminar the next Monday, Elaine informed me, "That guy Doug asked more about you after you left. Uh, Are you okay? You just turned green."

I dropped my head into my hands, feeling queasy.

"Too soon?" she asked apologetically.

"Um, yeah. No. I don't know. It wasn't too soon for Cameron to start thinking about other girls," I said with a hint of bitterness.

"Well, I didn't tell Doug about you being on the outs with your boyfriend or anything."

"Thanks." I managed a weak smile.

"But that same group of us are going to a movie Wednesday night, if you want to join us."

"I'll think about it," I replied, noncommittally.

* * * * * *

Meanwhile, each time I saw Michael in algebra class, I found myself looking at him in a different way. I became friendlier to him, and he reciprocated. We met in the library a couple of times to work on assignments together, but if there was any flirting going on, I was too dense to pick up on it. He'd even started sitting next to me in class instead of behind me. The first time he did it, I must have looked surprised.

He leaned closer to me and quietly said, "That girl who sits behind me—she opens and closes her Trapper Keeper about fifty times during every class period. I can't stand it anymore."

He tried to mimic the sound of Velcro being released, and his eyes lit up at the sound of my laugh. In a playful shove to my shoulder, he let his hand linger.

Trying to ignore what that could possibly mean, I pulled the zipper up and down on my jacket and told him about Zipper Guy from psych class. "He sits there doing this all class period. Drives me crazy."

Dr. Bow Tie arrived, and class began. It was a good thing too, because I needed a distraction. The thrill I got from Michael being so close—and leaning in to whisper near my ear—was confusing the heck out of me.

* * * * * *

I was planning to use the excuse of homework to avoid

the movie with Elaine and company. It was a poor excuse though because, after studying so obsessively for a couple of weeks, I was caught up on everything and had even gotten ahead in most of my classes.

I knew I should get out and go with them. What was I so afraid of? There were finally some genuine people I could become better friends with. So, shouldn't I take them up on their offer? But what if that guy Doug showed interest in me? What would I do?

Elaine called and said, "I'll be leaving in five minutes if you want a ride." She dragged out the last word to tempt me. "Come on. You know you want to. When was the last time you went to a movie?"

"Um, I don't even remember. What are you going to see?"

"*Shattered.* It's a suspense, or thriller, or whatever."

"Okay," I relented. "I'll meet you in the lobby."

"Awesome!"

The gang was all waiting for me in the lounge at the front of Bellamy. It was Elaine, Lisa, Jared, Tom, and Doug. On the way to the parking lot, I walked right past Cameron. We each turned around and made eye contact for about five seconds before he returned his attention to the girl he was walking with. At least they weren't holding hands. The girl was a brunette, so she wasn't Emily. *How many girls is he hanging out with these days?*

"What was that about?" Elaine asked me discreetly. Having never met Cameron, she didn't know that was him. I told her and she said, "Ohhh. Awkward, huh?"

"Yep."

I rode in her car with her and Lisa, and the guys rode in Doug's car. We all bought our own tickets and concessions. It was a casual group of friends hanging out at the movies. There wasn't any obvious flirting, and there were no signs of anyone coupling up. I breathed a sigh of relief and enjoyed the company.

Elaine was sitting on my right, and Doug took the seat

to my left, saying, "I want someone sitting between me and Elaine to protect my popcorn. She's an addict."

"Hey, I have my own," she said, holding up the large tub.

"Yeah, but when you're done mainlining it, you'll be reaching for everyone else's," he teased.

"Well, how do you know *I* won't try to steal your popcorn?" I asked him.

"I'll take my chances. I don't mind sharing, if you want some, but I don't have enough for that fiend over there."

He was a decent guy, personality wise. He'd played basketball in high school and would try out at NHU in the spring. I joked about him slumming it with the rest of us on the court in the rec center.

"I look at it as an opportunity to coach those less skilled," he said with a comical air of humility. Elaine heard him and leaned across me to slap him on the leg.

I couldn't get over how tall and muscle-bound he was. I'd never been interested in guys like him. Maybe because of the stereotypical meathead jocks I'd known in high school. But I wasn't in high school anymore, and I was judging this guy without knowing him. That wasn't fair, was it?

The movie was good and kept my interest. So well, in fact, that I didn't initially notice Doug's arm touching mine on the armrest between our seats. I was struck with indecision. Was he doing it on purpose to gauge my interest? Would he think I was interested if I didn't move away? If I *did* move away, would that send a definite message that I wasn't interested?

It turned out I didn't have to decide because he leaned away from me, whispering something to Tom who was on his other side. But then a few minutes later, we reached into the popcorn bucket at the same time, and our hands touched.

He intertwined a couple of his fingers with mine, making my heart skip a beat. But it was no comparison to the first time Cameron had held my hand. That had been electrifying and had taken my breath away. Doug's hand just felt like ... someone else's hand. Someone that didn't really matter to me. I didn't pull away though and tried not to feel guilty or weird.

When Cameron and I were at our best in our relationship, I never would have imagined that I'd be in such a situation with a different guy again. That was ridiculous though, because what did I think? Like, we'd get married or something? We were still teenagers!

Doug and I ended up holding hands *outside* of the popcorn bucket, too. I willed myself to be comfortable with it, but it still felt like something I was just going along with. After the movie, Elaine insisted we go to an all-night diner called Jack's because they had the best pie in all New Haven.

Doug acted like he wanted me to ride in his car with him, but I got in Elaine's instead. She asked, "Sooo, did I see some hand holding going on?"

"Yeah, sort of, I guess," I stammered. Lisa had gone in Doug's car, so it was just the two of us. "I don't know what I'm doing," I said miserably.

"Do any of us ever know what we're doing?"

"I don't know that, either."

At the diner, the six of us crammed into a booth like sardines. It was such a greasy spoon type of place, that I wondered how they could have anything remarkable. But Elaine was right, the pie was great. I was so glad Cameron had gotten me to try cream cheese, or I might have never given Jack's lemon cream cheese pie a shot.

They were all drinking coffee and talked me into trying some. Lisa said the only way she could drink it was with milk and honey and fixed a cup for me which was surprisingly good. It brought back memories of visiting my grandparents as kid. My grandfather used to give me a little bit of coffee with a whole lot of milk and sugar.

We had a good time joking around and cutting up. At

times I felt a bit like an outsider because they'd all been hanging out together since school started. They didn't exclude me though, and I was even asked questions about myself; something I hadn't been used to. On our way out, Doug walked alongside me and took my hand for a moment as we said goodbye. But that was it, and I was grateful.

I laid in bed that night trying to sort things out in my mind and fell asleep without making much progress. Sometime in the night, I awakened in a sweat and was crying from a sad dream. I couldn't remember any details other than I was lost, scared, and lonely. And I somehow sensed, deep down, that I'd probably ruined things with Cameron forever.

CH. 13 ~ FOILED

I stopped avoiding places where I'd run into Cameron. Therefore, I started seeing him more often. Sometimes he was alone, or with Gary or Scott.

Sometimes he was with Emily.

Sometimes he was with another girl I still knew nothing about.

Sometimes I wanted to run up to him and ask him if we could stop this nonsense, but the sadness and pity I saw in his eyes kept me from speaking to him. I didn't get the impression that he even missed me.

I got pulled into a double date with Doug, Elaine, and Jared. We went miniature golfing, which was the perfect setting for Jared to clown around. Elaine acted all serious and put out by it, but I could tell it was a game they were playing with each other. She was more interested in him than she was letting on.

Doug flirted openly with me. Ignoring my conflicted feelings, I flirted some too. It was physically weird— different anyway—to be with a guy who was so much bigger than me. One time, we were goofing around, trying to mess with each other's attempts to putt on the golf course, and he picked me up as though I was light as a feather and carried me out of the way. Setting me down, he kissed me on the cheek. It gave me a rush of something between excitement and fear.

In the car on the way back to our dorm, Elaine was driving, and Jared was in the front seat with her. He leaned over, quietly said something to her, and she nodded. Doug asked, "Hey, what are y'all whispering about up there? Didn't your momma ever tell you that's impolite?"

"I've been planning a prank on my roommate, and tonight's the best night for it. Elaine's helping me. We're wondering if you guys want in on it," Jared explained.

He'd been telling us about what a pretentious snob his roommate, Preston, was, so I wasn't surprised to hear that he had a prank in mind.

"That depends. What is it?" I asked.

"Nothing illegal," Jared replied.

"I'm in," Doug said. "How about it, Olivia?"

I shrugged and agreed. "Okay, what's the plan?"

"I'll show you when we get in the room."

Elaine giggled. Quite uncharacteristic for her.

Jared lived on the third floor. The same floor as Cameron. I tried not to think about that as we all snuck into Jared's and Preston's room like spies on a mission. He pulled a bag out of a closet. It contained about a dozen rolls of aluminum foil.

"Preston thinks he's so shiny. We're gonna make his *stuff* shiny, too," he said with an evil genius laugh.

Doug asked, "How are we going to do that?"

"Duh," Elaine said with an eye roll. "We're going to wrap all his stuff in foil."

"Ohhh," I said in understanding and laughed too. "What a cool idea."

We spent the next couple of hours wrapping practically everything of Preston's in foil; his TV, remote, bed, pillow, closet door, lamp, phone, shower caddy with shampoo, shaving cream, and razor. I did the desk and all the stuff on it. Each book, pen, pencil, and highlighter got securely wrapped in foil. I was worried Preston would show up, but

Jared assured us he was out of town for the weekend.

"You can't tell anyone I was in on this, man. I don't want any retaliation pranks," Doug warned.

"Don't worry about it. Your names will remain anonymous," Jared promised.

When everything was covered to Jared's satisfaction, and we all stopped laughing about how crazy it looked, he poked his head out the door to see if the hallway was clear. He gave us the signal to follow. The cloak and dagger routine wasn't necessary, but it was fun.

Elaine and I couldn't control our laughter though and started running for the exit with Jared and Doug hot on our heels. I almost missed seeing Cameron walking toward us. Our eyes met for the briefest moment, and I had the crazy feeling I'd been caught red-handed doing something wrong.

At the elevators, the laughter died down, and Doug kissed me on the lips. It made me nervous because of who might have seen it happen. Fortunately, Elaine and Jared were the only ones around. In a moment of spontaneity, I kissed him back. But then he tried to put his tongue in my mouth, and I pulled away and told him goodnight. I wasn't ready for that. Honestly, I wasn't ready for any of what was going on, but I was letting myself get swept away by it anyway.

* * * * * *

I slept late the next morning and was awakened by the phone ringing. It was Doug. He asked me out to dinner that night, and I said yes. *What am I thinking? It'll only be the two of us!*

Was I really going on a date with someone besides Cameron? Yes. Yes, I was. And I was going to try to enjoy myself, because that's what Cameron was doing, too. Isn't it what he'd practically told me to do?

The plan was for Doug to meet me in front of Bellamy Hall, and on my way there, I saw Cameron. He was playing his guitar in the lounge and had an audience again, mostly girls. He looked and sounded great. I indulged myself by watching him from a short distance away, hoping he wouldn't see me.

All of a sudden, I was startled by Doug who picked me up and threw me over his shoulder. I screamed in surprise and involuntarily started laughing. It caused Cameron and his groupies to look my way. Doug, grinning ear to ear, put me down and gave me a peck on the cheek.

Did Cameron see that? What would he think? Why did I care? I took Doug's arm and headed out the main doors as fast as I could. In the parking lot, he kissed me on the lips and opened the car door for me.

I was glad he suggested Pizza Hut. A romantic restaurant would have made me uncomfortable, but I could deal with sharing a pizza with him. We sat in a booth, across from each other. He provided most of the conversation and told me he came from a big family. He had seven siblings! And all their names started with D.

Oh, my gosh. Why hadn't it occurred to me that I was on a date with a guy whose name started with D? What are the odds of that? I'd dated a string of guys in high school whose names started with D, and I'd sworn to never do it again.

"Seven brothers and sisters. What was that like? Did you have a huge house?" I asked to get my mind off the D thing.

"Big, but not huge. None of us had our own rooms. I had to share with an older brother, and that sucked. He was always doing stuff that got me in trouble. I was an innocent bystander," he said with a mischievous grin.

"You expect me to believe that?"

"Yeah." He reached over and took my hand that had been idly fidgeting with the parmesan cheese and red pepper shakers on the table. He traced the lines of my palm with his fingertip. My stomach flip-flopped. Maybe it was the pizza. It had to be because I didn't like the idea of any guy besides Cameron having that effect on me. I sat there looking at our hands, momentarily paralyzed.

"You want to get out of here?" he asked.

"Um, sure."

Driving back to campus, he pulled over at a park-like area with a fountain in the center. We got out and took a walk around the place, talking casually, holding hands. The temperature had dropped considerably. He took his jacket off and draped it over my shoulders. It hung on me, several sizes too large, reminding me of how much bigger he was than Cameron. But at least it was warm, and I appreciated the gesture.

When we went to his car to leave, instead of getting in, he picked me up and set me down on the trunk. What was the deal with this guy wanting to lift me off my feet all the time?

I think he had in mind that he'd stand between my legs, but I crossed my ankles and locked my knees together. Putting his hands on my knees, he leaned forward and started kissing me. The stubble on his face was coarser than I was used to. I could feel my lips and face getting scratched up by it. It didn't exactly hurt, but I didn't care for it. Cameron was always so clean-shaven.

Doug was really sure of himself. He was practically sticking his tongue down my throat, and his hands moved from my knees up my thighs. An alarm in my head got louder when he slipped one of his hands up the back of my shirt.

I shuddered as if in revulsion and tried to come up for air from his energetic kissing. By placing my hands on his chest, I was able to push him back some. He got the message. At any rate, he took his hand out of my shirt and put it back on my thigh.

"Oh, baby, come on," he said and tried to kiss my neck. I was sick to my stomach and needed him to get his hands off of me.

I made a noise of protestation. "Um, wait. Please stop." He did and looked at me questioningly as he reached down—and of all things—made an adjustment to his crotch. He did it in the blink of an eye, but there was no mistaking it.

He saw my reaction and said, "Sorry, I can't help it. You make me so hard."

I squeezed my eyes shut and pretended I was somewhere else—*anywhere* else. He caught on that I was upset and asked, "What's wrong? You're not into it?"

"No, I'm sorry. I'm kind of on the rebound right now, or something like that, I don't even know what it is. You're a great guy, but—"

"Oh, damn, I'm sorry. Was I coming on too strong? It's just been a while since I've been with a girl, and I was really hoping ..." He didn't finish whatever he was going to say because I must have looked like I was about to be sick. He backed away, and I jumped down from the trunk.

Did he think he was going to get lucky with me? Did I somehow give him that idea?

"Whoa, no, I'm sorry. That's ... um ... No," I said as nicely as I could but shook my head adamantly.

"That's cool. I get it. I'm not into making girls do anything they don't want to. You want me to take you home?"

He was disappointed, but he wasn't a jerk. Thank God. What if he had been? That was something I had *never* had to worry about before—being with a guy that might force himself on me. And Doug was big and strong enough that he could have done whatever he wanted to me.

"Yeah, I think so. That would be good." He opened the passenger side door for me and offered a dejected smile. We made awkward small talk until we got to the dorm, where he walked me into the lobby and kissed my cheek goodbye.

Dazed and uneasy, I went to my room with the realization that, if I'd been willing, Doug would have slept with me in a heartbeat. That was the first time I'd been in a situation like that. Cameron would have been appalled if he knew what had happened. Sure, we both knew that kind of casual encounter was happening all around us. But now that we were independently available for such propositions from other people, was that happening to him, too?

I wanted to trust that, since we'd had an exclusive ten-month relationship and hadn't fooled around, he wouldn't go do it with some random girl. But was Emily random to him? Had he started to have feelings for her? What about that other girl? What if he drew a different line with them than he had with me?

The pizza I'd eaten was threatening to make its way back up. I had to think about something else. Anything else!

* * * * * *

NHU's homecoming brought an influx of people to campus for the football game. I didn't go to it. I knew I was such a stick in the mud, but at least I didn't try to make other people feel stupid for liking it, the way my dad did. I might have agreed to go to the homecoming game with Cameron, if we'd still been together, and if he'd asked me. That ship had sailed. I hid out in my room most of the weekend and had it all to myself because Ann had gone MIA.

A few days later, she finally returned, acting stranger than usual; almost cagey, and like she wanted to ask me something but wouldn't. I was tired of playing games and said, "What's your deal, Ann?"

"Olivia, I don't know what to do! I've got a problem, but I'm not sure who to talk to about it." Her eyes were huge with worry.

"About what?" I asked with caution. Did I really want to know what she'd gotten herself into?

"So, uh, what happened was, um, I stayed with these guys for a couple of nights and ... there was lots of sex—"

"Okay, no," I protested with a gesture for her to stop. "I don't want to know."

"But there's something wrong with me. It itches like crazy down there and—"

"Ann! This is *none* of my business."

"Just help me figure out what to do!"

"Go to the doctor, for God's sake. Maybe one of them gave you an STD."

"But we used condoms."

"That's not a guarantee."

"Oh, God, what am I going to do? Will my parents find out if I go to the doctor? My parents can't find out about this. They can't know that I'm having sex! Do you think the doctor would call them?"

"How should I know?" I asked in exasperation. I'd never seen her so scared and paranoid. Maybe I should have been more helpful and compassionate, but I just didn't care.

The next day, she made a "confidential" visit to student health services, and the mystery was solved. She came back with a couple of prescriptions and announced, "So, I've got a yeast infection *and* a urinary tract infection. I'm surprised you couldn't tell me that's what it might be. You had me so worried I had an STD."

"Why would *I* have been able to tell you what was wrong?"

"The doctor said it's common for women who are having sex. Hasn't it ever happened to you?"

"Uh, *no*," I replied sarcastically.

I almost blurted out something about the fact that I'd never even had sex. I was glad I didn't though. It was none of her business.

CH. 14 ~ NOT. GONNA. HAPPEN.

I'd been hearing about several Halloween parties that would be going on around campus. I wasn't usually into the whole costume thing, but I wanted to be someone else for a night. Elaine, Lisa, and I had a blast at a costume shop trying on some crazy stuff. I fell in love with a red, velvety Scarlett O'Hara dress. My best friend Lyla, the aspiring fashion designer, would have loved it.

It was cut low in front, and the sleeve design was off the shoulders which required a bustier-type strapless bra. I rented the dress and bought the bra. Elaine got a blue Marge Simpson wig and wore a yellow bodysuit with a lime green dress and Lisa put together a Madonna ensemble.

I was in my dorm room, alone, wearing just the bustier and underwear, experimenting with how I wanted to wear my hair, when Ann burst into the room. I grabbed my robe and put it on because I wasn't comfortable parading around half naked the way she and a lot of the other girls did. I still hadn't even gotten in the habit of changing clothes in front of anyone.

"God, Olivia, you're so modest," Ann chided me and giggled. She was either drunk or high, or both.

"Oooh, what is that?" she asked about the dress that was laid across my bed.

"A *Gone with the Wind* dress."

"What's that? I don't even know what you're talking about," she said. That didn't surprise me at all. "So where are you going tonight?"

"I don't know. I guess there's a few different parties to drop in on."

"Me too." She pulled a box out from under her bed and kept her back to me so I couldn't see what she was doing. Standing up, she shoved something in her pocket and said, "Well, have fun," and left. I was becoming more and more curious about what she kept under there, but I wasn't a snoop.

I put the finishing touches on my hair and makeup, stepped into the dress, and took a final look at myself in the full-length mirror on the back of the door. I had a fleeting thought that I wished Cameron could see me in the dress, but it was interrupted by a knock on the door. It was Elaine and Lisa. We all congratulated each other on our costumes, and Lisa made a comment about me "busting out" of the top of my dress, thanks to the bustier.

"Is it too much?" I asked.

"No! Girl, if you've got it, flaunt it! I had to stuff this thing," she said, pointing at her Madonna bustier.

"So where should we go first?" Elaine asked.

"You two lead the way. But please don't desert me anywhere tonight, okay?"

"No way. We go everywhere together, and we come back together," Elaine stated.

"Promise," Lisa concurred.

Whew, that was a relief. I didn't need a repeat of the experience with Ann. And I knew that with if being Halloween, parties would get crazier and there would be way more people to get mixed up with.

We started out at the house of some girls Lisa knew. One of them was old enough to legally buy alcohol. I got a cup of beer from the keg. It tasted awful.

The costumes were anywhere from simple and lame to

elaborate and spectacular. Some people were playing pool. I played one game but leaning over to take my shots was revealing even more of my chest than I was comfortable with. A short guy—barely my height—dressed like a French painter, came up to talk to me.

He was an art major named Pierre. I found the name hard to believe and figured it was part of his costume persona. I played along and told him my name was Scarlett.

Elaine and Lisa came around to tell me they were ready to go visit a haunted house they'd heard about. "I guess I'll see you around," I said to Pierre.

"I was gonna check out that haunted house too. Maybe I'll see you there. Scarlett, right?" He put his hand out for me to shake.

"Yeah. See ya," I said and was dragged off by a giggling Lisa.

"Scarlett, darling, whatever am I to do with you?" Elaine asked in a southern drawl.

"For starters you can find me something other than beer to drink. Are you okay to drive?"

"I'm fine. I don't drink."

I was curious about that but didn't want to be rude by asking why.

"So, we can always count on her to be the designated driver," Lisa said in a sing-song voice.

At the haunted house, I got a few feet in and retreated. I went back out and waited around with some other chickens. The screaming and horrific sounds coming from inside were enough to put me on edge. That wasn't my thing. Pierre showed up with two other guys who went in, but he stayed outside.

"Aren't you going in?" I asked him, motioning toward the house.

"Nah. I'd rather stay out here and talk to you." Great. A charmer. He mentioned another party down the street that he was going to next and asked if my friends and I would consider going.

"I'll mention it to them."

"Cool. It's walking distance from here. That way," he said and pointed down the street.

Elaine and Lisa came out laughing. Jared and Tom were with them. I hadn't even known they were there, but hey, the more the merrier. They looked all disheveled and talked over each other at the same time, telling me about a guy with a chainsaw. Glad I missed that.

They agreed to go to the party Pierre had suggested, and we walked together. He talked to me about art stuff but asked me hardly anything about myself. The group was rowdy and loud by the time we got to our destination—a house decorated to the max with Halloween stuff.

The front lawn was a graveyard, and there were cobwebs in the trees with bats and spiders stuck in them. Inside was less macabre. There was a disco ball and laser lights and people dancing. Pierre told me it was the house of a buddy of his and asked if I wanted something to drink.

"What are the options?" I asked.

"Jello shots," he answered and took a tray out of the refrigerator with tiny lime green concoctions. That drew a crowd, and they were grabbed up fast. Pierre snagged a couple and handed one to me. I'd never done a Jello shot. He showed me what to do, and it was good. I wanted another, but they were all gone.

"I know where some more are," he informed me, leading me to the garage where there was a refrigerator with lots more. We each took a couple and went back inside to a room that was lit with a black light. Some people were dancing, others were standing around talking, and there was a couple making out on a couch. He motioned toward a sofa chair where I sat down, and he perched on the arm of it.

I couldn't get a feel for whether he was truly hitting on me or not. Then the alcohol helped me loosen up, and *I* was flirting with *him*. Every so often, I'd see Elaine or Lisa walked by and peeked into the room. I appreciated them checking up on me.

"Have you ever seen what highlighters look like under a black light?" Pierre asked. He ran the back of his hand against my bare arm, giving me goose bumps.

"Do you mean highlighter *pens?*"

"Yeah." He opened a drawer in a desk nearby and pulled out a yellow highlighter. How handy, almost like he staged it. He took the lid off and reached for my hand.

"May I?" he asked, poised to write on the back of my hand.

"I guess so." I watched him draw some abstract shapes in an intricate pattern that went up my wrist. The yellow highlighter ink glowed in the black light as he drew. It was mesmerizing.

"That's so cool."

"Let it dry so it doesn't smear," he advised. He stood up and pulled my other hand to have me stand up, too. "Dance with me?"

"Sure."

He put his arms around me, and we danced to a slow song. If he'd been taller, I would have leaned my head on his shoulder because I was light-headed. Instead, I closed my eyes and pressed the side of my face against his. I heard him talking to someone else and opened my eyes in time to see a guy hand him something which he then slipped into his back pocket.

Not much caring for the knowing look the guy gave me, I curiously reached around to Pierre's back pocket. Feeling something flat and round, I put two and two together. His encouraging smile told me I'd given him the wrong idea by groping his backside. *Ugh.* I took the condom out of his pocket and held it up between us.

"Really?" I asked, sobering up.

He shrugged and took the foil packet out of my hand. "Can't blame a guy for wanting to be prepared."

"Not. Gonna. Happen." Walking away, I heard him call me a tease, only he put another word in front of it that I won't repeat. I found Elaine and Lisa. To my relief, they were ready to go. They asked about Pierre.

"He wasn't really my type," I replied but didn't feel like explaining.

A new hopelessness set in that night. *What is the point of it all? Life sucks!*

CH. 15 ~ ROOMMATE FROM HELL

I laid low for a few days, keeping to myself and listening to Ann's Nirvana and Pearl Jam albums. The music suited—and perpetuated—my mood. It made me uncomfortable how easily I'd fallen into that situation on Halloween. I was embarrassed and angry at myself, and I became more guarded and wearier of guys. Were they all just looking to get laid?

Algebra was a big fat albatross around my neck. I predicted I'd be lucky to pull through the semester with a C. I had never made a C for a final grade in my entire life! My dad would be so disappointed. The self-pity that I'd managed to set aside by being more sociable found its way back in and made itself comfortable.

I was losing patience with Ann. Living in the same room with her and her mess grated against my orderly nature. She was such a slob! And she was unpredictable and flaky. She'd started acting sketchy and dishonest *all* the time. I found one of my shirts wadded up at the bottom of my closet and asked her if she knew how that happened.

"God, I don't know, Olivia! Maybe you should take better care of your stuff," she suggested. I knew she must have worn it and left it there because, on closer inspection, three was a nicotine stain on it.

One day I was certain I could smell my perfume on her. My expensive, custom-formulated perfume. I hit the roof! She denied that, too. I bought a lockbox and started keeping my small valuable items in it hidden away under my bed. When I discovered she was helping herself to my food too, I didn't even confront her about it. Instead I seethed and plotted revenge.

I studied her, her habits, and her things for a couple of days and decided on a way to mess with her. She had a retainer that she wore at night. It was one of those big, torturous-looking things that she couldn't wear during the day because she wouldn't be able to talk with it in. I considered giving it a toilet dip, but chances were, she'd never know. I needed to do something to it that she'd notice.

Wandering the aisles near the pharmacy at the store, I looked for something that I could put on it that would be a bother, but not harmful. I settled on Anbesol, the over-the-counter topical oral pain relief gel. It was perfect. It was clear, and she never even saw it on there before popping the contraption into her mouth.

I watched her closely the first time. Other than making a funny face and opening and closing her mouth a few times, she didn't have much of a reaction. So, I put the Anbesol on there a couple of nights in a row. It was gross that I was touching the nasty thing that had been in her mouth, but I'd had the presence of mind to buy some latex gloves at the store, too.

One night, she finally commented about a strange taste and said her mouth was numb. I said, "What kind of drugs have you been doing? Maybe you're having a bad reaction."

She thought about that and look worried. *Ha ha!* I couldn't believe how dense she was. If it had been me, I would have figured out it had something to do with the retainer, but she didn't make the connection.

There was an incident that finally put me over the edge with her. I was studying alone in our room and heard a key in the door. It wasn't Ann. It was some grungy guy she'd loaned her key to. She'd asked him to come get something from the room. I was livid!

I went straight to Gina and asked her if I could switch roommates. She was unsympathetic. Acting like I was a brat, she handed me a request form which I filled out right then and there. It was a meaningless exercise because chances were, it ended up in the circular file by her bed.

Storming back into my room, I wanted to hit something. I punched my pillow. That helped some, but I looked around the tiny room, feeling the walls closing in on me. My eyes landed on the framed photo collage Kate had made with the pictures of me and Cameron. It had been there since the day I moved in, but I'd trained myself to *stop* looking at it. Right then, it was mocking me. I grabbed it and was tempted to break it—that's how bad off I was. Instead I shoved it under my mattress.

I was spinning out of control. Too many thoughts were crowding into my mind. Too many feelings were surfacing that I'd been pushing down and ignoring. Elaine had told me she'd seen Cameron walking with a girl holding hands earlier that day. At the time, I'd chosen to not think about it. But in full-on psycho mode, I couldn't *stop* thinking about it. I was so angry at myself for letting the best thing that had ever happened to me fall apart.

If I hadn't been so whiny and self absorbed, none of this would have happened! He and I would be together, and everything would be fine. A lot of good this idea of a break had been. I was worse off than before.

I changed into my running shoes and went out for a run in the cold. It helped, but I was reminded of why I didn't usually go running in the winter. My ears ached for hours, compounding my misery.

Elaine called to see if I wanted to go out with her and Lisa. I declined, needing more time to fight the demons in my head. The rage that I had earlier over Ann, and then Gina, scared me. Was I turning into my dad? My reaction to them had more to do with the way I was feeling about *myself.* Was that why my dad had such anger problems? Did he feel like crap about himself all the time, and was that why he flew off the handle so much? What made *him* feel like crap about himself?

I tried to chill out and turn my mind off. I was over-analyzing stuff and making life harder than it should be. Wouldn't it be easier if I could go along with the flow of things and not let stuff bother me so much? Who cares if I had no idea what I was doing half the time? Did anyone else know what *they* were doing, either?

* * * * * *

Michael offered to help me study for an upcoming algebra test. We met in the library a couple of times. He may have been starting to flirt with me, but I talked myself into thinking it was my imagination. Only, it wasn't.

We were sitting across from each other at a library table, and I was focused on a homework problem but sensed that he was watching me. He slid his foot along the floor to where it brushed up against mine. I tried not to think about why butterflies were invading my stomach and, without looking up from what I was doing, slid my foot closer to his.

Oh, my gosh, Olivia, you gave him an invitation. What are you thinking? Hadn't I already learned my lesson about encouraging guys? The physical contact was so comforting though. And I needed comfort. More than I was willing to admit.

He moved his leg closer to me, and a few minutes later, his other leg was on the other side of mine. My calf was nestled between his. It was oddly intimate. My heart was racing, but I kept pretending to work on algebra. Neither of us said anything about it, and the rest of our study "date" was uneventful.

The next time we got together in the library, something *did* happen. I was in a particularly good mood because I'd managed to get a B on a quiz. Michael was in a good mood too, and we were cutting up, making jokes about the professor and his bow ties and Velcro Girl and her Trapper Keeper. We laughed too loud, and someone at a nearby table shushed us.

Michael whispered, "Hey, can I show you something over there?" and nodded his head toward the stacks.

I was naive and clueless, thinking there really was something he wanted to show me, so I followed him. Out of sight of anyone else, he kissed me. A quick kiss on the lips. He searched my eyes to see what I thought of that.

I thought it was nice and kissed him back. It was slow and tentative, reminding me of the first few times Cameron had kissed me. I lost myself in it. Michael was gentle and respectful, unlike Doug had been.

We returned to the table and proceeded to work on our homework as if nothing had happened. I was okay with that. *Maybe I can just enjoy these little moments and never have to analyze what they mean.*

CH. 16 ~ CAN I DRIVE?

Michael asked me if I wanted to meet him and his friends for a pre-grand opening at a new go-cart track. It sounded fun, and he said to bring a friend. That told me it wasn't a date. It was by invitation only, and he told me he'd put my name down plus one guest. I asked Elaine to go with me, and we went in her car.

We got to drive the go-carts for about an hour on an awesome, elaborate track. I was hooked! I wanted to drive that co-cart around forever. I loved going fast and being in front, ahead of everyone else. Michael and Elaine laughed and teased me for my competitiveness.

Another group of people arrived for the event, and I reluctantly gave up my go-cart. Elaine had already gone into the building that housed an arcade and cafe. Michael and I went in for something to drink and found her at a table with some of his friends.

"Olivia, are you about ready to go?" Elaine asked.

"I can give you a ride back to campus," Michael offered, "If you want to stay and hang out, we could get something to eat."

"Okay, thanks. That'd be great. I need to get my purse from her car, though."

As Elaine and I walked out of the building, she asked,

"How well do you know this guy? Are you sure you're okay with him giving you a ride back to Bellamy?"

"I'm sure. He's a good guy. I appreciate your concern, but I'll be fine," I replied, glad to know that someone had my back.

Michael and I shared a plate of nachos, and he did the foot and leg thing under the table with me again. The more time I spent with him, the more I felt like he was someone I could fall for. I was all too aware that the reason for that was because he reminded me of Cameron. *Should I feel bad that I might just be using him to help me get over Cameron?*

In the parking lot, he walked toward a red sports car. "That's your car?" I asked, pointing at it.

"Yeah," he answered.

I liked fast cars, and after zipping around in a go-cart earlier, I wanted to drive. Fast! "Can I drive?" I asked excitedly.

He looked at me in surprise. "Can you drive a stick shift?"

I smirked and rolled my eyes. "Oh, please. Can I drive a stick shift? My dad wouldn't even let me get my driver's license until I knew how to handle a standard transmission."

"Well ... okay," he said and tossed me the keys. We got in, and I started it up. He told me stuff about the car; the make and model and size of the engine and other stuff that didn't mean anything to me. All I cared about was getting it out on the road.

We were in a rural area off a main highway, so I got up to a high speed right out of the parking lot. It was such a rush! The car handled like a dream. I was in a zone, where it was just me, the car, and the open road. Reaching eighty miles per hour, I glanced over at Michael, wondering if he was alarmed about that. He was watching me instead of the road. *Wow, he sure is trusting.*

He suggested I turn onto a particular road if I wanted

to keep driving, so I followed his directions. The road was great for the kind of driving I wanted to do. It had straight stretches and then meandering curves that the car handled beautifully. I drove for about twenty-five miles and turned around, heading back the way we'd come.

On one of the straight stretches, I got it up to one hundred miles per hour. It made me feel so free. I wanted to keep going forever but figured I'd pushed my luck enough already. A speeding ticket was the last thing I needed.

"You want to drive now?" I asked.

"No, I don't mind if you want to keep driving."

"Okay, but you'll have to tell me where to go. I'm terrible with directions and since Elaine drove, I have no idea where to go." He pointed out where to turn to get back to campus, and I took it slower, wanting to draw out the experience.

"I love this car!" I exclaimed, putting it in park. I had a ridiculous grin plastered across my face. He was still watching me, but I had no idea what he was thinking. I asked him, "What? What is that look for?"

"I hope you don't take this the wrong way but ... I gotta tell you something ... Watching you drive my car—" he laughed nervously, "That was one of the *sexiest* things I've ever seen." He laughed again and looked away, embarrassed.

I started laughing too and said, "Thank you ... I guess."

"The only other time I've let a girl drive this car—or try to drive this car—she had no idea what she was doing. It was terrible!"

"I'm surprised you trusted me."

"I had a feeling you knew what you were doing." He leaned over and brushed his lips across my cheek. Then, near my ear, he quietly added, "And you looked amazing doing it."

I turned my face toward him, and his lips found mine. The kiss started out gentle, reminding of that kiss in the library, but it slowly deepened. I wondered if he was going to be like Doug and expect more. Thankfully, he didn't start pawing at me.

He was content with the kissing, and I was too. That is, until I started thinking about Cameron and feeling guilty for letting another guy get my heart racing like only he had ever been able to. What was I doing? Michael was such a great guy, but I didn't want to give this part of myself to anyone but Cameron.

A tear rolled down my cheek. He reached up and wiped it away but didn't look surprised. In a gentle voice, he said, "I can't figure you out, Olivia. You're cold and then hot and then cold again."

"I'm sorry." I squeezed my eyes shut and tried to stop the tears.

"Don't be sorry." He put his hand on my shoulder, opening his arms to me. I let him embrace me and cried silently into his chest. "Who broke your heart?" he asked.

I thought for a long moment and then replied. "There's a guy ... that I love more than I've ever loved anyone or anything, but I screwed it up. I'm sorry if I've led you on. I didn't mean to. I've been trying to move on, but—"

"Shhh." He put a finger over my lips. "I get it. As much as I'd like to be the one to help you get over him, I can't. Not in good conscience anyway. You should go back to him and try to work things out."

That brought on a new bout of tears for me. How could I try to work things out with Cameron? We weren't even talking to each other, and he'd been able to move on from me fine. How pathetic was it that I couldn't do the same?

Trying to regain my composure, I said, "Thank you. I hope we can be friends. I do enjoy hanging out with you."

"Of course."

"That won't be awkward at all, will it?" I laughed.

"Maybe, but it's okay. I'm a big boy. I can handle it."

"Thank you."

CH. 17 ~ SURENDER

"What the hell is going on, Olivia?" Lyla demanded over the phone which had awakened me from a deep sleep.

"What do you mean?" I asked. It was late Friday afternoon. I had fallen asleep with a headache from reading my psychology book.

"*Why* did I just run into *your* boyfriend with another girl at Taco Bell in Cambridge?"

"What?"

"Did I wake you or something?"

"Sort of. Wait, what? Cameron is in Cambridge?"

"Yes! Have you guys broken up or something?"

"Sort of. I don't know. Why were they there?"

"I was too stunned and confused to ask."

"Were they ... did they seem to be ... together?"

"Well, yeah, they were together. They came in together and left together."

"No, I mean, did they act like they were—damn it, Lyla! Were they holding hands or anything?" I asked in frustration.

"Not that I noticed," she replied. "What happened? Why haven't you told me anything about this?"

"It started out as a break, whatever that's supposed to mean, but we've been seeing other people for a few weeks."

"That is so not cool, Olivia! This can't be happening. You're perfect for each other."

"Oh, Lyla, don't," I pleaded, and my throat constricted with emotion.

"I can't help it. I'm shocked. Are you okay?"

"I'm trying to be."

"I'm hurt that you didn't tell me."

"I'm sorry. I've been trying to sort things out and ... I guess I was embarrassed. And delusional that we might get back together. But we haven't even talked."

"Well, I sure stepped in it," she said with regret.

"How? What do you mean?"

"I asked him where you were."

"What did he say?"

"He said he didn't know and that maybe I should give *you* a call."

I hung up and bawled my eyes out. Grabbing the Bible Mrs. K had given me, I searched in desperation for something, *anything*, that would make me feel better. I clung to it like it was a lifeline, but my eyes were too blurry with tears to make out the words. There was a dark pit yawning open, threatening to swallow me whole.

In the same box under my bed where the Bible had been stored, was the T-shirt I'd sprayed some of Cameron's cologne on the day before we moved. I buried my face in it, hoping it would still carry his scent. If there was any trace of it, I couldn't smell it because my nose was stuffy from crying.

I missed him so badly, my heart and mind ached.

I missed his voice, his smell, his touch.

I missed his thoughtful gestures.

I missed what we had together and hated myself for messing it up.

Wiping my face with the shirt, I looked at what Mrs. K had handwritten inside the cover of the Bible. Seeing her familiar handwriting made me start crying harder. I got out my calling card and entered the five hundred *freaking* numbers required to use it and called her house.

She answered, and I said, "Mrs. K?" in a shaky voice.

"Olivia?" she asked with instant concern. "Uh, oh. What's wrong? Are you okay?"

"I'm okay," I said, not wanting to alarm her. "But I'm miserable, and I don't know what to do."

"What happened? Can you tell me?"

"It's a bunch of stuff, but right now it's mostly that Cameron and I broke up."

"Oh, no! I'm so sorry. Do you feel like talking about it?"

"Yes, I want to. But I need to get away from here. Can I come see you?" I would go crazy if I didn't get out of there.

"Of course. In fact, I've got the whole house to myself this weekend. Billy is out of town. If you're sure you can get here safe, come on."

"Okay, thank you," I sighed with relief, feeling better already.

"Promise me you'll drive careful."

"Yes, I will. I'll be there in a couple of hours."

"And I'll be praying for you the whole way." Somehow that helped me feel better, too.

I quickly packed a bag, feeling a new sense of purpose. I had the presence of mind to grab the stuff I needed to register for next semester's classes by phone on Saturday. Remembering my promise to Mrs. K, I drove safely and didn't cry on my way to Cambridge.

It did not escape me that I was rushing off to the same place Cameron had gone for the weekend. But I figured if I stayed at Mrs. K's, I wouldn't have to worry about running into him. I didn't want to do anything to make him think I was chasing after him. I wasn't even planning to let my parents or friends know I was in town.

"Come in here," Mrs. K said, opening her door and pulling me into a hug. "Welcome to the Lawson Retreat." She showed me into her home and asked if I was hungry.

"Actually yes, I'm starving."

"Let me see what I can rustle up."

She made me some of the best comfort food—a grilled cheese sandwich and tomato soup—and I relayed my pitiful tale of woe. I started from the beginning and added details that I'd left out in my letters to her. She listened, paying close attention, and asked questions at appropriate times. I managed to keep from crying by pretending I was telling her a story about someone else.

"I'm sorry it's been so rough for you," she sympathized.

"Thank you. Is this normal? I've got to be the only person this kind of thing is happening to."

"Well, I don't know what's normal and what's not. I suspect that part of what you're dealing with is that you're just young and inexperienced. You haven't had many opportunities to learn resilience."

I was tired and emotionally spent, so I had to ask, "What do you mean?"

"You haven't had enough life experiences to practice getting back on that horse after it bucks you off. A bunch of things have made you feel like your feet have been kicked out from under you."

"Yeah, and some of those things I brought on myself."

"You've been really hard on yourself, haven't you?"

"But if *I'm* not hard on myself, then *who* will be, and how will I learn from my mistakes?"

"Is it possible that while you've been away, you've started making yourself play the critical role your dad did when you were still living at home?"

Whoa. Was that what I'd been doing? There were tapes that played in my head *all the time* of things my dad had said in the past, as if he were right there beside me all the time. Since he wasn't there with me at NHU, was I being extra hard on myself and having unrealistic expectations imposed on me ... *by myself?* How messed up was that?

"Maybe that's what I'm doing. I don't know. I'm confused. I've made so many mistakes, and I feel like ... I need to punish myself."

"But you don't, honey. You don't need to act as judge,

jury, and executioner. Do you think you can forgive yourself for all these mistakes you *believe* you've made?"

"I hadn't thought about ... needing to forgive myself."

She told me about a time in her life when she'd held onto a bunch of emotional baggage. It was making her miserable and was changing who she was and wanted to be when she finally surrendered it all to God. She learned to forgive herself and was able to ask for God's forgiveness, too.

"And then something almost magical happened. I experienced a peace that passed all understanding," she said wistfully. "That kind of peace can only come from God."

I wanted that. I wanted peace.

She added, "The key was surrendering. You've got to let it all go."

On the nightstand in the spare room I slept in, there was a small book called *God's Promises For Your Every Need.* I thumbed through it and found that it had a handy index in the back. You could look up different things you might be feeling or need, such as comfort, and it gave a page number that provided applicable scripture.

I spent some time looking up the different things I'd been feeling over the last few months. Reading the scriptures, I sensed that God was talking to me. Especially in 1 Peter 5:7 which said, "Cast all your anxiety on him because he cares for you."

I'd never had an experience like what Mrs. K had told me about. I had head knowledge about God, and I was a believer, but I'd never experienced a personal connection to him. The image I carried in my mind of what God was like, very much resembled the way I saw my dad; authoritative, strict, unyielding, and critical.

That idea was faulty. I started dismantling it and allowed for the fact that God could comfort me, ease my fears and anxieties, and guide me when I was so aimless. I just needed to ask. I'd been trying to work through all this stuff on my own. Could I do what Mrs. K had suggested and humble myself before the Lord and ask for help?

Down on my knees beside the bed—something I hadn't done since I was a child—I prayed. First, I asked God to help me forgive *myself* for the colossal pity party I'd been having. Then, I asked *him* to forgive my ugly thoughts and actions that had resulted from that pity party. Tired of trying to make sense of everything on my own, I asked him to help me surrender my troubles to him.

I felt some relief, and was able to go to sleep, but I wouldn't have described it as a "peace that passes all understanding". Maybe that would come later. Maybe this would take practice. And time.

CH. 18 ~ F.R.O.G.

Mrs. K went to work the next day at the CCC, the place where I'd worked and volunteered for several years during high school. She told me to make myself at home, including using the hot tub that was in an enclosed gazebo in the backyard.

I hadn't brought a swimsuit, but since I was the only one there, I went in wearing my bra and underwear. I spent about four hours soaking, reading, and listening to my Walkman until the batteries died. I relished every second of it. I wasn't sure how healthy it was to have stayed in the hot tub for that long, but it helped me feel like a new woman.

I registered for my spring semester classes by phone. I'd already met with an advisor to figure out what I should take and found out I needed a physical education credit. The thought of taking a PE class in college was dreadful, but she suggested something like dance. Since I'd taken a couple of dance classes in high school, I figured that was my best option.

The other classes I signed up for were life science, cultural anthropology, geography, and a couple of sociology classes. One was called Sociology of Work and Occupations, and the other was Collective Behavior. Those were the ones I was looking forward to.

Huh, imagine that. I'd finally found the subject I was interested in. That was at least *one* good thing I had managed to do during my first semester.

Mrs. K and I talked some more at dinner. I told her about how I'd prayed the night before, and she was encouraged by that.

"I see that you've relaxed a little and are getting some clarity. There's something I'm going to tell you, but I want you to keep your perspective, okay?" she said.

"Okay," I agreed, feeling hesitant. Then she told me the last thing I ever expected to hear.

"Cameron came to see me at the CCC today." She waited because I started choking on my drink. "I debated telling you, but I think it might help you to know what he said. He told me he was worried about you and asked me to call you and see how you were doing."

"You didn't tell him I was here, did you?"

"No, I didn't think you'd want me to. I hope that's okay." I nodded, thankful to her for that. "He also told me that the reason he came to town was to give his *friend*, Emily, a ride to a family event. He was afraid Lyla might call to tell you she'd seen them together and you'd get the wrong idea."

I sat staring off into space, stunned.

"Now, may I suggest you not let your mind run away with what this means? If he was trying to let me know—so that I could let *you* know—that he's not involved with this girl, you might be tempted to go patch things up with him. But I hope you'll ask yourself a very important question first."

"What's that?"

"Should you involve him in your life again before you've really figured things out for yourself? Because if you do, you might find yourself right back in this same condition."

Could I do that? Could I keep myself from running back to NHU and seeking Cameron out for a reconciliation? Yes, I could. I had to. It would be hard, but it was the right thing to do.

* * * * * *

Mrs. K talked me into attending church with her on Sunday morning. I was so glad she did. Hers was a refreshing change from the one I'd attended growing up. Instead of the old hymns, the music was contemporary, and the preacher was young and engaging, not fire and brimstone.

It was cheesy to think it, but the preacher's sermon seemed meant for me that day. He talked about how we can make a choice to seek God's help to overcome difficulties. Or we can allow ourselves to be overcome by them. That's what I'd been doing, letting my struggles compound and overcome me.

The preacher also said that in times of trouble, God may choose to either calm the storm, or he might choose to let it continue raging and calm you instead. In my mind, that circled back around to Mrs. K's advice about making sure you know what you stand for so that you won't fall for anything.

I initially thought that was about not falling into false beliefs, and that was part of it, but that wasn't all. If I didn't learn to stand strong in my faith and look to God for what I needed, I'd fall into that pit again that nearly swallowed me up.

Diana, the person who had taken over my job at the CCC, approached me at the end of the church service. We hugged and chatted for a few minutes, and then she asked if I could come to the CCC with her that afternoon.

"There's some things I've needed help with that I was holding off on until you came home for Thanksgiving, but since you're here, do you mind?" she asked.

"Of course, I don't mind," I replied. Mrs. K waved goodbye to me and said she'd see me back at the house later.

Stepping back into the building at the CCC was like coming home. I got all nostalgic and thoughtful, feeling like I'd been away for longer than four months. The things

Diana needed help with were no big deal, almost trivial. Then she asked me to walk over to the food pantry with her to drop off a box of items someone had brought in, and I soon found out the real reason she'd asked me to go there that day.

She unlocked the door to the portable building that housed the food pantry, and I followed her in and looked around. It was cold outside, and the heater wasn't on in the building, so it was chilly in there, too. But in the quiet stillness, I had the sensation of a warm blanket being placed over me, or at least over that indefinable part of me that had been so lost for the last few months. Being there somehow soothed the painful places in my heart and mind.

Since freshman year of high school, the food pantry had been where I'd spent countless hours working, volunteering, and honing my organizational skills into something Billy, Mrs. K's husband, used to call a fine art. The place hadn't changed, other than a few things that had been rearranged. Billy had done well taking care of the place. I wondered if he'd gotten a volunteer replacement for me.

I walked around, dreamlike, looking at all the familiar things; Billy's desk, the place I used to stash my purse when I was working there, the cabinet where supplies were kept, the shelves that had been added when we'd started stocking personal care items, the racks of donated clothing. It all held a certain magic for me.

I loved it, and I had missed it so much. Only, I hadn't known *that* was what I'd been missing. The CCC had given me my purpose, helped define who I was. And since I'd moved away, I'd lost it. *Why couldn't I see this before?* Working and volunteering there had been the things I was good at, the activities that had been the most rewarding and gave me confidence.

"You okay?" Diana asked and put her hand on my shoulder. I turned to her and began to feel tears streaming down my face. But they weren't sad tears. They were tears of relief.

It was an epiphany, and I started laughing. I hugged her, and she laughed too. I bounced up and down on the balls of my feet and twirled around in a circle. I finally knew what I needed to do to "find myself" or whatever it was that I'd been searching for.

"Oh, thank you, thank you, thank you, Diana! You have no idea what you've done by bringing me in here," I said. "Or do you? Did Mrs. K put you up to this?"

"Well," she said with a guilty grin, "Mrs. K *did* suggest I bring you to the CCC. She thought it might help you feel better to see the place, but it was my idea to come in here. I remembered how important all this was to you." I hugged her and thanked her again, and then we locked up and left.

She gave me a ride to Mrs. K's house, and as I packed to leave, I was so happy to tell her about my revelation. A weight had been lifted off me.

"I'm so glad. I guess you can take Olivia out of the CCC, but you can't take the CCC out of Olivia."

"But I can't drop out of college and go back to working there."

"No, but there's gotta be volunteer opportunities at NHU, or in the New Haven community."

"You're right, as usual."

"The best medicine for self-pity is to get busy serving others. It takes the focus off you and puts it on someone else who might need it more. So, go back to school, and get plugged into something you find meaningful. You know, churches are often a great place to find volunteer work, and it wouldn't hurt you to start spending time with fellow believers," she said in a sing-song voice.

"Yes, I know. I should be going to church."

She held her hands up and shrugged. "I'm just sayin'."

* * * * * *

On the drive back to NHU, I discovered a small package Mrs. K had slipped into my purse. It was a silver necklace with a little frog charm. The note card had a picture of a garden and said, "Bloom where you're planted".

Inside the card, Mrs. K had written "F.R.O.G." which was an acronym for "Fully Rely On God". It was special, and I was so blessed to have Mrs. K in my life. My decision to go to her had proved to be the smartest thing I'd done in a long time.

She hadn't judged me. She hadn't even offered much advice. What she *had* done was ask me questions and make observations to get me thinking in a certain direction. Then she'd orchestrated a way for me to come to my own conclusion about what I needed to do. That made it all the more meaningful for me. Mrs. K was a genius!

Almost as a dare for myself, I pulled off the highway at Suzy's Southern Cooking. I went in and was shown to a table. Sitting quietly, sipping a soda, I let my mind go down memory lane. I allowed myself to think about Cameron and, for the first time, acknowledge and feel the deep loss of him.

There were so many things I missed about him. His sense of humor, gorgeous smile, and how, whenever he pulled change out of his pocket, there was always at least one guitar pick mixed in with it. I missed his voice, his laugh, his touch, his candid compliments, his sweet and thoughtful gestures, his honorable integrity. Such rare things to be found in one guy, and I'd been so careless with it.

"You okay, hon?" the waitress asked, bringing me back to Earth. She handed me a napkin to wipe the tears that were rolling down my cheeks. I thanked her and assured her I was okay.

"I recognize you, you know. You were here a few months ago with that handsome young man. I watched y'all in the parking lot. The two of you were so happy together. I'm guessing something didn't work out since you don't look so happy now." I nodded and she added, "I know it's cliché, but I'm gonna say it anyway. If it's meant to be, it'll come back around. Have faith." I thanked her and pulled myself together and got back on the road.

Driving the rest of the way, I tried to pray but couldn't quite organize my thoughts into what I should pray for. I wanted to be careful, like Mrs. K had suggested, about not rushing into working things out with Cameron. There wasn't any real reason to think he'd want to anyway. Just because he had been worried about me and wanted to make sure I didn't think his visit to Cambridge with Emily meant anything, didn't mean he wanted me back.

I began to feel panicked about what I should do. But then I started to see a lot of cars on the road with bumper stickers and emblems with the Christian fish symbol. And by a lot, I mean four out of five. Not coincidence. God was showing me that he was with me, and I didn't feel so alone. For the first time in a long time, I believed that I was going to be okay.

CH. 19 ~ GOODY TWO SHOES

I dug out the welcome week folder from the first week I was on campus, vaguely remembering there was a flyer in it with information about volunteer opportunities. I found it. It was a green sheet of paper with a phone number that said to call Volunteer Coordinator Jenny Hernandez if interested in "serving our campus and the New Haven community". Sounded like providence to me. Why hadn't I paid attention to that when I'd first arrived? Probably because I never imagined how miserable I'd become if I stopped being involved in some type of community service. I'd been so focused on trying to fit in and get ready for classes, that volunteering never crossed my mind.

Over the next couple of weeks, I got plugged in, as Mrs. K had suggested. The volunteer coordinator, Jenny Hernandez, was a junior at NHU. She was instrumental in helping me figure out where I was interested in working and how best to use my talents. Mostly what I did those first few weeks was manual labor which suited me fine. I was out of shape and spent a few days with aching muscles, but it was a good ache. It meant that I was doing *something*. I joined various groups of other volunteers to pick up trash at a local park, clean playground equipment at a daycare, paint some outbuildings at a church, and put together emergency aid packages for missionaries to take all the way to Bangladesh where they were still trying to recover from a cyclone earlier that year.

I started to feel like my old self again. Not entirely, though. It wasn't a magical fix. I still had weak moments, but then who doesn't? I still missed Cameron, but the ache lessened. It didn't hurt quite so much to see him on campus. We'd even started smiling tentatively at each other from time to time. I hadn't worked up the nerve to try to talk to him yet.

He still did impromptu mini concerts in the lounge at Bellamy. It was usually the same girls hanging around him, but I didn't hear from Ann or Elaine that they'd seen him holding hands with other girls anymore. I prayed a lot and did a bunch of soul searching about what to do. I knew I wanted him back if that's what he wanted, but when would be the right time to make that move?

I was getting to know other service-minded students who shared the crazy passion I did for community involvement. Even though I was a late comer to the group, they welcomed me, and I became part of something bigger than myself. That was exactly what I wanted and needed.

I enjoyed an easy camaraderie with them. There was Cassidy, a sophomore who lived at home with her parents and April, who was a freshman living in Carter Hall. Zachary and Franco, a couple of guys in the group, were like big brothers to the girls and did a lot of the heavy lifting.

I went with a few of them to an animal shelter. They worked cleaning dog kennels, and I helped the manager, Paula, streamline her paperwork process. She was so grateful. I was more grateful to her for affording me the opportunity to be in my element.

She told me that her church, New Haven Bible Church, aka NHBC, had recently acquired a building that they were planning to renovate into a soup kitchen. She asked me if I wanted to help, and I nearly cried with joy, telling her I was definitely interested. The plan was to start working on it following Thanksgiving break. We exchanged phone numbers, and I promised I would come help if she'd let me know the time and place.

Meanwhile, I kept up with my schoolwork, but with less obsession than before. In psychology, we finally came to the section on social cognition. It was intriguing, and I was excited about how well it tied in with my sociology interests.

I stopped "dating" or whatever that was that I'd been doing. I uncovered my old sense of humor and gave up on the facade that I had it all together. It was okay to show vulnerability. Sometimes college life sucked, and it was okay to admit that. It turned out other people felt that way sometimes too. I wasn't alone.

Ann started calling me GTS. I had to ask her what that was. She answered me like I was an idiot, "It means Goody Two Shoes." The complaint was that I used to be fun but wasn't anymore. I tried not to let it bother me. She was a serious challenge to live with. And I mourned the fact that I hadn't gotten a roommate that I could consider a good friend.

Overall, things were turning a corner for me. That didn't mean God didn't allow a couple of storms to come my way. The week before Thanksgiving, I got a call from Emma. She was upset because our mom had forgotten to pick her up from school. Again. She told me that since I'd been gone, our mom had gone downhill.

"What do you mean?" I asked. "I just saw her five weeks ago for family weekend. She looked about the same as she always does."

"Yeah, she *looks* about the same. It's stuff she *does* that's gross. Dad's been gone on business trips a couple of times, and when he's gone, if she's not sleeping then she's eating. I've seen her polish off a whole pizza by herself. And you know that nasty imitation brand ice cream she eats?"

"Yeah."

"She ate nearly the whole container. With a bag of Cheetos!"

"Yuck!"

"I know. She's sick. You remember how Dad used to brag about working so hard in his career so that Mom could be a stay-at-home mom? What was the point? So, she could sleep all the time and eat herself to death?"

"Emma," I sighed. "I'm sorry. I'll be home next week. I'll see if there's anything I can do."

So, driving home for Thanksgiving, I had that hanging over my head, and a string of problems nearly took their toll on my newfound happiness. I dreaded having to be around my parents for any length of time. I dreaded the possibility of having to explain that Cameron and I weren't together anymore. I dreaded what the "Check Engine" light meant that came on in my car about thirty minutes from home. I stopped and called my dad from a payphone. He had me check a couple of things which were inconclusive and told me to go ahead and drive it home.

At home, the first thing I noticed was that Emma had lost weight, even though she'd already been thin. I hardly ever saw her eat anything and asked her about it. She insisted, "I'm fine, but I'm trying to keep from getting fat like mom." Then she admitted to having doubled up on the kickboxing video workouts we used to do.

She was exercising too strenuously and not eating enough. It scared me, but I couldn't talk to our parents about it. I called Mrs. K. She suggested I talk to Mrs. Davis, Kate's mom, who was a professional counselor.

CH. 20 ~ INTERVENTION

I invited Mrs. Davis to our house one day when my dad was going to be gone for a while. I had already explained to her what was going on and asked if she'd come facilitate a talk with my mom. I was uncomfortable and nervous, knowing my mom wouldn't appreciate me having involved someone else in our family's business. Something needed to be done though.

My mom, Mrs. Davis, Emma, and I sat down at the kitchen table. I started the conversation. "Mom, I'm concerned about some things. Emma is too. I hope you don't mind that I've asked Mrs. Davis to be here."

"What is this, an intervention or something?" she asked, her defenses building.

"I don't know. Maybe. Let's just say it's time to deal with some stuff that's been ignored for too long. I'm not trying to hurt your feelings with what I'm going to say, so please don't feel like I'm being mean."

With her face looking pinched, she nodded for me to continue.

I told myself it was now or never and took a deep breath. "There's been way too many times that you've been late to pick Emma up from school because you've forgotten about her. You did the same thing to me more times than I can remember, and I understand how it's making Emma feel like she's—"

"Neglected," Emma interjected.

"And we need you to understand how much that hurts," I finished.

Emma added, "And stop laughing me off when I get upset with you about it."

Silence.

"Mrs. Miller, do you have anything you want to say in response to that?" Mrs. Davis asked gently.

"I'm sorry. Last week when that happened, I had fallen asleep," my mom replied.

"Do you sleep a lot during the day?" Mrs. Davis asked.

"*All the time.* It's all she does besides eating *ungodly* amounts of *disgusting* food," Emma said angrily. I put my hand on hers, trying to send her a subliminal message to keep her cool.

My mom looked away, somewhere off in space, avoiding eye contact with any of us. I knew she was embarrassed, and I was embarrassed for her. My dad had complained to her for years about her eating habits and about being overweight, but she'd been unable or unwilling to do anything about it.

"Do you have any idea why you sleep so much?" Mrs. Davis asked.

"So, I can escape my miserable life," she admitted. There were tears in her eyes.

"Why do you feel that your life is miserable?" Mrs. Davis prodded further.

My mom looked at her and shrugged. "I wouldn't even know where to start. I guess I'm unhappy ... about a lot of things ... but I don't know what to do."

I had to know, so I asked, "What are you unhappy about?"

"My life ... You're right, Olivia. And Emma. I *am* a terrible mother. I've neglected both of you, but I can't even bring myself to do anything about it. I'm too lazy and ... fat.

I feel like ... there's no point in trying to change. I want to, and I know I need to, but I can't."

"How long have you felt like this?" Mrs. Davis asked.

"About twenty years," she answered, staring off into space again.

Interesting. My parents' twentieth anniversary was a few months ago, and she hadn't always been overweight. In fact, from wedding pictures I'd seen, she was quite thin. What had happened?

"Is it Dad's fault?" Emma wondered.

"Is *what* his fault?" my mom asked defensively.

"That you're so unhappy. Is it that he sucked the will to live right out of you?"

"Emma," I said in warning. I didn't want this to turn ugly.

"No, Olivia!" she protested. "If we're going to do this, we're going to do it right, okay? Mom, did you give up on taking care of us and yourself because Dad is such a control freak and criticizes everything?"

"If you're asking me to blame my sorry state on your dad, I'm not going to," my mom said, her voice hollow and her expression vacant. I worried we were losing her attention, thanks to Emma's insistence on being confrontational.

"You're not denying it though," Emma shot back.

Mrs. Davis cleared her throat and asked my mom, "Have you ever been treated for depression?"

My mom scoffed, "No family member of John Miller's is allowed to be depressed. Certainly not his wife."

We took turns explaining to Mrs. Davis about the monumental stigma that my dad associated with mental health problems. My mom sighed wearily and said, "We're supposed to pull ourselves up by our bootstraps."

"How's that working out for you?" Mrs. Davis asked, being blunt, but in a polite way.

"It's not. But what can I possibly do?"

"See a doctor who can determine if antidepressants

would be helpful," Mrs. Davis suggested.

"How? My husband would find out." She sounded almost frightened, and fresh tears rolled down her cheeks.

"He would only find out if *you* told him," Mrs. Davis said. "I know it would seem like lying, but what if you could take medicine that would help you feel better? Give you more energy, help you get up in the morning and not sleep during the day so much? Maybe even lose some weight?"

My mom broke down and sobbed into her hands, and I found myself having emotions for her that I wasn't used to. Other than occasional animosity, I was usually indifferent to her. But through this whole conversation, my heart started opening up, and I was able to empathize with her situation.

I put my hand on her arm and assured her, "Mrs. Davis is right. Dad wouldn't even have to know. Can we please get you some help? I'm not around much anymore, but Emma's still here, and she needs a mom."

"Mrs. Miller, I hope you don't mind, but I took the liberty of making an appointment for you this afternoon with a psychiatric colleague of mine named Dr. Cunningham," Mrs. Davis said.

I added, "If you would go and hear what he has to say, I think it could be a positive step for you. I'll even drive you there myself."

"I don't know," she sobbed and shook her head. "Do you really think there's medicine that could help me?"

Mrs. Davis said, "Yes, I do. I've seen medication and counseling help people overcome the kind of long-term depression I suspect you've been dealing with. It takes time, but wouldn't it be worth it for a better quality of life for you. And your family."

"Okay, then," my mom said in defeat. "I guess I've got an appointment to get ready for."

Breathing a sigh of relief, I tried to express with my eyes to Mrs. Davis how much I appreciated her help.

I took my mom to the appointment, and Dr.

Cunningham believed she could definitely benefit from antidepressants along with counseling. My mom paid him in cash and didn't submit any insurance information. She was terrified of my dad finding out. She made me swear to never breathe a word of it. I made her swear she'd see Mrs. Davis for counseling at least once a week, and take Emma sometimes, too.

* * * * * *

That was one issue dealt with, but another presented itself. The next day, I walked in on Emma and her boyfriend Tyler making out in her room. On her bed! Our parents had been gone for a few hours, and I didn't even know Tyler was there. I tried not to cause a scene in front of him, but I asked him to please leave and then chewed Emma out. She said they'd only been kissing, but I'd seen Tyler's hand whip out from under her shirt.

Emma was furious that I had walked into her room without knocking, and I apologized for that, but she got dramatic and called me Goody Two Shoes. That struck a raw nerve. She then proceeded to pile on a guilt trip, telling me how much she resented me for having left her at home to deal with our parents by herself. What was I supposed do, delay my college plans to stay home and babysit her? Her irrationality made me angry, and I caught myself treating her the way my dad did.

The pit that I'd worked so hard to pull myself out of was yawning open, and I was in danger of getting sucked back into it.

On top of all that drama, my dad decided my car wasn't worth fixing. I was faced with making a big financial decision for myself. He offered to loan me some money to buy another car and let me use the Mustang for a trade in. We spent an unsuccessful day car shopping and ended up at Kate's dad's dealership. As we drove onto the lot, I was discouraged and had started to wonder how I would get back to NHU.

Then, I saw *it*.

It was a little maroon Nissan, and it got my heart rate up. My dad started looking at the "sensible" cars, but I gravitated toward the Nissan. It had a sporty body, dark tinted windows, and T-tops. I was running my fingertips over the hood, admiring the deep rich color, and Mr. Davis approached.

"Hello, Olivia. Nice car, huh?"

"Oh, hi, Mr. Davis. Yes, it is. What can you tell me about it?"

"This is a Nissan NX2000 sports coupe. It's only got about fifteen thousand miles on it, electric windows, power steering, CD stereo. I probably shouldn't tell you this, but I will because you're like family. A guy brought it in and asked us to take it off his hands for blue book value. He's going through a divorce and needed the cash."

My heart sank when he told me what year model it was. There was no way I'd be able to afford a newer model car, but oh, I was itching to drive it. My dad walked up, and Mr. Davis said, "Olivia's got her eye on this sports car."

"You can't be serious, Olivia," he admonished. "It's not practical." My back stiffened. Why did everything have to be practical?

"I know," I said, trying to make my voice sound light. "But let me dream for a few minutes." I turned to Mr. Davis and asked if I could take it for a spin. He went to get the key.

My dad scrutinized the car, bumper to bumper, and discouraged me against buying foreign. I knew it was a pipe dream. I just wanted to drive it. See if it gave me the same thrill I'd gotten from driving Michael's car. Of course, having my dad in the seat next to me would put a damper on the fun, but I couldn't exactly ask him to stay behind.

It was a standard transmission, so my dad at least approved of that. He tried out the A/C and confirmed that it worked great. The interior was clean and well cared for. I made sure to keep my speed in check and drove the sporty coupe with comfortable confidence. I loved it!

"It handles well," my dad commented.

"Beautifully," I murmured. It was every bit as fun to drive as Michael's had been.

Returning to the car lot, I asked Mr. Davis, "How much are you looking to get for it?" He told me a price that was quite a bit more than what I'd planned to spend. My mind started calculating what that would do to my savings account.

"I can tell you like it," my dad commented. He was being uncharacteristically ... nice.

"I really do," I nodded.

"Would you like to come in and see what kind of deal we can come up with?" Mr. Davis asked.

I expected my dad to take charge and decline, but he looked to me for the next move. Was this a test? Was he trying to see if I'd do the responsible thing? Responsible according to whom?

"Sure, let's see what the bottom line would be with the trade-in," I suggested.

Sitting at Mr. Davis' desk, I could see the car out the window over his shoulder. I had to have it! There had to be a way. Some numbers were discussed, and I looked at my dad. He held up his hands and shrugged. He was really leaving this all up to me.

What bizarre dimension had I entered, and since when did he miss an opportunity to tell me what to do? My mind was spinning with the weight of the decision, but it felt good instead of overwhelming. I didn't freak out with indecision like the old me would have.

I negotiated the price down a little, got a better trade-in for the Mustang than the other places had offered, and made a hefty down payment. My dad paid the rest with the agreement that I'd pay him back over time. It was impulsive, but I knew that if I left without that car, I'd regret it.

I'd been dreading the drive back to NHU, worrying that I'd have Cameron on my mind. My new car helped my mood. Was I trying to replace him with a car? No, I didn't think so. It was just a car. An awesome car! I thought about stopping at Suzy's but didn't because I was done being sad.

* * * * * *

I hadn't gotten to see my friends over Thanksgiving break. Lyla and her mom were visiting family out of town, and Kate had gone with Josh and his family to their lake house. I missed all of them, but it was actually a relief to *not* see them. That way I didn't have to talk to anyone about why Cameron and I weren't together anymore.

CH. 21 ~ FANCY MEETING YOU HERE

I met Paula, from the animal shelter, at NHBC early Saturday morning and rode with her to the building that was being renovated for the soup kitchen. It was in a not-so-great part of town. Not that New Haven had *terrible* parts of town, but like in Cambridge and Leeville, there was an area where lower income housing and poverty existed.

Paula worried it would bother me, but I told her about the CCC and my experience working with people in need. She was fascinated and said it sounded like what NHBC was planning.

"I love the idea of a food pantry. The soup kitchen is one thing, but a food pantry ..." she said in wonder. "Olivia, I'm going to have to introduce you to my pastor. I think he'd like to hear your ideas."

"Oh, Paula, I don't know that I have any ideas. I didn't start the food pantry at the CCC. I only volunteered in it."

"But you know what it's supposed to look like, how it's run, right?"

"I guess."

"Then don't underestimate yourself."

I chuckled at her optimism and thanked her.

The soon-to-be soup kitchen was in a big building that was formerly a cafeteria-style restaurant. It was cool that someone had donated it to the church. A middle-aged man named Mr. Barnes was in charge and rallied the twenty or so volunteers together to give instructions.

I teamed up with a mother and daughter named Barbara and Brittney. Brittney was about fifteen. She had a good relationship with her mom, which I thought was cool. We were asked to start clearing out debris from a wall that had been knocked out. Fortunately, someone had brought a bunch of gloves. I found a pair that fit and got to work. About an hour later, I was laughing at something Brittney had said and heard Paula call my name.

"Olivia, come meet my niece, Emily. She goes to NHU, too."

Well, what do you know? Cameron's Emily was the last person I expected to see that day, but it was her all right. Did she know who I was? If so, she didn't let on that she did. I took my right glove off to shake her hand. Then— strike what I said before about *Emily* being the last person I expected to see that day—because guess who walked out from behind the building and was coming toward us. Cameron.

We looked at each other in equal surprise. Paula proceeded to introduce *him* to me, too. It was some comfort that she introduced him as Emily's "friend" and not "boyfriend", but it would have been a lie if I'd said it didn't bother me that they were there together.

Cameron and I shook hands and exchanged pleasantries as if we were meeting for the first time. It didn't feel fake though. It felt like a new beginning. And the brief contact from the handshake made me jittery.

Willing myself to stay on task, I pretended that Cameron was just another volunteer. I continued working on various projects with Brittney and her mom. We worked well together, finding things to joke and laugh about. One time, I looked up and saw Cameron watching me. He smiled in a way that I hadn't seen in a long time. It wasn't a big smile, but if I used my imagination—and wishful thinking—it was almost ... wistful.

Later, I ended up working alongside Cameron. We were on our hands and knees cleaning tile grout on the kitchen floor. We weren't alone though, so there were other people to keep up conversations with. A lady named Nancy was asking me about myself. I was glad that the questions she asked had to do with recent things I'd been doing, such as volunteering with a group of NHU students. It was a way to let Cameron know what had been going on with me without directly telling him. I got the impression he was listening intently.

Being that close to him had a physical effect on me, and trust me, it wasn't the grout cleaner making me light-headed! I definitely still had the hots for this guy. Even without our past, if we had just met that day, I would have wanted to get close to him.

It started getting dark, and we all began wrapping up the operation, bringing tools inside, and gathering trash for the dumpster. Mr. Barnes announced there would be pizza for everyone back at the church.

Cameron approached me, looking nervous, and asked, "Are you going to the church to eat?"

"That's where my car is, so yeah, I guess so. I rode with Paula. Are you going?"

"Yeah, I think so." He was trying to be casual.

"Okay," I said and smiled to encourage him. "I hope to see you there." He smiled bigger, and there were those dimples. I fought the urge to reach out and touch his gorgeous face.

* * * * * *

Paula talked about all kinds of things on the way to the church. I had trouble paying attention because I was thinking about Cameron. Did he ask me if I was going to join the rest of them for pizza because he *hoped* I would? Should I try to talk to him, or should I wait for him to make that move? Wow, it was like the calendar had been turned back to January when we'd first met. It was exhilarating, but I was nervous. I didn't want to get my hopes up for nothing.

Pizza boxes were set out on a big table in the church gym, and everyone helped themselves. I got a couple of slices and a drink and found a place to sit on the bleachers. Cameron arrived with Emily. I watched them. There was no sign of them being anything other than friends, so I allowed myself to relax about that. But then I remembered Elaine had seen him holding hands with a brunette. What if he was, in fact, involved with that other girl?

He got some pizza and approached me. "Can I join you?" he asked.

"Of course," I replied, more eagerly than I'd meant to. He sat down, leaving about two feet of space between us.

"So, you've gotten back into the community service mode?"

"Yeah, I have. I'm enjoying it."

"Good. I'm glad." He opened his mouth to say something else but stopped himself.

"How about you?" I asked. "What got you involved in this project today?"

"Emily goes to this church."

I nodded and took another bite to keep from asking something about Emily.

He asked, "How have you been?"

"I've been good. Really good." My eyes searched his. I was trying to convey so much with a look; a look that said, *I'm better now. I did what you said and found what makes me happy.*

His eyes held mine, and he said, "I can tell. You seem—"

"Olivia!" someone called my name. We looked in the direction it had come from. It was Brittney. She was holding a basketball and motioned for me to come join her and a few other people who were playing. I had finished eating and remembered how much fun I'd had with Elaine and the others that day at the rec center.

I hesitated for a second, worried about walking away

from Cameron since we were finally having a conversation after seven and a half long weeks. He smiled at me, but it was a smile that said, *Who do they think you are? You don't play basketball.*

Setting my plate down, I called to Brittney that I'd be right there. Cameron looked surprised and gave me a curious smile. I asked if he wanted to come. "Um, sure, maybe in a minute. I'm going to finish eating."

"Okay." I left the bleachers to go join the group of about six people on the court.

I told myself to have fun and forget that Cameron was over there watching me. It got rowdy, and I laughed a lot at a couple of the guys' antics. At one point, Brittney and I even ended up on the floor, laughing so hard we couldn't breathe. I was sure that, to anyone watching, it all looked ridiculous, but I didn't care. I was having fun, and that was okay. That was my new motto, "It's okay."

Cameron never did come play with us, but every time I looked over at him, he was watching me closely. We got applause from him and a few others for our comedy act. I walked back over to him, smiling one of those uncontrollable smiles. The smile he gave me was, again, wistful.

What was up with him? Would we get to a point where we could talk about what had happened between us? And about what had happened with each of us *since* then? Did I want to know? Or, the bigger question for myself was, did I want to tell him about my journey back to being in a better place? Parts of it weren't pretty. If we were going to try to be friends—or more—again, maybe we could start totally fresh. Maybe he didn't need to know all that embarrassing stuff.

CH. 22 ~ HAVE MERCY

The volunteers were all telling each other goodbye and heading for the parking lot. Cameron asked me, "Can we talk?"

"Sure." I welcomed the butterfly invasion in my stomach.

"How about we go ... um, somewhere ..." He was trying to think of where we could go that would be neutral territory but not outside where the temperature had dropped.

"I know where there's a cafe with excellent pie. You want to follow me there?"

"Okay," he agreed, and we walked outside. He looked around at the few cars left in the parking lot. "I thought you said your car was here."

With my face beaming, I pointed at my new car. "It is." He looked surprised again. I'd never seen as much surprise on his face as I did that day.

"For real? When did this happen?"

"Over Thanksgiving. The old Mustang bit the dust."

"This is awesome. It totally suits you, too."

"Thank you. You want to ride in it?" I asked without thinking it through. That was dumb. Too much too soon?

"Yeah," he answered right away. Oh, okay, maybe it

wasn't such a dumb suggestion.

"Cool! Hop in." I tried to hide my shaky hands as I put on my seatbelt and started the car.

"How many speeding tickets have you gotten?" he teased.

I laughed and said, "None. I've been careful."

"You do like to go fast though, don't you?"

"Love to!"

"You seem ... happy," he suddenly blurted out. "It was good to see you today ... in your element ... doing the volunteer stuff. And then with the basketball." He laughed. He *actually* laughed. Oh, God, how I'd missed that sound.

"Hey, don't make fun of me," I said, feigning embarrassment.

"No, no, no," he said and put his hand on my arm. He quickly pulled it away though, and continued, "I'm not making fun. I'm ... trying to tell you that it was great. I loved it! I loved watching you have so much fun. It was like watching the old Olivia, the one who ..." About five seconds of silence followed. "The one I used to know."

"Thank you," I said quietly, wondering if he'd been about to say, "the one who I fell in love with". To cover the awkwardness, I asked, "You still want pie?"

He smiled and nodded.

I drove us to Jack's, and we made small talk about school stuff, including what classes we'd signed up for in the spring. I sat there listening to him, thinking I should pinch myself to be sure I wasn't dreaming. Waiting for our order, I tidied up the napkin holder and condiment containers on the table, rearranging them a couple of times. It was a nervous habit I'd developed. I realized how silly I looked fiddling with all that and tucked my hands under my legs until the waitress arrived with our pie.

I had ordered the lemon cream cheese, and Cameron got pumpkin. He took a couple of bites and swore it was the best pumpkin pie he'd ever had. He offered me a bite. I must have looked doubtful because he quoted *Green Eggs and Ham* for old time's sake. "You do not like it, so you say. Try it, try it, and you may."

We laughed together, and it felt so comfortable, so familiar. Could I be blessed by a second chance with him?

He extended his fork toward me. I opened my mouth and let him feed it to me. It was incredibly intimate. He watched me intently with his amazing brown eyes, the color of which made me think of Hershey's chocolate kisses.

I'd never tried anything pumpkin flavored before. The spices and the texture of the pie, mixed with the rich whipped cream, were heavenly. I smiled and nodded to let him know I liked it.

He got a serious look on his face and reached across the table to touch my hand. Our fingers intertwined, sending sparks through me.

"You cannot *possibly* imagine how much I've missed you, Olivia."

My heart was about to burst, and I said, "Yes, I can, actually. I've missed you, too. Can you forgive me for the way I messed things up?"

"Olivia, it wasn't just you—"

"But it was. I take full responsibility."

"That's not fair. I could have been more understanding and patient."

"You were a saint."

"That's not even close to being true." He was thoughtful for a moment, shook his head, and asked. "But can we put that behind us?"

"I'd love to."

"Did Lyla tell you she saw me with Emily in Cambridge a few weeks ago?" I nodded, and he continued. "I was just giving her a ride."

"So, was there ever anything ... between the two of you?" I dared to ask.

"Well, yeah. I'm not going to lie to you. There kind of was, but only for a couple of weeks. It started about a week after you and I ..." He was reluctant to define *what* exactly had happened between us.

"Okay," I said and swallowed hard, feeling tormented. There were things I wanted to ask but didn't know how and was scared of what the answers might be.

"We're just friends now," he reassured me.

"A friend of mine saw you ... holding hands with a girl. A brunette?"

He turned red. "That was Carrie. She's in one of my classes. We went out a couple of times, but she wasn't really my type. Wait a minute. Why is all the focus on me? What about you and that guy I saw carry you out of Bellamy over his shoulder?" He wasn't angry, but he was uncomfortable and saw a way to deflect the attention back on me.

"That was Doug. A friend of a friend. We went out, but it was nothing. He wasn't my type, either."

Clearing his throat, he asked, "What about Michael?" Then it was my turn to blush. "Uh, oh," he said and pulled his hand away. He sat back in the booth, studying my face carefully. I could tell that he was letting his imagination fill in the blanks about what could have happened between me and Michael.

"Um ... we spent some time together and ... kissed, but all I could think about was *you*."

He put his elbows on the table and covered his face with his hands. "Okay, full disclosure ... I kissed Emily." His voice was muffled, but I understood him. It stabbed me in the heart, but who was I to judge?

I told him, "I kissed Doug, too. Or, actually, it was more like I let him kiss me." He peeked at me between his parted fingers. "But it was a terrible mistake ... trust me."

"Let's talk about something else," he suggested, sitting up straighter. "Did Mrs. K ever call to tell you I went to see her?"

"Yes. In fact, I was in Cambridge at her house that weekend."

I told him about my weekend renewal at the "Lawson Retreat". I even shared with him about the preacher's sermon, the *Book of God's Promises*, and about how much I'd been praying.

Then I told him about going to the food pantry at the CCC and having the revelation about what had been missing in my life at NHU. I explained how it had led to volunteering at the animal shelter where I'd met Paula who then got me into the NHBC project.

"I couldn't believe it when I saw you there this morning," he said.

"I know. I couldn't believe it when I saw you there, too."

"At first, I thought it would be awkward. I figured I'd just try to stay out of your way. But as I watched you—sorry if this sounds corny—I saw a changed person. A person I wanted to get to know and get close to. Can I do that, Olivia? Can we try to start over?"

A dream come true! I stood up and moved to his side of the booth. Sitting down next to him, I took his hand, kissed it, and said, "Yes, I would love that."

I kissed him and got to enjoy a second taste of the pumpkin pie when he kissed me back. His lips were so soft, warm, and familiar; truly the only lips I ever wanted on mine again.

The waitress rounded the corner. "Oh, sorry, I was just seeing if you wanted coffee or anything else this evening."

"Yes, coffee sounds great. Thank you," I replied.

Cameron turned to me and asked, "What? You've become a coffee drinker?"

I shrugged and smiled. "Yeah, but I'm not like one of those die hard, gotta-have-my-coffee people. So, tell me, what's new with you?"

"I'm in a blues band. It's called Have Mercy. We haven't performed anywhere yet, and we've only practiced a few times After Christmas break, we'll try to get some gigs scheduled."

"That's great! I can't wait to come see you."

"Thanks. Yeah, there's pretty good chemistry with us. The singer's a bit of a wild card, but they usually are."

CH. 23 ~ WILD HORSES

I drove Cameron back to the church where his truck was. He wasn't in any hurry to get out of my car. I didn't mind. I wasn't ready to be away from him now that I had him back.

He was relaxed, leaning back in his seat with his head turned toward me. Looking at his gorgeous face, knowing that he was happy to be with me, and that I wasn't screwing it up, gave me the warm fuzzies in the cold December air.

"You're so beautiful. I couldn't stand being apart from you. I worried I'd never get to be with you again ... or touch you or kiss you." He reached for my hand, intertwining his gorgeous long fingers with mine.

"I felt like more than half of me was missing without you."

"I know exactly what you mean. You're what makes my world go 'round, Olivia."

"Are you sure?" I asked, remembering the times he'd appeared to be doing fine over the last several weeks. "I mean, sometimes it seemed like you were ... happier. Better off without me."

"I think I was trying to make it look like that, but in reality, I was dying inside." He put his hand on my face, curling his fingers around to my neck. "I'm so sorry I pushed you away when you were struggling. I was such a jerk for doing that."

"No, you weren't. It's okay. I don't blame you. It was probably the push I needed in order to figure things out."

Was it too soon to tell him I loved him? My brain told me yes, it might be, but my heart told me to go for it. "I love you," I said quietly.

"I love you, too. I never stopped loving you. Thank you for coming back to me."

"You're welcome. Thank you for giving me the chance to show you that I'm back to being my old self."

"Not your old self, your new and improved self," he insisted.

"Okay, if you say so. I'm glad you made the move to talk to me again."

"Wild horses couldn't have dragged me away from you today, Olivia," he admitted and chuckled.

"Me either."

What followed was the kind of tender and sweet kissing that I remembered from the early days of our relationship. We were getting to know each other again except this time we knew the value of what we had and didn't take anything for granted.

Getting out of my car, he said, "Hey, I've been going to church at NHBC. You want to go with me tomorrow?"

"Okay. Yeah, I'd like that."

He'd kept busy while we were broken up, or on a break, or whatever it was. It didn't matter anymore *what* it was, because it was over. I had my second chance, and I thanked God for it.

* * * * * *

We met at NHBC the next morning and sat in church together for the first time. It was a non-denominational church. I liked it a lot and even looked forward to going again. That wasn't something I ever expected.

I'd been calling Mrs. K every other day since the

weekend I spent with her. She loved hearing from me about how much better I was doing. I called her that afternoon and updated her that Cameron and I were getting back together. I told her how it all happened, and she was happy for us. She said she'd keep praying, and I was grateful for that.

Cameron and I didn't pick up right where we'd left off. But that was a good thing. We took it slow, and I made sure to balance my time with him and the other things and people in my life.

* * * * * *

Final exams were the next week. I wasn't stressing too much about mine, but Cameron was sweating over a couple of his. He'd maintained good grades all semester and wanted to finish strong. I had resigned to the fact that I'd probably get a C in algebra, and that was okay. I could say that I'd done the best I could and wasn't going to beat myself up about it. Math wasn't my thing, so it was good that it was the last math class I'd probably ever have to take.

My nineteenth birthday was December tenth, during finals week. Cameron took me out to eat at the barbeque place, which was fine with me, but he apologized for not having planned something more special. I told him not to worry about it. He had a good excuse. How could he have known we'd be back together?

He'd made cassette tapes for me from a couple of new CDs. One was U2's *Achtung Baby*, and the other was a Stevie Ray Vaughan album called *The Sky is Crying* that had been assembled and released after his death. We went to my room to listen to them. Thankfully, Ann wasn't around, but he acted nervous about being in my room. Did being alone with me in a bedroom remind him of what we were doing right before we had that terrible fight?

He sat in my desk chair, and I sat on the edge of my bed, facing him, our knees touching. The music of U2 played from my boom box, and we listened quietly. I was holding a cup from the restaurant and was playing around with the straw in my mouth, not even aware of what I must look like. That is, until he said, "I sure wish I was that straw right now," in a low, sexy voice.

"What? Why?" I asked coyly.

"I think you know why."

"No, I don't. Tell me," I teased.

He took the cup from me, set it on the desk, and pulled me onto his lap, whispering in my ear, "Because then your mouth would be all over *me*."

Being in his arms again was such a relief, like coming home from a long and painful journey, and his kisses turned me into melted butter.

"I've missed you so much, Olivia," he sighed, holding me close. "Your lips, your hands touching me, the way you make me feel, your smell. Oh, my gosh, I've missed that. Every time I smell vanilla, it makes me think of you." He'd always been addicted to my vanilla scented perfume. His cologne was equally intoxicating to me.

"I've missed you, too. Unbelievably so."

He laid his ear against my chest and whispered, "Your heart is racing. Mine is, too."

I pressed my palm over his heart, and he started kissing my neck, letting his lips make their way down to my collarbone. It felt so good, and I wanted more, but it wasn't meant to be because suddenly, we heard someone unlocking the door.

I jumped off his lap guiltily as Ann came in, surprised to see us. I should have put a hair scrunchy on the door handle, but that required forethought that I hadn't had.

"Whoa, sorry you guys," she said. "I need to get something, and then I'll be out of your way." She pulled a box out from under her bed and acted sneaky. Whatever she was doing or looking for, it was taking forever. Finally, she slipped her hand into her coat pocket, shoved the box back under the bed, and left.

"By the way, she's turned into a total wackadoo," I said.

Cameron laughed, and it was contagious. Our intimate moment was over, thanks to my crazy roommate.

"You know she smelled like marijuana, right? In fact, the room smells of it too. I noticed it earlier."

My eyes went wide. "Is that what that smell is? I had no idea. I thought it was the cigarette smoke and that she never does her laundry."

"Yeah, it's weed, and I'm willing to bet that box under her bed has something illegal in it."

"Oh, my gosh. How do *you* know what pot smells like?"

"I guess from smelling it at concerts and stuff, and there's some guys on my floor that smoke in their room."

"Have you ever tried it?"

"Once. About three years ago. I was at a friend's house, this guy named Blake. We tried it, but it didn't do anything for me. And then something crazy happened," he chuckled and shook his head. "I haven't thought of this in a long time."

"What happened?"

"I walked back to my house afterward, and when I got home, Blake called me. He was all upset and freaking out. He said that about five minutes after I'd left his house, he got this random phone call from someone who told him I had been in an accident and was *dead*."

"What the heck?"

"It was so bizarre. I was fine, obviously, and we never did figure out who it was that called him. I'm guessing *you've* never tried pot."

"Well, no, and I didn't even know what it smelled like."

CH. 24 ~ THAT WASN'T MICKEY MOUSE

Thursday night, I wanted to celebrate being done with my finals, but Cameron still had one more scheduled for the next morning. He was meeting with a study group to cram for it. So, I went out to eat and to a movie with Elaine and Lisa.

In packing up what I wanted to take home for the month-long semester break, I came across a book I'd bought months ago and had forgotten all about. It was John Grisham's *The Firm*.

I fell asleep reading it and was awakened past midnight by Ann and some guy who had come into the room. I stuck my earbud headphones in my ears, so I didn't have to hear them and hoped they'd leave soon. With my back to them, I fell asleep again. I shouldn't have done that. And I sure as heck shouldn't have gone back to sleep.

I was awakened again, but this time by someone pulling the covers off me and putting a hand on my hip. The hand grasped the waistband of my pajama pants and started to pull them down. Alarmed, I tried to sit up, but I was pushed back down. It was dark in the room. I was caught completely off guard. I didn't know who it was or what was happening.

An attempt to scream out for help was muffled by a

hand that flew up to cover my mouth. With his other hand, the guy held one of my legs down and used his knee to pin my other leg. No matter how much I struggled against him, I was no match for this guy's strength.

I couldn't get free from him. My earbuds got jerked out of my ears, and I was pretty sure he was saying something because I could hear a voice. But there was such a loud, rushing sound in my ears, I couldn't understand him.

Trapped and helpless, I thrashed my hands around, searching for something to grab onto. The Walkman. Not exactly an ideal weapon, but it was better than nothing. I raised it up and hit the guy, landing a solid blow to the side of his head. At least I thought it was his head, it was too dark to tell for sure. I was only seeing silhouettes.

It took him off guard and bought me the precious seconds I needed to get my foot up and shove him away with a kick. He cussed and stumbled back some. My hand reached for my lamp, and I turned it on in time to see him pulling his pants up over his hips as he ran for the door and out of the room. I never saw his face, just his back.

Scrambling out of bed and to the door, I locked it with shaking hands. Ann was in her bed, sound asleep. How did she sleep through that?! I shook her by the shoulders, screaming, "Who was that? Who was he?" She wouldn't wake up. She was passed out cold from God only knew what.

Nothing like this had ever happened to me. I paced the room anxiously, feeling like I was going to throw up, and waited for my heart rate to go down from the adrenaline rush. What if Ann gave him a key to our room, and he came back? There was no way I was going back to sleep, even if I'd wanted to.

All kinds of thoughts raced through my mind. Should I call the cops? And tell them what? Some guy who I couldn't even describe had been in my room and tried to do something horrible to me. There wouldn't be anything they could do about that. Calling campus security seemed useless too. What could they do? They wouldn't know who to look for.

I thought about calling Cameron, but it was only three o'clock in the morning. Besides, he had a final at eight o'clock in one of his most important classes. I didn't want to be the cause of him blowing it. So, I got back in bed and sat there, huddled under the blanket, keeping a eye on the door. It felt like my skin was crawling, and I was still shaking. I replayed the incident over and over in my mind.

I wanted to remember something, anything, that would help me know who the guy was. Otherwise, how would I know if I ran into him on campus. Would he know *me? Oh, God, help me!* I sat there and prayed until eight o'clock. Then, I changed clothes and brushed my hair. Another attempt to wake Ann up was unsuccessful, but I did at least confirm that she was breathing.

Creeping out of my room as if somebody might jump out at me, I went down the hall to the bathroom. I brushed my teeth and washed my face without looking at myself in the mirror. This was the most humiliating thing that had ever happened to me. Jerry, Cameron's mom's boyfriend, had grabbed my butt one time, but that was no big deal compared to what had just happened.

I sat on a couch in the lounge to wait for Cameron to return from his test. I had my coat on and got too hot, but I couldn't bring myself to take it off. It helped me feel safer. From where I was sitting, I could watch all the people coming and going, though there weren't that many. A lot of students had already left for the break. I was starving, and I was sleepy, but I stayed awake. Finally, around ten o'clock, Cameron walked into the building. I got up and went to him.

"Hey, Olivia," he said and smiled in surprise, but his face fell when he saw the condition I was in. "Is something wrong?"

"Yes. Can we go to your room?" I asked, trying to not break down until I could be alone with him.

He put his arm around me and led me to the elevator. Someone else was getting on it at the same time. We rode in silence. He held my hand tightly. I could feel the worry emanating from him. In his room, I collapsed in his arms and sobbed.

"Oh, my God, Olivia. What's wrong? You're really scaring me."

Knowing that I was probably making him think the worst, like someone had died or something, I tried to pull myself together and speak clearly. But after holding in the horror over the last several hours, I was just babbling nonsense. He let me cling to him until I calmed down some and became more coherent.

Finally, I was able to explain what happened in a logical sequence, ending with my unsuccessful attempts to wake Ann up. His face turned white, and he gripped my hands so hard it hurt. He suddenly darted out of his room, seething mad.

I caught up with him at the locked door to the west wing. The security guard saw me and released the lock for us to go through. Cameron started banging on the door, yelling, "Get your sorry ass up, Ann! Open this damn door!"

"Here, let me use my key. Calm down, please," I said. He was causing a scene for a couple of girls who had peeked out of their rooms at us.

He rushed into my room, went straight to Ann, and shook her roughly by the shoulders. It scared me, and I yelled at him to stop, but he was screaming at her so loudly that he couldn't hear me.

Her head lolled around, and she started to wake up. Understandably, she was shocked and scared by the rude awakening. She held her head as if in pain—probably from a hangover.

The interrogation began. Her only response was, "I don't know."

"Think, Ann," Cameron said in a more moderate tone. "Who were you with last night? Who did you bring in here?"

"I don't remember. I don't even know how I got here. What happened?"

"You brought a guy in here," he spat the words out, "who tried to *assault* Olivia!" His anger ramped up again. He got up and stormed out of the room. She sat there in bed hiccupping and cringing in pain.

He came right back in, insisting, "This has to be reported. Where is your RA?"

"Don't bother with Gina. She won't care. I think she's already gone for the break, anyway," I said, and he left again. I was exhausted, my nerves were raw, I was hungry and full of dread. This was so *not* how I wanted the semester to end.

"You're such a train wreck, Ann," I said. "I can't believe you did this—let this happen to me."

"I'm sorry," she whispered. "My life is over. I'm flunking everything. I can't even remember the last time I went to class. I'm drunk or high all the time, and now ... I don't even know who I was with last night." She was pale and looked like she might pass out.

Cameron came back again. This time, he had Lauren, the cool RA from the third floor, with him. He rapidly finished telling her about my ordeal.

"You're Olivia, right? Are you okay?" she asked, putting her arm around me. I nodded and swallowed hard, not wanting to get emotional again. "Do you need anything. Are you hurt or injured?"

"No, he didn't do anything." Though I had already started to feel bruised in a couple of places where the guy had kept me pinned down.

"But he tried?" she asked me quietly. I nodded. She then went over to Ann, and with less sympathy, asked her all the same questions we had already asked her. Ann stared off into space, practically catatonic.

Lauren asked, "Olivia, do you have her parents' phone number by any chance?"

I knew it was on a slip of paper somewhere on my desk.

Turning around to look for it, I heard Ann start saying, "Oh, no," over and over again, getting louder and more hysterical sounding. I looked at her in time to see her leap out of bed and race out of the room with more energy than I would have thought possible.

Lauren went after her, but Cameron and I stayed there. He looked at me. The fear and pain in his eyes made me get choked up again. Why did this have to happen? Especially when we'd only been back together for such a short time?

His expression changed to compassion, and he helped me over to my bed where I laid down. He sat next to me and rubbed my arm and back, talking softly and soothingly. Lauren came back in and said she hadn't been able to catch up with Ann.

She used my phone to call campus police. We listened to her explain that Ruth Ann Schubert had run off and needed to be found for questioning about an attempted sexual assault on her roommate, Olivia Miller.

Attempted sexual assault. Is this really happening to me? I had an out of body sensation where I imagined I was high up above, looking down at the scene, watching this happen to someone else—not me.

Lauren hung up and said to me, "They want you to come in and give a statement and file a report before you leave for the break. Are you done with finals?" I nodded and she added, "I'm so sorry this happened."

"*How* did this happen?" Cameron suddenly asked. "*How* did the guy get in here? Ann would have had to sign him in and escort him in, right?"

"I thought of that too, and I checked the record a minute ago. She signed someone in, but she wrote down that his name was Mickey Mouse," Lauren said.

A giggle escaped me and turned into laughter at the ridiculousness of it. They looked at me with concern.

"I think she needs to rest," Cameron said to Lauren. *Great, now I'm going to be treated like a mental patient.*

"No, I don't need to rest. I need to eat. I'm about to die

of hunger." My stomach growled for further emphasis. I didn't have any food in the room, and I figured the dining hall and food court in the Haven would be closed already.

"I'll be right back," Lauren said and left. We waited in silence. Cameron looked at me, squinted, and turned away. Did he see me differently? Nothing had happened! I hated that look on his face. I swore right then that I would *not* be treated like a victim.

Lauren returned with some peanut butter crackers and a cold can of Coke from the vending machine. *Duh.* Why hadn't I thought of that?

"Okay, so here's the deal," she said. "A couple of students on my floor aren't returning in the Spring. I've shuffled some of the girls around and that resulted in a vacant room. Room three twelve. There's a transfer student coming next semester who has been assigned to it, but you could be her roommate. What do you think about putting all your stuff up there now, so you'll already be moved in when you come back from Christmas break?"

"Oh, God bless you, Lauren," I said and hugged her. "I'll do it right now."

"Wait. First, you should go file a report, and I'll work on the paperwork for your room change."

"Yeah, Olivia. I'll go with you," Cameron offered.

At the campus police office, I had to repeat the whole horrible thing *again* to a stranger who took notes. I did finally remember what the guy was wearing, jeans and a plaid flannel shirt. That wasn't much to go on. The best I could do was to tell the officer that the guy smelled of cigarette smoke and had dark hair, but I never did see his face.

The officer said he would speak with the person who was supposed to be at the security desk overnight to find out if he remembered anything about the guy who was with Ann or if he'd seen a guy run out unescorted. The problem was, the guy could have left from a different, unmanned exit-only door, which was probably what he did. The officer told me exactly what I'd expected. There wasn't anything they could do without a better description of the guy.

"Has security found Ann?" I asked.

"I'm not at liberty to discuss that with anyone," the officer said apologetically.

* * * * * *

Cameron and I were packing up my stuff, and he said, "I can't stand it any longer. I have to know what's in that box under Ann's bed. Do you mind?"

"No, go ahead."

He pulled it out and, underneath a bunch of wadded up clothes was a smaller box with a stash of assorted pills and marijuana joints. The pills were in clear bags. We couldn't tell what any of them were.

"Oh, my gosh," I said. Cameron shook his head and put it all back under the bed. I was convicted about the part I might have played in Ann's degradation—or rather the part I *hadn't* played in preventing it.

"Maybe if I'd been a better friend, she wouldn't have gotten mixed up in all that. I was so focused on myself and my own problems that—"

"Olivia don't blame yourself. She was hell-bent on screwing her life up. I doubt anything you could have said or done would have stopped it."

"Yeah, I guess."

I still felt partially responsible though.

CH. 25 ~ BEAR TRAP

Our moods lightened considerably once we got my stuff moved to room 312.

"I have an idea," Cameron said as he took a floppy teddy bear he'd given to me several months before out of a box and set it on top of my dresser. "Let's not go back to Leeville today like we planned. You're probably going to be too exhausted to drive. I would take you home in my truck, but we shouldn't leave your car here over the break. That's too long, and you'll want it when you're in Leeville, right?"

"Yeah."

"So, you should spend the night in your new room." He came over and wrapped his arms around me. I snuggled against him, enjoying the sense of well-being he gave me. Then he added, "And I'm going to stay right here with you. I'm not leaving your side."

"Thank you," I whispered, feeling such appreciation for him.

"Come with me to my room so I can grab a few things, and then let's order a pizza."

He'd left the teddy bear on my dresser with its foot stuck in the top drawer which was open just a crack. "What's going on with the bear?" I asked, pointing at it.

He looked over and casually replied, "Bear trap."

I laughed, and the warm fuzzies spread all through me. "That's adorable! I love you!" I exclaimed and planted a big kiss on his mouth. He patted me on the head like I was a kid, but I could tell he was happy that he'd made me smile.

He humored me by agreeing to watch a chick-flick while we ate. I picked *Can't Buy Me Love*, and we snuggled up together on my bed. We ended up dozing off, and I had a nightmare.

It was so real. It started out with me being awakened by the unknown guy pawing at me. I could almost feel his hand covering my mouth again. This time he managed to pull my pajama pants down and was climbing onto my bed. I was trying to fight him off with ever fiber of my being, but I was helpless.

I awoke to the sound of my own strangled scream and sat straight up, flailing my arms around to ward off the imaginary perpetrator. Cameron sat up too, startled from a sound sleep.

"What's wrong? It's okay. I'm right here, Olivia." He put his hands on each side of my face, helping me focus on his. I gulped for air and quickly pulled the bedcovers away to verify that I was still fully clothed. The nightmare slowly gave way to reality, and I was so relieved.

You're all right, Olivia. That dream—that's not what actually happened.

"Are you okay?" Cameron asked. I saw that look on his face again that I'd been seeing off and on all day, and I couldn't stand it anymore.

"I'm okay. I don't want you to treat me like a victim," I blurted.

His eyes opened wide in surprise. "I'm sorry. Is that what you feel like I'm doing?"

"Kind of. I think. I don't know. There's this look you keep giving me."

His face contorted in pain, and he got choked up. "If that's what I'm doing, I'm not meaning to. I'm worried about you."

"I know. I'm sorry. I didn't mean to snap at you."

"When you were telling me this morning about what happened—when I was finally able to understand what you were saying, and it sunk in—it reminded me of this girl I know named Amanda. Our moms are good friends, and a few years ago, I overheard them talking about something horrible that had happened to Amanda. They didn't know I was listening, and I shouldn't have been, but it was like … morbid curiosity or something."

"What happened?" I asked but wasn't sure I really *wanted* to know.

"Amanda and her best friend had gone to a party and were supposed to have each other's backs, but they both drank so much they didn't even know what was going on. Amanda ended up alone in a room with a guy who raped her—" He covered his face with his hands and cleared his throat. My throat constricted, and my stomach tightened in a knot at the mention of that word.

He continued, "It was awful. It messed her up bad, mentally and emotionally. I wish to God I'd never heard that conversation. It's haunted me ever since. Olivia, I know this whole thing scared you, but it scared me, too. I keep thinking … what if that guy … what if he had … taken what I've been so careful to protect for you?"

Oh. My. Gosh. Now I understood better why he'd gotten so angry at Ann. What he'd said made me love him more than ever. He viewed his commitment of sexual purity with me as his way of protecting my innocence. I suddenly recognized the threat that he had experienced, too. He buried his face against my neck and stifled a sob. It was my turn to comfort him. He squeezed his arms around me so tightly that it almost hurt.

"But what happened to Amanda *didn't* happen to me," I reassured him in a calm voice. "We can thank God for that. *And* for the fact that I woke up in time and was able to fight him off."

He slowly repeated, "Able to fight him off." He sat up,

and with some urgency, said, "I forgot to tell you. When we were at the campus police office, I saw a poster for a self-defense class. Students can take it for their required PE credit. Would you do that please?"

"Well, I don't know. I already signed up for dance. I wonder if they'd let me change it."

"Can we look into it? That would help me feel so much better."

"Me too. That's a good idea."

"I mean, you know some kickboxing stuff, and I've seen you beat the crap out of a punching bag at the CCC," he chuckled, "but self-defense is about more than that. Don't you think?"

"Yeah, you're right. It is different. With the kickboxing and the punching bag, I'm on the offense, but last night ..." I started to say but didn't finish because of the lump in my throat.

"Are you going to tell your parents about what happened?"

I slowly shook my head at the thought of that. "No. I don't see what the point would be." He didn't argue.

"Can we do something we've never done before?" he asked. I looked at him suspiciously. I could think of some stuff we'd never done, but those would be strange things to suggest right then. "Get your mind out of the gutter, Miller," he teased. He got up and went down on his knees beside the bed. "Can we pray?"

"Oh, okay," I agreed and got down next to him. He took my hand in his, and we bowed our heads.

I wasn't sure what to expect. Were we going to pray silently? Or should I pray out loud? This was totally new to me. I'd *never* had a guy want to pray with me! I was working up the nerve to try it, but he started speaking first.

"Dear Lord," he began in a quiet voice, "Thank you for keeping Olivia safe. Help her to not have any more nightmares. Forgive me for how angry I got and how I acted. Help me know how to be ... the kind of guy that you want for Olivia. Thank you for giving her to me ... for giving her *back* to me. Amen."

I would have tried to pray too if I hadn't started crying. "Oh, no. I'm sorry. Don't cry. Was that too weird. It felt weird," he said nervously.

"No, it was perfect." I assured him with a smile. "Thank you."

"You're welcome."

We fell asleep, holding each other in that narrow twin bed. I slept like a baby.

* * * * * *

On the way to Leeville the next morning, we stopped at Suzy's for a late breakfast. The same waitress spotted us as we walked in. I smiled at her, and she winked at me. It was sweet that she remembered us.

At home, I looked for changes in my mom. I was hopeful that her medication had started to help. There were subtleties that I picked up on in the first few days. She had more energy, and she'd gotten a somewhat more stylish haircut. That was a sign to me that she was taking better care of herself. Emma was looking better, too. Apparently, they had taken a cooking class together and were planning to take more. That was so cool!

My mom and I were in the kitchen alone together, and I was helping her wash and dry the dishes. I asked, "How are things are going? Are the meds working?"

"Yeah, some. Dr. Cunningham and Mrs. Davis said it could take several weeks to get the full benefit. It's certainly not happening overnight, but I'm doing better about some things."

"Like what?" I prodded. I could tell she was uncomfortable with talking about this stuff. I was too, but in the wake of the Thanksgiving "intervention", I thought it was important to keep up an open dialogue.

She shrugged, "I've gone from taking naps every day to once every couple of days instead."

"That's good!"

"I guess so. I still have trouble getting up in the morning. And I ... well ... It's helping to meet with Mrs. Davis a couple of times a week, but none of this has been easy."

"I know it's hard. There'll be days when that soul crushing, deep, dark pit will threaten to pull you back in. But you'll get stronger, and it'll get easier to fight it off."

She stopped drying the dish she was holding and looked at me thoughtfully for a moment. "Sounds like you're speaking from experience."

"Well ..." I paused and tried to decide if I wanted to share my problems with her. I still didn't feel comfortable with my parents knowing that much about my life. "Let's just say I've had my own struggles too ... my own pit. But I've managed to get out of it, and I'm a better person for it. You will be too."

"Okay. Hey, your dad still doesn't know anything about the medication or the counseling. Please, let's keep it that way."

"I will. How do you think Emma's doing? Has she gone to see Kate's mom for counseling?"

"Only twice. I think she's okay though. She broke up with that boy Tyler. It may be my imagination, but she *seems* happier now. Before they broke up, there was lots of drama."

"As there usually is with Emma," I said, and we laughed lightly. "She hadn't mentioned to me that they'd broken up. What happened?"

"I don't know. She didn't necessarily tell me either. I had to ask. I noticed she wasn't on the phone with him as much anymore, and he hasn't come around for a couple of weeks."

"Well, maybe it's for the best," I speculated.

CH. 26 ~ FROM SANTA

"Okay, so when are you going to tell me about what happened with Tyler?" I finally asked Emma because she still hadn't said anything about it to me.

"Tyler's a jerk," she mumbled.

"What happened?"

"Promise you won't tell Mom and Dad?"

I sat down on her bed where she was sprawled out, studying for a final. "I promise."

"We broke up because of sex."

Eeek. I tried not to jump to conclusions and said, "Okay, you're gonna have to give me more than that, Emma."

"He kept wanting to go all the way, but I wouldn't let him. So, I guess I'm the Goody Two Shoes you wanted me to be after all."

"Oh, Emma." I thumped her on the leg. "Well, I guess I want to say I'm proud of you, but you'll probably roll your eyes at me." She obliged with a mega eye roll but couldn't keep from smiling. "Being a GTS isn't so bad, you know? It'll save you from a bunch of emotional baggage and other yucky stuff I'm sure you've heard about already."

"You mean like STDs?"

"Yep, and other stuff," I said, thinking of Ann's misadventure.

"I know, but that's not why I wouldn't do it with Tyler. He's never had sex either, so I wasn't worried about catching something from him."

"Hmmm. Then why didn't you do it? If you don't mind me asking."

She shrugged. "It just didn't feel right. I'm not going to let a guy pressure me into it because he says he loves me. Or because he says he'll break up with me if I don't do it. Besides, I'm only *fourteen*."

"Ahhh, music to my ears, little sis."

"Mom's doing better, don't you think?" she asked, changing the subject.

"Yeah."

"One day, Dad had been yelling about something, and she came and asked me if I wanted to go out with her for a while."

"What for? To get out of the house, away from him?"

"Yeah, I think so. We didn't go do anything in particular besides go to Sonic for drinks. And we didn't even talk about why we'd left. It was weird. But it was kinda cool, too."

"Good. I'm glad."

"I never told you thank you," she said.

"For what?"

"For finally getting Mom to acknowledge that there was a problem and to start doing something about it. Thank you for that."

"You're welcome. You helped too. I'm sorry we waited so long to do it. It's the kind of thing that sets in and builds up over time. If it goes unaddressed for too long, it becomes entrenched. I learned that in psychology," I finished in a know-it-all-tone and tossed a stuffed animal from her dresser at her. She caught it and threw it back.

"Oh, go away, you college student. I've got a *high school* test to study for."

"Fine. Love ya," I said.

"Love you, too. You want to do a kickboxing workout

later?"

"Sure. Come find me when you're done studying."

* * * * * *

Emma poked her head into my room and asked, "Are you still up for a workout?"

I'd been unpacking a few things and had let my mind wander onto thoughts of Ann, wondering if she was okay. I didn't like it that I was worried about her. I wanted to just be mad at her for what she'd let happen to me.

"Yeah, let's do it," I replied and tried to shake off the bad feelings.

But as we got into the workout, I allowed the memories of the near assault to take over. No matter how hard I punched and kicked, I couldn't get any satisfaction from it. I kept remembering that helplessness; being trapped and silenced with a hand over my mouth.

"What's your deal?" Emma asked.

"What do you mean?"

"You've got a lot of pent up anger or something."

"Oh. I don't know," I said evasively, but suddenly I *had* to get out of the house.

I went straight to the CCC. They'd already closed for the day. Thankfully, someone who knew me was there and let me in. I made a beeline for the punching bag, hoping that hitting it would bring more relief than punching the air had with the video workout.

I allowed the events of that night to fully play out in my mind again and took out my anger and fear on the bag. The guy without a face took a symbolic beating, and while I was at it, so did Ann. Then I threw in my dad for good measure and old time's sake.

Completely exhausted, I put the gloves away, and made my way out to the parking lot. I felt much better and thought about going to see one of my friends or Cameron, but I was a sweaty mess. Instead, I went back home and found Emma. Our time together had been spoiled by my moodiness. I wanted to make it up to her.

"You want to go out? Do something fun?" I asked her. She was sprawled out on her bed again with books all around her.

"I'd love to!" she exclaimed and slammed a book shut. "Did you forget that you're back in Leeville though? There's nothing fun to do around here."

I gave her a mischievous look. "Grab your coat and come with me."

We went to my room, and I showed her the rolls and rolls, *and rolls*, of wrapping paper that our mom had brought down from the attic for the holidays. Our mom was, shall we say, an impulsive shopper and sale addict. She couldn't pass up a good deal and habitually hit up all the after-Christmas markdowns every year. Before us stood the spoils of her shopping sprees. I was counting on the fact that she wouldn't miss a couple dozen rolls. Besides, I knew she had more in the attic that I figured I'd bring down to cover the shortage.

Emma got caught up in the suspense and excitement of whatever I had planned and helped me gather a couple of flashlights, wrapping paper, and rolls of tape. We had to be careful to not draw our parents' attention, but we managed to get out of the house unquestioned.

Our "neighborhood" was in the country. Houses were half a mile or more apart, and there were no privacy fences or streetlights. An old nemesis of mine from high school, Tasha Breckenridge, lived on the other side of the neighborhood. That's where I was headed.

Tasha and I had been good friends, but a few years ago, she had lured a boyfriend away from me and dumped him shortly thereafter. Then she'd tried to cause problems between me and Cameron earlier that year around the time of prom. I'd heard that Tasha was taking classes at CJC, so I was counting on the fact that she'd still be living at home with her parents. It wasn't that I necessarily had a vendetta against her, I just wanted to pull a prank, and she was the most obvious victim. Mind you, this was not something I was in the habit of doing, and I was nervous.

Thrilled to see her crummy green Chevrolet Chevette in the driveway, I turned off my headlights and cautiously approached. She liked to tell people that she drove a Vette to give the impression that she had a Corvette.

I laughed maniacally on impulse, and Emma asked, "Um ... what ... exactly are we doing?" with some reservation, though I could tell she was still up for whatever I had in mind. I told her about foiling Preston's stuff in his dorm room, and she thought it was hilarious. So, she understood what we were about to do to Tasha's car.

We snuck up to the Chevette and wrapped it—or most of it—in wrapping paper. Since it was dark, and we had to take turns holding the flashlight, it took longer than I'd expected. And of course, there was the ever-present risk of being detected. I had told Emma that if we were approached by anyone, to keep her mouth shut, and let me do the talking and take the rap.

We managed to hold off the hysterical laughter until we'd driven away. I'd never seen Emma laugh so hard. I was seriously afraid she was going to hyperventilate. Or pee her pants.

"I loved the tag you left on the door handle!" she squealed.

"From Santa!"

Maybe Tasha would see the hodge-podge wrapped car and think Santa had brought her something new, but underneath, it would be the same old green Chevette. Poor Tasha.

It was childish, I know. And it may have even been stupid to involve my sister, but it was worth it. Emma and I swore we'd never tell anyone about it. Even if questioned, we'd have to deny everything. She said that meant I couldn't tell Cameron or Lyla or Kate, either. I think she liked having a secret between the two of us.

* * * * * *

I got together with Cameron and our friends at Josh's house. It was great to see everyone. We were all a bit different since the last time we'd seen each other. I couldn't put my finger on what it was. It may have been that we were stuck in that stage between being teenagers and adults.

I overheard Lyla ask Cameron, "Is Olivia doing okay? She doesn't seem like herself." They were in the kitchen. I was outside the door about to go in but stopped when I heard that. *God forgive me for eavesdropping.*

"Yeah, she's okay. I think the first semester didn't go quite as she expected. You should talk to her, though. She's missed you and Kate a lot, especially since her roommate turned out to be such a disaster," he said.

"Oh, yeah, she told me about that crazy girl."

"There was ... a *whole lot* of crazy. You have no idea," he said. I didn't particularly care for the fact that they were talking about me, but I was thankful to Cameron for not giving Lyla any details.

I did finally tell her about the incident a few days later. We spent a whole day trying to catch up on *Beverly Hills, 90210* episodes, and then she spent the night at my house. We stayed up late talking. It was therapeutic for me to tell her about it.

She consoled me and said, "I admire you for wanting to make sure you don't get labeled a victim, but don't discount what happened simply because the guy didn't accomplish what he was planning to do. The fact that he had the *intention* is bad enough, in and of itself."

I got what she was saying and told her I'd be looking into a self-defense class. I voiced my biggest concern, which was that I might very well run into the guy in a class or on campus and never know it. How was I going to keep from being suspicious of every guy I encountered?

CH. 27 ~ WRAP IT UP

I was able to make some money over semester break at the CCC because Yvette and Diana took some time off. It was good for my dwindling bank account. I was loving my new car, but I still owed my dad for it. The sooner I could get him paid back, the less time he'd have to figure out how to attach strings to it.

I also got a chance to do some community service over the holiday. The CCC always did an annual Christmas project of some kind. That year, I was late coming in on it, but I was able to help some, and Cameron joined me.

Billy and Mrs. K had worked closely with their church to identify a few families in the area that had fallen on hard times and were struggling financially. They arranged for item and cash donations to be collected at the CCC to provide them with something for Christmas. With the cash donations, Mrs. K sent volunteers to shop for gifts for the children of those families. Volunteers paired up and randomly drew family names. Cameron and I drew the Robinsons.

The Robinsons had recently lost their home, and almost everything in it, from a fire. Since then, they'd been living in a travel trailer on a family member's land, waiting for an insurance check so they could figure out how to start recovering.

"So, do you know the Robinsons?" Cameron asked me. We were walking into Walmart, and he was pushing a cart.

"Never heard of them. Mrs. K's notes say there's an eight-year-old girl, Betsy, and a ten-year-old boy, Rusty. We've got their clothes and shoe sizes. Let's look for those first, and then maybe a couple of toys or games. What do you think?"

"Sounds like a plan. You want to get in the cart and let me push you around?" he asked.

I rolled my eyes. "Not a chance!" I put my arm around him and hooked my finger through a belt loop on his jeans.

"Hey, what are your plans for Christmas day?"

"We're going to my aunt and uncle's in Silsby. You remember Rachel and Carl?"

"Oh, yeah. Uncle Carl. He's funny. Silsby? Where's that?"

"It's only about forty-five minutes west of here, so it won't be overnight or anything. What are your plans?"

"James and Jasmine are coming over. I was hoping you could, too. What time do you think you'll be back?" James was Cameron's older brother, and Jasmine was his girlfriend. They were students at Aberdeen University and had an apartment together near campus.

"Hard to say. My family doesn't exactly try to follow a schedule. If I drive my own car, I could leave there sometime around two o'clock and come over to your house."

"That would be great. You'd get there in time for dinner."

"I can't wait," I said and grinned at him. He pulled me into his arms, right there in the kids' clothing section at Walmart and kissed me long and hard.

"That was nice," I said in surprise.

"I'm so glad we're back together. When we weren't, and I thought about not being with you at Christmas, it sucked. This is my favorite time of year, and I'm *really* excited to get to spend it with you."

"Thank you. I'm excited, too. I even have one of your Christmas presents already. I got it before we ..."

"Before we took a break," he filled in for me.

"Yeah, before that."

"Hmmm, I wonder what it could be. I helped you move to the new dorm room and didn't see anything that looked like it could be a gift for me."

"Don't do that," I playfully admonished. "Stop trying to figure it out. I had it tucked away someplace you wouldn't see it."

"Where? In your underwear drawer?"

"Cameron!" I laughed and blushed.

"Because if *that's* where you had it, I would have seen it," he said with confidence. "Remember, I set that bear trap. I discovered that the top drawer of your dresser is where you keep your—shall we say—delicates."

"Oh, my gosh!" I reached around him in an attempt to hit him on the butt, but he scooted out of the way. "You didn't go digging around looking in that drawer, did you?"

"No. It took considerable restraint, though, I will tell you that."

"Your gift wasn't in there anyway. It was in my suitcase. I wanted to make sure I didn't forget it when I got ready to leave for break."

"What were you going to do with it if we hadn't gotten back together?"

"Probably give it to my uncle Carl. He likes ugly Christmas sweaters, too," I said and clapped my hand over my mouth as if I'd told a secret.

"What?!" He pulled my head down under his arm like he was going to give me a noogie.

"Don't you dare!" I squealed and managed to escape his grasp.

"Hey, you guys!" someone called out, and we looked over and saw Mrs. K and Billy. We laughed like a couple of kids who had been caught misbehaving.

"Hello," Cameron said and waved.

"Hi," I said. "We were taking a break." I held up the list and added, "Back to shopping! See you later." They waved and smiled, and we turned the other way and cracked up again.

"Okay, we need to get busy. Stop sidetracking us, Olivia," Cameron joked. "We've still got to go wrap everything we buy, don't we?"

"Yeah. Let's do that at my house. We've got lots of wrapping paper. My mom stockpiles it like there's going to be a shortage someday."

We found a few clothing items and shoes for each of the kids and then checked out the toy aisles. We settled on a Lego set for the boy and a Spirograph set for the girl. I threw in a book that was something I would have read as an eight-year-old, and we also got a board game for the whole family.

"It's hard shopping for kids you don't even know," I said. Of course, I had trouble gift shopping for anyone. I always second guessed myself about whether the person would like it or not.

"I know," Cameron agreed. "Who's going to deliver all this stuff to the families?"

"I think it'll be some people from Mrs. K's church. They'll do it on Christmas Eve."

"We should go with them."

"That's a good idea."

At checkout, the total was more than we had cash for, which I expected, but Cameron pulled out a credit card and paid for the rest of it, saying it was his personal contribution to the cause. He wouldn't even consider letting me help cover the shortage.

* * * * * *

We got to my house, and nobody else was there. In the past, my parents had a strict rule about not having boys over without an adult present. I debated if I should be there alone with Cameron but decided we had a job to do, getting those gifts wrapped. And we were nineteen, for crying out loud! If we couldn't be trusted there, how could my parents have trusted me the last several months I'd been away from home?

"Where is everyone?" Cameron asked.

"Emma's not out of school yet, Dad's at work, and Mom's ... I don't know where she is." Actually, I did. She was at a counseling appointment, but I didn't feel like explaining any of that right then.

"Ahhh, so we're alone?" he asked and pulled me toward him. I allowed myself to fall under his spell, even more so as he began kissing me. His hand cradled my face, and his tongue darted between my lips. "Hmmm," he hummed, "you taste so good."

"What do I taste like?"

"Like *you*. You're one of a kind, Olivia," he said and let his teeth graze the skin on my neck. My breathing sped up, and I got light-headed. "Just seeing you ... thinking about you ... smelling you, touching you," he whispered lovingly between totally tantalizing kisses. "Everything about you turns me on until I feel like ... like I'm going to lose my mind if I can't have you ... all of you."

My lips and face tingled from oxygen deprivation, and I was practically panting in anticipation of more. But he pulled away and nonchalantly asked, "So, where's that wrapping paper?"

I gasped in surprise and fell against him. "What the heck, Cameron? You can't do that to me."

"What? What did I do?" he asked, feigning innocence.

"No fair." I slapped him playfully on the arm and tried to rein in my hormones.

"I know. I'm sorry. I couldn't help it," he said guiltily and grinned at me.

"Okay ... wrapping paper."

"Yeah. Where is it?"

"In my room."

"What?" he asked teasingly. "Are you trying to lure me to your bedroom?"

"No!"

"I'm kidding!"

"It's in my room because my mom put all the Christmas stuff there when she brought it down from the attic."

I headed for the stairs and turned around, giving him a coy look, which made him race after me. His hands cupped my butt cheeks, and I squealed, collapsing in laughter at the top. I rolled over and was delighted when he started to lower himself on top of me.

"You are being so *bad*, Cameron," I said. The smile on my face let him know I loved it.

"I know, but you're irresistible," he said in a low, gruff voice and kissed me passionately. Then, instead of lying fully on top of me, he jumped up and said, "Let's get to work. Quit fooling around or we're never going to get this done."

"Ahhh!" I groaned in frustration and beat my fists on the floor. He laughed and helped me to my feet.

We grabbed a few rolls of wrapping paper and carried them downstairs. The living room was a good place to work; safe territory should anyone arrive home to find us there alone.

"So, how do you to this?" he asked.

I couldn't help but laugh at him. "What? Wrap presents? Are you serious? Don't tell me. The maid does this kind of thing for you, too."

"No. My mom," he admitted, pretending to be shy.

"Okay. Lesson number one," I began and proceeded to show him how to expertly wrap gifts. I'd learned from a pro; my mom, the wrapping paper connoisseur.

"You're the coolest girlfriend ever, Olivia," Cameron announced out of the blue.

"Awww, thank you," I cooed and paused what I was doing to look over at him. "You're the most amazing boyfriend ever."

We were sitting on the floor about two feet apart with wrapping paper scraps and ribbons and bows all around us.

He reached out his hand toward me, and I took it, pulling him down onto his back.

Hovering over his face, I lowered my lips to his. His hands on the back of my head held me in place as his mouth did amazing things to mine. Then he picked up a bow and stuck it to my forehead. I giggled but left it there and laid down perpendicular to him with my head on his stomach.

Sighing in contentment, I said, "Right now ... with you ... I'm happier than I've ever been." I rolled over onto my stomach and propped my chin up in my hands so I could look at him.

"Me too. Have I told you lately that I love you?"

"Yes. But you can tell me again."

He reached over to push some hair behind my ear and said, "I love you so much, Olivia." He patted the bow on my forehead and added, "Bow and all." I'd forgotten it was there and reached up to whip it off and throw it at him.

We heard someone unlocking the front door, and I sat up quickly, wanting to make it look like we were working hard cleaning up the mess we'd made.

"Oh, hello, Olivia. Hi, Cameron," my mom said.

"Hello, Mrs. Miller."

"You can call me Sheila." She looked around and asked, "What's going on here?"

"Christmas community service project," I replied.

"Oh, yeah? What's the project?" she asked. I explained to her what it was all about, and she was genuinely interested.

"I'd like to help with that. Do you think that would be okay?"

"Sure," I said in surprise. My parents had never shown much interest in what I was involved in at the CCC. But this was my *new* mom. The one who was on medication that was helping her live a more normal life.

* * * * * *

Lyla, Kate, and I went Christmas shopping in Aberdeen. I asked Kate how things were going with her and Josh, and she said they were great. Apparently, she spent a lot of nights at his apartment at AU.

"Your parents aren't freaking out about that?" I asked.

"They did at first, but on nights when I have an eight o'clock class the next morning, it's nice to be closer to campus."

"You signed up for an eight o'clock class?" I asked. "Didn't anyone warn you not to do that?"

"Yes, but it was a prerequisite for a class I need to take this coming semester. It was my only option."

Lyla turned to me and said, "Olivia, would you get her to admit that she and Josh are—" and she made a gesture with her hands that spoke for itself.

"Lyla! I'm going to take you down, girl, and don't think I can't. You're a lightweight," Kate warned and gave her a semi-playful shove.

"Geez, Lyla. It's their business, not ours," I chided.

"She's jealous because she's been pining away for Brian."

"I have not," Lyla retorted. "We broke it off at the end of the summer, and I haven't heard from him since, so let it go, okay?"

"You didn't even try to stay in touch?" I asked.

"No. He knew he wouldn't be coming back for any holidays or breaks because his parents moved too. There's nothing in Leeville for him to come back for."

"There's you," Kate suggested.

"I told you to let it go," Lyla warned.

"Okay, so wait. You haven't dated *anyone* since August? What? Are there *no* guys worth dating at Cambridge Junior College?" I asked.

"It's not necessarily that. I've been busy with work and school. But I'm fine," she insisted. "I don't need a guy to slow me down right now anyway."

Suddenly overcome with sentimentality, I said, "I sure have missed you guys."

"Awww, we've missed you too, Olivia," Lyla cooed

sappily, and they both hugged me. We were in the middle of the mall and got some funny looks, but I didn't care.

We finished our shopping, ate dinner at Casita Jorge's, and then spent the night at Lyla's. We talked about all of us getting together with the guys to do something on New Year's Eve.

I started wondering what my parents would expect from me regarding curfew. Wasn't it time I should be able to make plans without having to second guess what I was "allowed" to do? We were in that vague area of me still being a dependent kid and an adult who could make decisions for myself.

CH. 28 ~ SURPRISING ANNOUNCEMENT

On Christmas Eve, Cameron, my mom, and I went with some other volunteers to deliver food and gifts to the Robinsons and one other family, the Brewsters. We went to the Brewsters first. They were a retired couple that was barely making ends meet on a fixed income. To complicate matters, their son, who had a thirteen-year-old daughter, had recently gone to prison for selling drugs, and they had taken the daughter in because her mom wasn't in the picture anymore.

Wow, and I thought I had problems sometimes. The situations some people find themselves in, whether from their own doing or not, were heartbreaking.

The Brewster's granddaughter, Chelsea, had already turned into an angry teenager. I sensed that she resented having to live with her grandparents, and she wasn't welcoming to us dropping by with "charity". Mrs. Brewster corrected her and said this wasn't charity, it was blessings. She said, "If the good Lord sees fit to have these nice people do this for us, who are we to turn it away or turn our noses up at it?"

Then we went to the Robinsons, and their kids were much more receptive to our visit. They had put up a little Christmas tree—and I mean little—in the tiny living room of the trailer. The kids spent lots of time trying to put the packages under it and rearranging them several times.

Their beaming smiles pulled at my emotions. I couldn't imagine being that age and losing everything in a fire. But they had each other, and they were making the best of things. Mr. and Mrs. Robinson were extremely grateful. It was a good feeling to have helped them out.

We met up with the other volunteers at the church for hot chocolate and cookies and to hang out until time for a candlelight Christmas Eve service. I doubted my mom would stick around for that since the church wasn't Baptist, but she actually stayed.

"Our church decided not to have a service tonight. Last year's got such poor attendance," my mom commented.

"Well, we're glad to have you join us," Mrs. K said.

"Thank you. I know I've never been involved with the stuff Olivia does at your center, and I'm sorry for that. This was a good experience for me."

Mrs. K put her hand on my mom's arm and said warmly in that way that she had of making a person feel truly special, "You are so welcome, Sheila. I'm glad the Lord gave you an opportunity to experience it."

It crossed my mind that I should pass on Mrs. K's advice to my mom about the best medicine for self pity, because maybe what some of my mom's depression boiled down to was exactly that.

* * * * * *

Christmas Day, I spent a few hours with my family in Silsby and then drove to Cameron's house. Luckily nobody gave me a hard time about leaving. Since we'd been together for almost a year, everyone understood that I didn't want to miss out on spending some time with him and his family.

Walking up to his house, I carried two presents for him. Uh, oh. I should have brought something for his dad and James and Jasmine. I was so stupid for not thinking of that! What if they got something for me? How embarrassing. But it was too late to do anything about it then. I needed to start thinking like an adult and plan better.

Cameron answered the door and said, "Merry Christmas."

"Merry Christmas!" I kissed him. "Hmmm, do I taste wine?"

"Yeah, uh, we've been having some *before* dinner drinks. Well, most of us anyway ..." he said vaguely and looked over his shoulder toward the kitchen. "Come in here with me for a minute." He took my hand and led me into the game room.

"What's going on?" I whispered.

"You're not going to believe this, but James and Jasmine made an announcement about an hour ago. She's pregnant." My jaw dropped, and my eyes got wide. "Yeah, and things are a *little* strained right now."

"Oh, no. Should I go? Maybe I shouldn't be—"

"No way," he said and wrapped his arms around me. "You're not going anywhere."

"Okay. How is your dad taking the news?"

"Stunned. Disappointed. But he's trying to be cool about it, you know, what else can he do?"

"Yeah ..." I said thoughtfully. This *was* a surprise. James and Jasmine were so young, and they weren't done with college yet. "When? I mean, when is the baby due?"

"I think they said sometime in June. Come on, we better get in there or they're going to start wondering where we are."

We went to the kitchen, and I greeted everyone. They all acted like everything was completely normal, but I think the look on my face gave away that I knew. I hugged Jasmine and could tell she was already showing a little. Though, if I hadn't known she was pregnant, I wouldn't have guessed it.

We had a wonderful dinner that my amazing boyfriend had helped his dad prepare. How cool was it that I was dating a guy that knew how to cook and liked to do it? There wasn't too much awkwardness around the table, but there was something below the surface. I hoped my being there wasn't making things more uncomfortable for the rest of them.

"How about us girls clean up the kitchen since you guys did all the work making everything?" Jasmine suggested after dessert.

"That's a good idea," I agreed.

"But *I* didn't do anything," James said, meaning he hadn't helped cook.

He stood up to gather his dishes, and I heard Mr. McClain say something under his breath that sounded like, "Oh, but you *did* do something."

My eyes darted to Cameron. He was shooting his dad a dirty look. Feeling uneasy, I stood up and started gathering dishes to take to the sink, and Jasmine followed.

The guys went into the living room, and Jasmine and I got to work putting leftovers away and loading the dishwasher. From beside me at the sink, she quietly said, "I'm guessing Cameron told you."

"Yeah. Congratulations."

She chuckled lightly. "Thank you, I think. Oh, I don't know what we're going to do." She shook her head and added, "This was *not* in the grand plan."

"I'm sorry. What happened?"

"I was sick a few months ago and on antibiotics which apparently interfere with the effectiveness of birth control pills. I sure didn't know that. Did you?"

"No," I said and filed that away for future reference. "Cameron said you're due in June. At least the spring semester will be over by then."

"And that's the saving grace. I'll actually graduate with an associate degree in nursing in May. But James has another year left. We'll have a couple of months to adjust before his classes start again."

We joined the guys in the living room, and the gift

exchange was totally different than the way my family did it. With mine, it was a free-for-all; everyone opening gifts at the same time, paper and ribbon flying. Cameron's was more deliberate and thoughtful. The giver of the gift watched the recipient open it while everyone else waited their turn.

I handed Cameron one of his gifts, and he asked, "Is this the ugly sweater?"

"I guess you'll have to open it and see for yourself." I was nervous, the way I always was with gift exchanges.

It was an antique-style cigar box that had been decorated with paper printed with music notes and pictures of guitars. "Wow, did you make this?" he asked.

"Are you kidding? I'm not that creative."

"It's cool. Thank you," he said and leaned over to kiss my cheek.

"I found it at an arts and crafts fair that I went to with my mom and sister in Aberdeen last week."

"Oh, so this wasn't the ugly sweater?"

"No, that's this one," I said and handed him another package. I remembered the day that I'd gotten it, back in early October, from a music store in New Haven. I hadn't even been looking for anything in particular, but they had some framed photographs of bands that I started flipping through.

"First, I want you to open one of yours, and then we'll go around the circle," he said. He handed me a small box that I opened to find a pair of tiny silver earrings in the shape of frogs.

"They're so cute, Cameron. Thank you. They practically match my necklace."

Jasmine came over to look at them. "Those are pretty. Why frogs?"

"Frog is an acronym for Fully Rely On God," Cameron answered for me. I had told him about Mrs. K's note.

"Okay, somebody else's turn," I said and started putting the earrings on. I was self-conscious with everyone watching me.

Jasmine, James, and Mr. McClain each took turns opening gifts. It was Cameron's turn again, and he opened the framed picture I'd gotten him. It was an eight by ten print of Jimmie and Stevie Ray Vaughan, Eric Clapton, and Robert Cray. He really liked it, especially because it had the two brothers together.

"Olivia, you're spoiling me," he said and hugged me.

He gave me another gift. It was a new Sony Walkman. He knew my old one had broken from falling on the floor after I'd hit that guy with it.

"Awesome. Thank you," I said, and quietly added. "You spent too much on me."

"No, I didn't. I could never spend too much on you," he assured me, but even so, our gift exchange had been terribly lopsided.

It didn't turn out to be too embarrassing that I hadn't gotten gifts for anyone else. They hadn't gotten anything for me either. Except for Mr. McClain. He gave Jasmine and I each a gift certificate to a spa in Aberdeen. We were both surprised and thankful and talked about getting appointments to go together.

"Thank you, Mr. McClain," I said. "I'm so embarrassed I didn't get you anything."

"Don't worry about it. I wanted to do something special for the two ladies who are making my sons so happy," he said. He smiled and reached over to pat Jasmine on the shoulder. I saw it as his way of letting her know he accepted the situation and would be supportive of them. "Now if you kids will excuse this old man, I've got a date to get ready for."

"What?" James asked incredulously.

"Oh, yeah, James. Dad's become quite the man-about-town," Cameron joked.

"Is it the lady you brought to Cameron's gig last summer?" I asked. I had forgotten all about that.

"No, this is someone different," he chuckled and ducked

out of the room.

"That's so weird!" James whispered and shook his head in disbelief.

"Tell me about it," Cameron laughed.

James asked Cameron, "How do you think he's taking the news about being a grandfather?"

"Hard to tell. I guess it's still sinking in."

"He gave me a hard time when we moved in together, and I feel like he predicted this," James lamented.

"Let's give him time," Jasmine said.

"Have you told Mom?" Cameron asked.

"No. We're going to call her tomorrow."

They told us goodnight and left, leaving Cameron and me with the place to ourselves. He poured us some more wine, and we listened to music on the living room stereo. We were on opposite ends of the couch and had our legs up, overlapping each other's.

"I can't believe I'm going to be an uncle," he said.

"Uncle Cameron," I chuckled. His hand that was on my leg squeezed my calf, and it tickled. I tried to pull it away, but he held onto it.

"Say 'uncle' again," he dared me and slipped his fingers up the leg of my jeans past my ankle. He pulled it back out like he'd been stuck by a cactus. "Ow, woman, when was the last time you shaved those legs?"

"Oh, my gosh, Cameron. You're embarrassing me." I squealed and tried to get free of him. "It is wintertime, you know?"

He tried to tickle me, and we rolled onto the floor laughing. I got my legs on either side of him and squeezed him around the waist between my thighs.

"Wow, your legs are strong. It's kind of a turn-on, but you're making it hard to breathe," he chuckled.

"Say 'uncle'," I demanded.

"Uncle!"

I loosened my grip, and he laid down beside me. "Uh, oh. We're lying down. We get in trouble when we do this,"

I said and sat up.

"No, come on, it's okay. I'll be good," he said seriously and gently pulled me back down. I nestled under his arm, and we laid there and talked for a long time. It was the most amazing way to spend Christmas evening, and we even fell asleep together on the floor. Mr. McClain coming in the front door woke us up.

"Well, hello, there," he said in surprise.

Cameron sat up and stretched. "Oh, hey, Dad. I guess we fell asleep," he said sleepily.

"It's after midnight!" I exclaimed and jumped up. "My parents are probably freaking out."

"Wait, slow down. Do you want me to drive you home?" Cameron asked.

His dad stood nearby with his hands in his pockets and smiled at us. I'm sure we looked like a couple of teenagers—which we were—getting caught having a sleepover.

"No, I'm okay to drive," I said and put my shoes on. "Goodnight, Mr. McClain," I called as we walked out to my car.

"Be careful. I love you," Cameron said and kissed me goodbye.

"I love you, too."

"Merry Christmas."

"The merriest," I said dreamily.

I drove home quickly and found that everyone had gone to bed already.

Should I wake them up to tell them I'm home? Oh, darn, why hadn't we discussed what the "rules" were? I decided to just go to bed. If they were able to go to sleep without worrying about me, there wasn't any sense in waking them up.

* * * * * *

I slept late the next morning, and my parents and Emma weren't even there when I made my way downstairs. They'd left a note that they went to do some after-Christmas shopping. I spent the next several hours in a luxurious, hot bath reading completely non-educational fiction for fun. It was blissful.

Later, my dad said, "In the future, I'd appreciate a call if you plan on staying out past midnight."

"Okay, sure. I'm sorry about last night. I got home about a quarter to one," I said.

"That's okay, I guess. We weren't too worried since we knew you were at Cameron's house."

Okay, that's cool. Maybe he was chilling out some.

CH. 29 ~ HAPPY NEW YEAR!

"There's a New Year's Eve party in Aberdeen that Josh wants to go to. Do you guys want to come?" Kate asked from behind her camera lens. She was photographing Lyla in outfits and dresses she'd made for a portfolio she was building. I was acting as Lyla's fashion assistant. It was fun—like playing dress-up.

"I guess so. Where is it?" I asked, handing Lyla a belt she was pointing at on her bed.

"No, not that one. Give me the brown one for this dress," Lyla instructed.

Kate said, "It's somewhere in that ritzy neighborhood, Toscana Villas. Josh knows this guy named Serge. It's his parents' house."

Fastening the brown belt around her petite little waist, Lyla asked, "Will his parents be there?"

Kate shrugged. "How should I know. Who cares? Josh said the alcohol will be plentiful."

"Count me in!" Lyla said and struck a pose.

"And this guy won't mind that you're inviting other people?" I asked.

"I guess not," Kate said and shrugged again, shooting a few pictures of Lyla who was hamming it up for the camera.

"Okay, since you have so many *concrete* details, it

sounds like such a good idea!" I teased.

"Let's go, and if it's lame, we'll take off and do our own thing," Lyla suggested, and we agreed.

"But ... I've got to figure out what to tell my parents."

"Oh, geez, Olivia, *still* with the curfew?" Lyla asked and was already changing into a different outfit.

"I don't know! They haven't said, and I haven't asked. There's this unspoken ... weirdness about it, like I don't know how they feel about me staying out half the night."

"Well, figure it out, and make sure you can go with us, whatever you have to do. We're gonna ring in 1992 in style!" Lyla announced.

* * * * * *

I settled on telling my parents that my friends and I were going to go to a party at the house of a friend of Josh's and that I would "probably" spend the night at Lyla's. It was vague, and I wasn't sure if they picked up on that and let it pass, or if they'd decided to give me free rein, but they didn't make a big deal out of it.

Lyla rode with Cameron and me, and we met Josh and Kate there. Serge's place in the Toscana Villas neighborhood was beyond posh. Josh knew Serge from one of his business classes at AU. Serge's parents were in New Zealand for the holiday. The place screamed of extravagant wealth.

Counting us, there were about twenty people at the party. My friends and I were the youngest, but we didn't feel out of place. Or at least I didn't. As far as I could tell, Cameron was having a good time.

There was a bartender who only spoke Spanish. Cameron ordered a Long Island Iced Tea for me, but the guy made something that more closely resembled a watered-down Coke with too much of something that was lemon flavored. It was okay, but not what I remembered the drink *should* taste like. Heck, for all I knew, that first one I'd had could have been something else entirely, and I'd never know!

Serge, or more accurately Sergio, was suave and good-looking. He flirted with all the single girls and even with some of us who weren't single. He paid special attention to Lyla. I started to wonder if she would still need a ride home that night or if she'd stay there with him. Maybe even run off and elope or something with the way they were acting.

A guy and girl who were salsa dancing got a few of us to try it out. Kate, Lyla, and I had had enough to drink that our inhibitions were relaxed, and we had a lot of fun learning. There was more laughing than dancing going on. Cameron didn't want to try it, so he got the enjoyment of watching. Sergio danced with several girls, but with Lyla, she didn't have to do anything because he picked her up off her feet, held her incredibly close, and did the moves by himself. I could almost see her swooning for him.

Close to midnight, we turned the TV on to watch the ball drop in Times Square. I was sitting on Cameron's lap in a sofa chair, and we were making out before the countdown even ended. Everything around us faded away, and it was just the two of us.

"I want to spend every New Year's Eve with you," I whispered in his ear and breathed against his neck. His arms tightened around me, and he pulled me closer, which didn't even seem possible for how glued together we already were.

He moved his lips close to my ear and whispered, "Me too. I'm never going to be without you again." That was a declaration, not just an *I don't ever want to be without you.*

Getting lost in my love and desire for him, I wondered if there was somewhere we could go to be alone. Lyla joked, "You two get a room," which brought my attention back to the party. I looked up and saw that she was cradled in Serge's arms, and he was headed toward the back of the house.

Wait a minute. Where is he taking her?

"Lyla?" I said protectively and got up from Cameron's lap to try to check on her.

"I'm fine, Olivia. We're coming right back," she giggled. Serge came back about fifteen seconds later, still carrying Lyla who now had a big gift bag hanging on her arm. He set her down on the bar and pulled miniature champagne bottles out of the bag. They were party favors which he and Lyla started handing out to everyone.

Cameron and I were getting ready to leave, and I half-jokingly asked Lyla, "Sooo, do you still need a ride home, or are you going to stay here with Serge?"

"Are you kidding? He's fun. And hot! Oh, my!" she said, giggling and fanning herself. "But we're only flirting. He's totally not my type. I couldn't pin down a guy like that to save my life."

"Okay, good," I said in relief. "I was going to have to talk you out of it if you'd said anything else."

"You must think I'm an idiot."

"No, I don't! But I saw lots of ... chemistry between you two."

"Yeah, it was nice," she giggled again. "But I need to go home tonight. Take me home!" Then she added in a whisper, "Before I change my mind."

I grabbed Cameron's hand and chased Lyla toward the door. We waved goodbye to everyone and thanked Serge profusely for a wonderful evening. Josh and Kate were right behind us.

"Are you okay to drive?" I asked Cameron.

"Yeah, I stopped drinking about two hours ago. All I had was a couple of beers anyway."

"Okay, what about you?" I asked Josh, paranoid about everyone's safety.

"I'm driving tonight," Kate said and held up the keys to Josh's Corvette. "Don't worry, Olivia, I'm fine."

"Okay, then. Goodnight, and happy New Year," I said and hugged Kate and Josh. "Thanks for taking us to a fabulous party."

"You're welcome. You guys be careful," Josh said.

Cameron, Lyla, and I got in the truck. She lounged

against the passenger side door and closed her eyes. I asked her if she was okay.

"Yes, drive me away from this place, or I might change my mind," she said and whimpered. "Oh, Serge! You hunka hunka burnin' love!"

We laughed at her and Cameron asked, "Was he *that* good looking?"

Uh, oh, is this a test?

"In a ... European sort of way, I guess. But totally not *my* type," I answered safely and scooted closer to him. I nibbled his ear to reassure him that only *he* was my type. He made that low humming sound that I loved and squeezed my thigh.

I leaned my spinning head against the seatback and looked over at Lyla. Her eyes were still closed, and a slight smile was on her face. Cameron put on some music and drove us back to Leeville. Pulling up to Lyla's house, I looked over at her. She was sound asleep.

"I hate to wake her," I said quietly.

"Yeah, I know. Don't do it yet. Come here," he said and put his arm around me. He quietly suggested, "Come home with me tonight?" and kissed me deeply, making sure I got his meaning.

I moaned softly into his mouth, and he slid his hand inside my jacket. My mind played out what it would be like to do what he'd asked. His lips and tongue were trying to convince me it was a good idea, and my body was responding in the affirmative.

Lyla stirred and woke up. "Oh, geez, if y'all are going to do that, let me get out first." She opened the door and practically fell out because of the way she'd been leaning on it. That led to a fit of laughter. From her. Cameron and I were trying to calm our hormones.

"I want to ..." I said to him.

"But ..." he said expectantly with a look of frustration and resignation.

"I'm sor—" I started to say.

"It's okay ... for now. Goodnight, Olivia. I love you," he said and kissed me again. He called to Lyla, "Goodnight, Lyla."

"Goodnight, lover boy. I love you too!" she called to him, giggling all the way to her front door.

I kissed Cameron one more time, told him I loved him, and hopped out of the truck before I had a chance to change *my* mind the way Lyla had been afraid she might. What was Cameron thinking, trying to tempt me like that?! And what did he mean by, "It's okay ... for now?"

CH. 30 ~ MEETING MONIQUE

Getting switched from dance to self-defense was the first thing I did after getting back to campus. Thankfully, it was an easy schedule change. Next, I met my new roommate. As I entered my room, she whirled around in surprise from where she was sitting at her desk.

"Hi, sorry if I scared you," I apologized. "I'm your roommate."

"That's okay. Olivia, right? The RA told me about you," she said and got up and helped me roll my suitcase into the room because my hands were full of other stuff. She smiled easily and introduced herself as Monique Bryant. She was friendly, and I was struck by how beautiful she was. Her hair was long, dark and wavy, and her skin was a smooth, golden brown color and flawless. I assumed she must be bi-racial, and the more she spoke, the more I picked up on an accent I wasn't familiar with.

"So where are you from?" I asked and started unpacking.

"New Orleans." She pronounced it "ore-lins" which was different from the way I thought it was pronounced, "ore-leenz".

"You transferred here, right? What brings you to Texas?"

She sat down on her bed and fell back with a big sigh. "Long story. Yes, I transferred here from a small school in Louisiana, but NHU is where I should have come in the first place. I got accepted here and even *wanted* to come here because NHU's got a great education program. I want to be a teacher. But I screwed up and stayed in Louisiana because of a boyfriend. *That* was a mistake. We broke up about two months into the semester, but I was stuck there."

"Oh, that sucks. I'm sorry, but welcome to NHU. What do you want to teach?"

"Early childhood, elementary. I love kids." She smiled wistfully. She was gorgeous. I hoped I wasn't making her uncomfortable with my staring, but she had this enchanting quality about her that made it hard to look away. She was about the same size as me, and we had similar figures, but her face and hair were way better than mine.

"Forgive me for asking, but what's your accent?" I asked.

"Cajun. Ma mère, sorry, my momma is Cajun. My daddy was a black man from Mississippi who took off when I was a baby."

"Oh, you speak French?" I asked. "I know some. Well, I've had two and a half years of classes, so I should know more, but I read it and understand it better than I can speak it."

"Cajun French is a little different, but you'll probably understand me fine. I don't talk that way often. Though I do slip into it sometimes. Especially if I'm tired, or when I've been drinking," she giggled. "But enough about me, tell me about yourself, Olivia. I love your name, by the way."

"Thank you. I love yours, too. Um, let's see," I began and sat down on my bed. "I'm a social science major. I haven't decided on what field I'm most interested in yet, but I'm leaning toward sociology. I'm from Leeville which is a small town two and half hours northwest of here."

There was a knock on the door, and I heard Cameron

call my name. "Oh, and that's my boyfriend, Cameron," I said and jumped up to open the door.

"Hey, baby," he said and pulled me into an embrace, kissing me as if we hadn't seen each other earlier that day in Leeville. I blushed and smiled at Scott who was standing nearby rolling his eyes at us.

"How'd you get through security?" I asked.

"I've got my ways." He winked at me and laughed. "Nah, Lauren saw us and buzzed us through."

"Okay. Hey, my new roommate is here," I said and introduced everyone. Scott was instantly mesmerized by Monique. I should have offered him a towel to wipe up the drool.

"Nice to meet you. Welcome to NHU," Cameron said.

"Thank you."

"So, we were wondering if you want to go grab something to eat. Join us, Monique?" Cameron asked.

"Yeah, come with us," I said and looked at her to see if she was interested. Scott looked hopeful. *Isn't he dating someone? I'll have to ask Cameron about that.*

She wavered and said, "I'm gonna be straight with you. I'm cash poor. It's taken all I've got to just be here, so y'all go on without me."

"No, come on, it'll be our treat. Sort of a welcome to New Haven," Cameron offered.

"Yeah, and besides, the dining halls aren't open until tomorrow, so you gotta eat, right?" Scott added.

"Y'all are too nice," Monique said.

"Please, come with us. It'll be fun," I insisted.

"Well, okay. I guess if you're sure."

"What do you like? Is pizza okay?" Cameron asked.

"Pizza's great. Thanks." We grabbed our purses and went in Scott's car.

I didn't want to get my hopes up too soon that Monique and I could become friends, but I had a good feeling about her. She was genuine, and there were no indications that she was there to reinvent herself like Ann had been. She asked me things about myself as often as I asked her stuff about herself. She laughed easily and had a good sense of humor.

I could tell that Scott was totally enamored with her. What I couldn't tell was if Monique picked up on it and would reciprocate that interest. She was nice and polite to him but didn't flirt. Not that what Scott was doing could truly be called flirting. Gawking, yes, but flirting? He would work up to that.

* * * * * *

On Saturday morning, Monique went to apply for a job at the campus bookstore, and I slept in. Then Cameron and I celebrated a late Christmas with his mom at her house. Fortunately, Jerk Jerry was away, driving his truck.

"Have you heard from James lately?" Cameron asked his mom.

"Yes," she replied and sighed. "He's going to go and make me a grandmother before I'm ready. How's your dad taking it?"

"Okay, I guess. I know he's worried about James finishing college. This may put a kink in their long-term business plans." James and Mr. McClain planned to someday have their own architecture firm.

"Well, sometimes things don't turn out like we think they will ..." she said thoughtfully and looked sad. Was she thinking about her own life?

"We all know that to be true," Cameron commented, sounding almost bitter.

She brought her attention back to us and said, "It'll work out somehow. I hope you two don't make the same mistake."

I blushed, and Cameron shook his head. "Excuse me," he said in disbelief.

"I just want to make sure y'all are being careful and don't find yourselves in the same situation."

"That's not something you need to worry about with us, Mom."

She raised her eyebrows in a questioning way but didn't ask any more about it. We didn't offer any further information, either. Why did everyone assume that we were having sex?

* * * * * *

On our way back to Bellamy Hall, I asked Cameron about his mom's comment. He got aggravated and said, "I can't believe she had the nerve to suggest something like that about us. She's the one living with her boyfriend."

"But *she's* probably not in any danger of getting pregnant. I think that's all she was getting at."

"Hmmm, that's true," he agreed and changed the subject. "So, it looks like your new roommate is a drastic improvement."

"Yesss! I think I really lucked out this time. She's cool."

"She's pretty too, or so Scott keeps telling me," he said as he parked, and we got out.

"Hey, you better not be thinking about any other girls being pretty," I pretended to be jealous. I wasn't going to fault him for noticing how beautiful Monique was. He just better not look too often or too closely.

"I'm only telling you what Scott thinks," he said innocently, taking my hand as we walked into the building and headed for the west wing.

"I know she's gorgeous, but isn't Scott seeing someone?"

"Stacey? He said she went away for a week over Christmas and has been acting different since she got back. He thinks maybe she met someone else." He held the main lobby door open for me.

"Uh, oh."

"Yeah. Hey, you want to go to church tomorrow?" he asked.

"Sure. Meet me in the lobby at nine thirty."

"See you then," he said. We were standing outside my dorm room, my back was against the wall, and he leaned in, giving me a long kiss goodbye. Ahhh, I'd never get tired of that!

CH. 31 ~ ROOM RULES

The preacher, Simon Mueller, announced to the congregation that there would be another workday at the soup kitchen that next Saturday. He asked for volunteers to meet with Mr. Barnes in the back of the sanctuary at the conclusion of the church service. Cameron whispered to me, "You'll have to go without me that day. I already committed to helping Scott at his parents' ranch."

Emily was among the volunteers. She and Cameron exchanged hellos, and she smiled shyly at him before looking over at me uncomfortably. He asked her something about Comp Sci club which put her at ease.

I knew they were just friends, but I struggled with being around her and making small talk. All I could think about was that she and my boyfriend had kissed. Of course, he wasn't my boyfriend at the time. At least not technically, I guess.

Had it only been a kiss? Or did they actually make out? I couldn't turn my mind off with all the wondering. Was it as weird for *her* to be around me as it was for me to be around her? Did she wish there had been something more between them? Did she resent me for being the one he wanted to be with? Did she wonder if I was wondering all the things I was wondering? *Oh, geez!*

"What are your plans for the rest of the day?" Cameron asked me on our way back to Bellamy Hall.

"I'm going to map out my class schedule, like we did back in August. I think I've got a good handle on it, but as you know, I'm still directionally challenged."

"I don't think I'll be able to go with you. Scott and I are going to go hang out with a couple of other guys. Friends from high school."

I shrugged and said, "That's okay. I won't get lost."

"Oh, I know. I didn't mean to imply that you would. But ... I'd feel better if you weren't alone."

"I'll see if Monique wants to go with me."

"That's a good idea," he said in relief.

"But you know I won't be able to have someone with all the time, right?"

"Yeah. I'm trying to come to grips with that," he muttered and furrowed his eyebrows. The incident was still be haunting him. "I wonder if campus police ever found anything out. Like if the person who was supposed to be at the security desk remembered anything?"

"Who knows?" I said and shrugged. "I guess I could ask them."

"It's worth a try." We got out of his truck and walked toward Bellamy Hall. "How have you felt about being back here?"

"Fine. I mean, it helps that Monique seems like she'll be a much better roommate."

"Good. What days does the self-defense class meet?"

"Monday, Wednesday, and Friday at ten."

"Okay. Please be careful. Maybe don't wear your headphones while you're walking around—"

"Cameron."

He put his hand on my face and apologized, "I'm sorry. I know you don't like me to make a big deal out of this, but your safety *is* a big deal to me."

"I know," I said and softened my voice. "And I'm glad. Thank you. I'll be *super* careful."

* * * * * *

Monique and I went around campus, walking out our class schedules. I knew my way around so much better than I had the first semester.

"How long have you and Cameron been together?" she asked on the way back to our room.

"Almost a year. Minus about seven weeks when we ... took a break and sort of dated other people."

"Oh, how long ago was that?"

"We got back together the week before finals last semester." I told her about that chain of events without going into too much detail.

"Y'all seem happy together."

"Thank you. I feel like we're in a good place in our relationship right now," I said, unlocking our door.

"Can we talk about some room rules? I know it's awkward and all, but I learned the hard way last semester that if these things don't get agreed on up front, it leads to more problems."

"Sure. That's a good idea. I learned some things the hard way, too. What rules do you have in mind?" I asked.

"Well, the biggest problem I had was getting kicked out of my room all the time when my roommate's boyfriend was there. Which, I don't have a problem with if it's every now and then, but this girl ended up expecting to have sleepover dates, and I was like, where am I supposed to go?"

I was shaking my head to assure her I wasn't going to put her in that situation. "That won't be an issue. I mean, we may occasionally want some privacy, but there'll be no overnight stays."

"Okay, cool. And I guess you're not a smoker. I'm not either, so that's not an issue, right?"

"Right. And no drugs in the room."

"Agreed. What else?" she asked thoughtfully. "Oh, I know, if we want to borrow each other's stuff, promise we'll ask first?"

"Promise. You can use my TV and VCR anytime you'd

like. I see you have a coffee maker. Do you mind sharing it, and can you show me how to use it? I only started drinking coffee recently."

"Sure. And I'm thinking that once I get some money, I might buy a small microwave and fridge. Would you want to go in on those with me?"

"Yeah, that's a good idea."

"Deal. Do you have any requests?" she asked.

"Don't loan your room key to anyone else *ever.*"

"Okay. Sounds like there's a story behind that."

"It's unnerving to be in the room and have someone use a key to let themselves in and it's *not* your roommate, and instead some random guy you don't know."

"I understand. No worries there."

"And ... did Lauren, the RA, mention anything to you about why I switched rooms?" She shook her head no. "My old roommate came in late one night with a guy. I woke up when they came in, but I went back to sleep. Well, she passed out drunk and probably high on drugs too. The guy decided to try something with me, but I woke up and was able to fight him off. The bad thing is, I don't know who it was, I didn't get a good look at him because it was dark."

"That's terrible! Couldn't your roommate tell you who it was?"

"Nope. She claimed she had no idea. She was so wasted, she didn't even remember how she got back to our room, much less who was with her. So, I guess what I'm asking is, please don't bring guys in late at night that you don't know well."

She held up her hands as if to stop me from saying anything more and said something that sounded like "mon shah". "You got nothin' to worry about there. First of all, I'd never get that drunk, and wouldn't be doing drugs. Second of all, I'm not into casual sex or one-night stands, and there won't be any guys coming in here late at night with me."

"That's good to know. Thanks. What was that you said,

206

'mon shah'?"

"What? Oh, mon shah? It means 'my dear'."

"Ohhh. It sounds like you're saying 'mon chat', like French for 'my cat'."

"No, that's c-h-a-t. I'm saying c-h-e-r." The words sounded the same to me when she said them!

"Cher?" I asked, pronouncing it the way I'd learned the French word for dear which sounds like 'share' or Cher, as in Sonny and Cher.

"That's my Cajun accent. We say cher like shah."

"Okay," I giggled. "I was trying to figure out why you were talking about your cat."

"Girl, I ain't got no cat." She picked up her pillow and hit me with it. "You cooyon. That's crazy person, in case you don't know." That word she'd used sounded like coo-yawn.

"What the heck? That's not the French word for crazy!" I retaliated by hitting her with my pillow. "How do you spell that?"

"C-o-o-y-o-n. Crazy person!" she said, and we had a good old-fashioned pillow fight. I was definitely glad I'd gotten a new roommate!

CH. 32 ~ SELF DEFENSE

The self-defense class met in one of the group exercise rooms in the rec center. There were about twenty-five women, no men, and a woman instructor who reminded me of a PE coach I'd had in middle school. She had a loud, booming voice and an abrupt personality.

She said, "Welcome to self-defense. You can call me Coach or Coach Saunders. Some of you may have signed up for this class because you've been a victim of assault. If so, I'm truly sorry for your experience. Don't get me wrong, I sympathize with anyone who that's happened to. But I'm telling you up front, I won't allow a victim mentality in my class. We're all here to learn self-defense. We're not here to talk about our problems. That's what therapy is for.

"Furthermore," she continued, "Those of you who think this will be an easy PE credit, think again. We're going to work, and we're going to work hard. I want all my students to finish this class stronger than when they came in. That means there will be cardio workouts and resistance training on a regular basis. So you'll need to dress appropriately and wear athletic clothes and shoes to every class."

I heard the girl next to me mutter, "Damn, I'm outta here," and she slipped out the door.

"If anyone else is having second thoughts about taking this class, feel free to go ahead and leave now. No hard feelings, no shame. But don't waste my time or your classmates' if you're not on board with how I run this class," Coach said.

A couple of other girls left. Personally, I didn't consider leaving for even one second. This lady was exactly what I needed. I had worried I would have to hear other students' tragic stories of assault and wasn't sure I was up for that. If Coach wasn't going to allow it, that was fine with me.

"All right then." She gave a girl a stack of papers and asked her to hand them out. "We're all women here, so I don't think any of you will be offended that the book I've chosen to have you read over the next few weeks is called *Self Defense: the Womanly art of self-care, intuition and choice*. I've made sure the campus bookstore has plenty of copies, and it shouldn't cost you much. This will be a requirement of the course. We'll have class discussions about it and, as you will see on the syllabus, there will be a report due at the end of the term."

With that announcement, two more girls quietly left the room. Then there were about twenty of us. Coach had us all sit down in a circle and introduce ourselves. "Tell us your name, year, major, and if you've ever taken a self-defense or martial arts class."

The answers to these questions were all over the board, from freshman to senior, and a wide representation of majors. A couple of girls had martial arts experience, but most of us had never taken any kind of self-defense class.

* * * * * *

I dropped by the campus police office and talked to the same officer who had taken my statement about the incident. It wasn't surprising that they didn't have any information for me. The person who'd been at the security desk that night didn't know anything. *Great.* What was the point of having someone sit at that desk all the time? Back at the dorm, I found Lauren and asked her if she knew what had happened with Ann.

"I don't know much," she said, "and I'm not supposed to talk about it. I *can* tell you that her parents came and got her, and she didn't return for this semester."

"Okay, thanks. I understand."

"How's it going? Are things okay with Monique?"

"Oh, yes. Absolutely. Big improvement."

"Good. I'm glad. Let me know if you need anything."

"Thanks!"

* * * * * *

Wanting to jump right back into volunteering, I called Jenny Hernandez. She had a few things I might be interested in and asked if I wanted to join her, Cassidy, and April for dinner in the Student Haven that night. I told her I'd be there.

There were a couple of books I went to the bookstore for and saw Monique working. She'd found out that morning that she'd gotten the job, and they'd already called her in. I also ran into Doug. He was standing in the checkout line, and I walked by and said hello. I didn't get the impression that he harbored any ill feelings against me, and we were polite to each other.

I got to the Student Haven early and found Elaine and Lisa in the lounge playing pool. "We're going to go get something to eat. You want to come?" Lisa asked me.

"I was about to go meet a few people about volunteer stuff," I replied.

"Like what kind of volunteer stuff?" she asked.

"I don't know yet. That's what I'm meeting with them about."

"If we join you, do we have to commit to doing something?" Elaine deadpanned.

"No, but it wouldn't kill ya, would it?" I teased.

"I don't know. It might," she retorted.

"Come on, Elaine, let's go see what they're doing. If you lifted a finger occasionally, it might look good on the scholarship applications you're working on for next year,"

Lisa chided.

We met up with Jenny, Cassidy, and April in the food court. I introduced Elaine and Lisa, and we talked about upcoming service options. Jenny told Elaine and Lisa that if they were interested, there were basically five types of service opportunities.

"There's the animal shelter, senior center and nursing home, childhood development center, troop support, and the environment," she said.

"So basically, dogs, old people, kids, soldiers, and the earth?" Elaine reiterated. She reached for her drink which was a cup with no lid, but it had a straw in it. As Jenny started to answer her, Elaine brought her cup up to her mouth to take a drink. She'd forgotten there was a straw, and it went up her nose. I busted up laughing, and she just sat there with the straw in her nose, keeping a straight face. My own face had to have been bright red with embarrassment for laughing at her.

"What? Is there something on my face?" she asked, trying to act like she didn't know. Then she took it out and started cracking up too. We all had a good laugh at her expense, but she was cool with it.

Hanging out with that group of girls gave me a much-needed sense of well-being. I fit in and was accepted for who I was, and I learned to accept others for who they were, quirks included. The lonely struggles I'd had back in October and November were in my past. Those dark days were over.

We didn't accomplish much in terms of volunteer planning, but we recruited Elaine and Lisa, and we all had a lot of fun getting to know each other better. Cassidy and Jenny had planned to go to a movie and invited the rest of us to go. I didn't have any homework yet, so I went along and was so glad I did. We saw *Fried Green Tomatoes*. It became one of my all-time favorite movies because, not only was it a great story, I was in the company of good friends.

* * * * * *

Michael was in my Life Sciences class. He motioned for me to sit next to him, and I didn't even hesitate. Fortunately, any awkwardness between us had been resolved soon after I'd spent the weekend with Mrs. K. We'd become comfortable with each other as friends. I hadn't talked to him since Cameron and I had gotten back together, and I was excited to tell him.

"Hey, how's it going?" I asked him.

"Good. How was your break?"

"Great," I replied and started grinning uncontrollably.

He smiled knowingly at me. "Huh. What is causing this beautiful glow that you have? Did you get back together with your ex?" I nodded and was relieved that he looked genuinely happy for me. There was no denying that he and I had been attracted to each other at one time, but we were over it.

"Yes, and things are better than ever."

"I'm glad. You seem happy."

"I am. How was *your* break?"

"Awesome. I met someone. Well, I already knew her, but not very well. She was in one of my classes last semester, and we figured out we're from the same hometown. I gave her a ride home for the break. Then we saw each other a few times over Christmas."

"Cool! What's her name?"

"Maria."

Near the end of the class period, we were randomly assigned to study groups of six people each. Michael and I were assigned to the same group. At least I already knew we studied well together.

CH. 33 ~ MINE

"Oh, by the way, Have Mercy is playing at Diversions Nightclub next Thursday," Cameron told me on our drive to the movie theater.

"That's so great, honey. I can't wait to come!"

"Thanks. Get the word out, invite your friends. The more people we can bring in, the more likely we'll be to get a set time slot every week."

"Are they paying you?"

"*That* remains to be seen. We get free drinks, but for me that means soda. I can't wait to be twenty-one."

"Yeah, me too. I'll tell everyone about the gig. So, how has your first week of classes been?"

"Fairly good. It's cool to be in the sophomore and junior level classes already. And Gary and I are in a couple of classes together. How about you? How is self-defense going?" Our conversation was momentarily halted as he got out of the truck and came around to my side to open the door for me. Always such a gentleman.

"Great, but I'm discovering how out of shape I am," I complained, moving like an old lady as I got out of the truck.

"Hey, I like the shape you're in," he joked. "Have you had a chance to show off your kickboxing moves yet?"

"No, and there will be no showing off, you big dork. So far we've done laps around the basketball court, lifted weights in the weight room and listened to the Coach talk about the five steps of defense."

"Which are ...?"

"Let me see. I'm supposed to know this for a quiz on Monday. Prevention, avoidance ... deterrence, escape and survival."

"Do you feel like you're learning anything?"

"Yeah. We haven't done much yet with actual physical self-defense though."

"How about your other classes?"

"Collective Behavior is going to be awesome," I said, and we entered the lobby of the movie theater.

"You're going to have to tell me what that's about. It sounds to me like you're studying mob mentality."

"Well, that's one form of collective behavior, but there's others. It's about group dynamics. Like, how social circumstances cause people to do things they normally wouldn't. The link to social psychology is fascinating to me."

"I'm glad you find that interesting, but I think I'll stick with computers. So, we're meeting Elaine and who else?"

"Jared. He's a lot of fun. I think you'll like him." Looking around for my friends, I spotted them and waved.

"Hey, I know you. You're on the same floor as me," Cameron said to Jared. He had met Elaine, but not Jared.

"Yeah, third floor, Bellamy Hall," Jared confirmed.

"You're the one who foiled Preston!" Cameron grinned and held his hand up for Jared to high five. "That was ingenious!"

"Yeah, that was me," Jared said. Elaine cleared her throat as a prompt for him to give us credit too. "I couldn't have done it without these two, though. They put the fine touches on it."

"What?" Cameron asked and looked at me in surprise. "Oh, was that the night I saw you in my hallway?" I smiled and nodded. He put his arm around me and kissed my cheek. "My little prankster."

"I never got to hear what Preston's reaction was," I said to Jared.

"He was mad at first, but he had to admire our work and the time we put into it. Would you believe there's stuff he still hasn't unwrapped?"

Elaine and I went into the theater to get seats, and the guys got drinks and popcorn. I asked her, "So, what's the deal? Are you guys finally dating?"

"I think so ..." she said vaguely. "He's hard to pin down. We've gone out a couple of times, but he still hasn't kissed me or even held hands with me."

"Well, this movie is a thriller, right? Maybe you'll need him to put his arm around you to help you feel safe," I suggested in a sappy voice.

"Hey, I hadn't thought of that. Tonight might be the night. If he doesn't make a move, I'm going to."

The movie was *The Hand That Rocks the Cradle*, and it provided moments of suspense that must have been the catalyst for one of them to make that move. I saw them holding hands by the end of it.

On our way back to the dorm, I was driving and wondered why Cameron had been kind of quiet.

"Did you have a good time?" I asked.

"Yeah. Your friends are cool. Are they the ones who introduced you to that guy? What did you say his name was?"

"Doug? Yes," I answered hesitantly. Where was he going with this?

"Do you ever see him anymore?"

"I saw him at the bookstore one day. Why?"

"Ahhh, it's nothing. I just don't like being reminded of you being with another guy."

"I'm sorry," I said and kept myself from saying anything about how I didn't like seeing Emily at church every Sunday and being reminded of him being with her.

I parked in the Bellamy Hall parking lot, turned to him, and said, "Cameron, I know it sucks for you that I went out with other guys when we were apart, but I gotta tell you, I'm glad I did it because it helped me figure something out."

"What's that?"

"That I don't want to be with anyone else but you."

He reached for my hand and said, "I'm so glad. That's what I figured out, too." He sat back and laid his head against the seat. I leaned over to kiss him, and his arms went around me. They tightened as my lips made their way to his neck. I let my teeth graze his skin and released my breath, making him shudder.

"Ohhh, you know what that does to me," he whispered. "Lately, I'm struggling to remember that line we agreed to not cross."

"Me too. I guess it's a good thing we're in my car right now," I replied with a smile.

"Yeah," he agreed. I laid my head against his shoulder, and he asked, "By the way, *where* is that line?"

I laughed softly and sat up to look at him. "That's a good question. I've wondered about that myself several times."

Suddenly, he said, "I need to ask you something," and the mood changed.

"Okay ... what?"

He squinted his eyes shut and hesitated, making me anticipate something terrible. "I'm sorry to even bring it up, but it's been eating away at me."

"What's wrong?"

"When you went out with those other guys ... Did anything happen?"

"No," I said in surprise. "What do you mean? I told you. There was kissing but nothing else. Why have you been worrying about that?"

"*Just* kissing?"

"Yes. Why?" My mind raced to figure out where this was coming from. "Do you have a confession of your own to make or something?"

"No. I promise you," he said. He looked into my eyes so intently, like he was trying to draw something out of me.

"Good. I promise you, too."

"Okay. I'm sorry that I even brought it up, but I needed reassurance that we're still ... um, that you didn't ... I mean, I know you didn't like, *sleep* with anyone, but ... has anyone ever ..."

He looked desperately at me, either afraid to ask what he wanted to know, or afraid to hear the answer. I was pretty sure I knew what he was getting at, and I thought it was sweet and humorous that the two of us—nineteen-year-old college students—were having this conversation. I was so crazy about this guy! God really knew what he was doing by pairing us up.

"Cameron," I said quietly and asked, "Are you wanting to know if anyone has ever touched me?" He nodded, looking anguished, and I told him, "No, nobody has."

His relief was visible, and before I could ask him the same question, he said, "Me, neither. I mean, I haven't either ... with anyone else, or the other way around. Oh, you know what I mean." He chuckled self-consciously.

"Yes,"

"Can we put all that behind us and forget about it?" he asked.

"I had. I thought you had, too. I'm sorry you've been worrying about it."

"I'm sorry, I can't help being jealous, I guess. I want you to be mine ... and *only* mine."

"I'm all yours, Cameron."

"Good, I'm all yours, too."

Trying to fall asleep that night, it occurred to me that we still hadn't defined "the line".

CH. 34 ~ THUNDERBIRD

Saturday at the soup kitchen was a lot of hard work, and my muscles were already sore from the weight room workout in self-defense class. I was exhausted by the time I drove back to the dorm and took a hot shower. Monique was out for the evening, so Cameron picked up dinner for us, and we ate in my room and watched TV. He was tired too, from working with Scott at his parents' ranch.

"Take your shirt off, and I'll give you a massage," I offered. He hesitated, and I teased, "What? Are you afraid I'll ravage you? I'll be good. You can trust me."

"Oh, I know. It's not that. Ahhh, there's something I did back in October that you don't know about yet. If I take my shirt off, you'll find out."

"Then you better take that shirt off, right now," I demanded, sort of playfully, but wondering what this could possibly be about.

"First, you have to promise you won't freak out."

"Okay ... now I'm more than a little curious. What are you hiding from me?"

He slowly took his shirt off, and I saw it. He had a tattoo!

"What?" I exclaimed. I couldn't help touching it. It was a southwestern thunderbird, and it was so cool. It was colorful and a decent size—not too large—on his upper right arm.

The old tape started playing in my head of what my dad thought about people with tattoos. That tape tried to tell me I should judge Cameron for it, but I told it to shut up.

"For the Fabulous Thunderbirds. What do you think?" he asked. "I hadn't mentioned it because I wasn't sure how you'd feel about it."

"It's cool." I ran my fingers over it, and added, "I like it. Did it hurt?"

"Yeah, but I'm glad I did it. It was something I'd been thinking about for a while, and I talked Scott into going with me. He chickened out on getting one himself, though." He laid down on his stomach so I could rub his shoulders.

I put extra effort into some tight spots, and he said, "Hmmm, you've got magic hands."

"My turn next."

"Are you going to take your shirt off for me like I did for you?"

I lightly slapped him on the arm, and he rolled over and grabbed my hands. "I'm kidding. Although, if you want to, you won't hear me complain. Here, lie down."

I lowered myself onto my stomach, and he gently gathered up my hair and moved it out of the way. It gave me goose bumps. I relaxed and enjoyed his hands on me.

"Tell me if I hurt you," he said and started massaging my neck, then my shoulders, making his way down my back. He worked my sore muscles with the perfect pressure.

"*You're* the one with magic hands," I murmured, feeling drowsy.

Pushing the hem of my shirt up, he brushed his fingers across the small of my back and quietly asked, "Is this a birthmark?"

"Yeah." It was one of those stork bite birthmarks that babies sometimes have on their foreheads, but I had one on the small of my back.

"I noticed it last summer at the river, when you wore that sexy bikini, but I didn't know how to ask about it."

"Does it gross you out?"

"No! It's adorable. I've even thought about it several times since then. There's nothing gross about you, Olivia."

"Hmmm. Thank you. Less talking, more massaging."

He worked both of his hands up the back of my shirt. His warm, smooth hands felt amazing. I became so relaxed that I nodded off to sleep. I barely woke up when I heard Monique come in. She and Cameron had a whispered conversation, and then he kissed my cheek and told me goodnight.

I had a dream. It was about Emily, of all people. I think it was triggered from having been around her earlier that day at the soup kitchen. In the dream, she and I became good friends, and then she seduced Cameron away from me. I woke up with a yucky feeling and told Monique about it.

"Who did you say this girl Emily is?" she asked.

"A friend of Cameron's. Well, they dated for a couple of weeks when we were apart. But I trust him that there's nothing between them now. I've seen them together, and I don't have anything to worry about. The dream was so real, though. Ugh!"

"Chill, mon cher. It was only a dream. It don't mean nothin'."

"I know."

But it stayed with me all day. Did it mean that I was threatened by Emily's continued friendship with Cameron?

* * * * * *

Opening my door to Cameron, I said, "Happy anniversary." It was exactly one year since our first date.

"You too, honey. You look great."

"Thank you. You do too. Are you going to tell me where we're going now?"

"Soon. Open this first." He handed me a box wrapped in foil. "I didn't have any wrapping paper, so I borrowed some foil from Preston."

"Ha Ha." We sat down on my bed, and I peeled the foil off to reveal a box from Zoe's Cafe and Bakery. It held two cream cheese brownies that had come all the way from Leeville. "What? How did you get these?"

"I had Mrs. K do me a favor."

"Wow. You arranged to have her send these to you in time for our anniversary?"

"Yeah, and I hope they haven't gotten stale."

"Well, here, let's try one," I said and broke two corners of a brownie off. I handed him one, and he fed it to me before taking the other for himself. I nodded and said, "Yum."

"You remember that day at Zoe's?"

"Of course, I do. It was the first time you and I got to have a decent conversation. I was so glad you asked for my phone number."

He chuckled and said, "I was nervous. I saw Daniel put his arm around you, and I was so disappointed."

"I remember the look on your face!"

"Was it that obvious?"

"Kind of. That's why I made sure to introduce him to you as a *friend*."

"Yeah, because if it had turned out that you and Daniel were together, I was going to chew Josh out for not warning me."

"Oh, that's right, you'd been asking him about me, hadn't you?"

"Yes." He looked at his watch and said, "But that's not your only gift." He handed me a card, and inside were two tickets to the theater. The live act kind of theater. I'd never been to a real stage performance and was excited.

"*Death of a Salesman*. Thank you so much!"

"Good, I'm glad you like it because the show is today, and it's the last one."

"It's perfect." I checked the tickets to see what time the show was. We still had time for dinner. "I've got something for you, too, but I didn't have any wrapping paper, either."

I handed him a scrapbook that I'd made with pictures from his band's gig. I was pleased with the way it had turned out, considering I wasn't very creative. Monique had helped me with the page layouts, and I'd spent hours decorating them; matting the photos and cutting out stenciled letters to spell out Have Mercy and the band members names.

"Oh, my gosh, Olivia. This is incredible. You got some great pictures. Was that the camera you got for Christmas?"

"Yeah. I especially like this one." I pointed to a close-up picture of him playing his guitar. I'd gotten an extra copy of it for myself.

"I love this. Do you mind if I show it to the rest of the band next week?"

"No, I don't mind."

He stood and pulled me to my feet and hugged me. "This is really special. Thank you so much."

"Thank you for my gifts too. Are you hungry?"

"Yes, and I know exactly where I'd like to take you. Is Italian okay?"

"Italian is always okay with me."

"Hey, is this the same thing you wore on our first date?" he asked.

"Yes. Thank you for noticing." I snuggled into his arms. "I'll never forget that night."

"It was the first time we held hands." He and ran his fingers down my arm and intertwined them with mine. I felt the same electricity between us the way I had three hundred sixty-five days before and lots of times since.

"And it was the first time you kissed me, which by the way, I've always wondered why that first kiss wasn't a French kiss," I asked with a self-conscious giggle.

"Wouldn't you like to know?" he teased.

"Was it because I had bad breath? How embarrassing."

"No, nothing like that. For one thing, I was nervous. But

it was also because I decided to take my time. I wanted every moment and every new experience with you to count for something."

"It worked. You make me feel cherished, Cameron. I love you."

"I love you too. When Josh introduced me to you, I knew right then that I wanted to get to know you. You were, and still are, the prettiest girl I've ever seen. The highlight of my days was seeing you and talking to you."

"Mine too. I got addicted to your smile and sense of humor, not to mention your impeccable manners and the sweet things you do. You're the whole package—good-looking, great kisser, romantic, and a perfect gentleman."

"Thank you. I thought moving to Leeville with only half of my senior year left was going to suck. I never expected to make such good friends, and I especially didn't think I'd meet a girl like you. You're the whole package, too."

CH. 35 ~ FOCUS GROUP

Professor Hennings, of my Collective Behavior sociology class, was looking for freshman volunteers to participate in a focus group about new student experiences. I didn't have any idea what a focus group was, but she said she'd give extra credit for it, so I signed up.

I arrived early, and she put me to work getting handouts ready. She was an interesting person. I'd only been in her class for a few of weeks, but I had already decided I liked her. In her thirties, married with young children, she was quirky and scatterbrained. She drank out of little kid sippy cups because they wouldn't leak in the backpack she carried when she rode her bike to campus every day. She was full of life and spontaneously recited famous quotes. I could tell she loved sociology, and it came naturally for her to make it fun and interesting for her students. She was the kind of person you wanted to be around because you knew it would be personally edifying to associate with her.

She was part of a committee that answered to the New Student Development Center, and the goal of the focus group was to get student feedback on the effectiveness of the university's freshman orientation, welcome week, Freshman Seminar, and any other freshman topics that came up. There were sixteen freshmen in the room as well as the professor and her TA, Isabel.

I hadn't put that much thought into the role that the university, in and of itself, had played in my initial college experience. I thought back to the reasons I gave my dad for why I wanted to go to NHU instead of AU. One of them had been that NHU advertised a better freshman program, and there I was being asked to evaluate my experience with that. It's cool how things come back around full circle.

I needed more time than anyone else to think about my answers to the questions. My rotten first semester experience couldn't be blamed on the university. At least I didn't think it could.

"Olivia, you've been quiet. Any thoughts on different topics that could have been introduced in Freshman Seminar that would have helped you become more assimilated into the college culture?" Professor Hennings asked.

"Well ... I've got to be honest with you. My difficulties last semester had more to do with my own problems. I can't say the class failed me in any way."

"Okay, that's fair. Let me ask it this way then, can you say that it *did* help you in any way?"

"In general, it did. But now that I think about it, I guess it didn't turn out to be what I had expected."

"Excellent segue into the next question," she said. "Let's go around the table and hear about what each of you expected when you signed up for it, and we'll talk about whether it did, or did not, meet those expectations."

The comments that followed prompted me to think more about what would have been helpful. For example, if I had been more encouraged to get involved in clubs and organizations, I might have gotten more plugged in from the start, which would have helped me feel less alienated. Of course, I had to own up to the fact that I'd done a bang-up job of alienating myself.

At any rate, my input was that if the instructors could

include in their Freshman Seminar more information about that kind of thing and the importance of getting involved, I might have paid more attention. Especially if they'd been more informative about volunteer opportunities.

My other input was about having RAs in the freshman dorm who cared about being helpful and about the well-being of the students on their floor. If I'd had Lauren as my RA that first semester, instead of Gina, I would have had someone I could go to with my roommate problems.

* * * * * *

I settled into a comfortable routine with classes, volunteering, church, and hanging out with Cameron and friends. Have Mercy brought in such good crowds for a couple of gigs that they were offered the same time slot every week. I didn't always get to go, but I tried to be there for most of the gigs. I wanted to make sure the girls didn't get the idea that Cameron was single.

He still did occasional mini concerts in the student lounge. It didn't worry me though, because he was so good at making sure everyone knew we were an item. That was accomplished with lots of PDA which we'd both become much more comfortable with.

Study groups became a regular thing for me too, and not only for the purpose of studying, but also for fun and camaraderie. There was a girl in my Life Sciences group who, once we got to know each other, I found out she'd had difficulties adjusting to college life too. Like me, she'd been afraid to admit to anyone that things weren't what she'd expected.

It turned out that Michael's Maria was the same Maria in my self-defense class. At first, I thought she and I could be friends, but once she found out Michael and I had sort of dated—if you could even call it that—she kept me at arm's length. That wasn't so easy, considering we got assigned as partners for practicing self-defense moves. Sometimes, she was even a bit hostile, but it worked well for me; gave me the opportunity to put more force into the exercises.

The book I had to read for self-defense class turned out to be beneficial. It helped me put my own experiences into perspective. I became more aware of situations that had the potential to create personal safety problems.

I had previously thought I was good at doing that, and for obvious hazards, I was. But I'd made the mistake of turning my back and going to sleep the night Ann had brought that guy into our room. If I could have gone back to that night, I would have done things differently. I would have stayed awake until he left, or I would have left the room myself. I would never let something like that happen again.

I still became fearful at times of the unidentifiable stranger who had attacked me, but I was determined to not let if rule my life. Occasionally, I had nightmares about what had happened, and sometimes variations of the same scenario. I tried to immediately turn my mind to prayer and remember the good feelings I'd had that night when Cameron had prayed with me. I was so thankful to God for giving me a boyfriend who wanted me to be safe and would never intentionally hurt me.

* * * * * *

"How are you going to top last Valentine's Day?" I asked Cameron.

"I don't know. The pressure's on though, isn't it?" he said and took his fingers off his computer keyboard. We were in his room studying, or at least that's what he was doing. I was distracted and couldn't bring myself to take anything seriously.

"It's next week. But we can do whatever you'd like. It doesn't matter to me, so long as I'm with you." I was lying on my stomach on his bed with my geography book and notebook spread out in front of me.

"How about I bring you flowers?" he asked with a mischievous grin.

"Don't you dare," I warned. I couldn't stand the waste of money on flowers being bought for me, and he knew it. I was *so* not the typical girlfriend in that regard.

"I know, I know."

"There is something that could commemorate our first Valentine's Day, though."

"White zinfandel?"

"Ding, ding, ding. We have a winner!"

"Hmmm. I don't know how I'll be able to swing that," he said doubtfully. "But, hey, *Wayne's World* starts showing in theaters that day."

I eyed him skeptically. "I'm game for that ... *if* you get me something to drink first to make it funnier."

"Wow! You really want to get your drink on, don't you?" He laughed and stood up to stretch.

"Hey, I've been working hard. I need a break." I rolled over and acted exhausted for dramatic effect.

"You do realize we're only a month into the semester, right?" He leaned down to kiss my forehead, and I put my arms around his neck.

"Yes."

"But I know you have been working hard. That's why I'm going to do whatever I can to get you your drink of choice for Valentine's Day next Friday night. I may know a guy who knows a guy who can get another guy to get it for us."

I started giggling and tried to pull him down onto the bed with me.

"What are you doing?" he asked. His teasing smile told me that he knew exactly what I was trying to do.

I released him, and in frustration said, "I was *trying* to get you to lie down with me."

"Olivia, dear, not tonight. I feel unusually capable of resisting your charm." Confident in his statement, he sat down on Gary's bed across from me.

"Oh, yeah?" I asked, rolling back over onto my stomach. "In that case, I'll go back to studying."

I reached for a soda that I had on the windowsill beside the bed. It had a straw in it. I shamelessly played with it in my mouth, knowing that he was watching me. He gasped. "You okay, honey?" I asked innocently.

"You little minx," he said, still keeping his distance. But then, he muttered, "You know exactly what you're doing to me."

And, as the saying goes, he was on me like a duck on a June bug. He pushed my books onto the floor, and I rolled back over, giggling at my success. On his hands and knees, he hovered over me. He looked me in the eyes with amusement as I wrapped my legs around him, trying to get him to lie down.

"You're asking for trouble, you know that?" he whispered, nestling his face between my neck and shoulder.

I was pushing the hem of his shirt up, and he raised up onto his knees and took it off. Leaning back down to kiss along my jaw line, he asked, "Is that what you wanted?"

The playful teasing was replaced with passion. I kissed his chest all over, tasting his warm skin on my lips and tongue. He finally laid down on me, and I clenched his hips between my thighs to keep him there.

"Olivia," he said breathlessly.

"No talking," I insisted, silencing him with kisses. My lips crushed onto his, and my tongue thrust into his mouth. He answered with equal desire while my hands ran down his back and onto his butt. He made that low humming sound and pressed his body onto mine for a glorious few seconds. But then he broke free of my grasp, got up from the bed, and knelt next to it.

"Nooo," I quietly protested.

"Baby, I'm trying to keep this PG."

"Forget about PG." I rolled onto my side and looked at him. "I want you."

"I want you, too. More than you could possibly know," he said, lowering his head to where his chin rested on the bed, and his eyes were level with mine.

We stared into each other's eyes for a minute. I imagined I could read his mind. He was thinking, *I'm trying to do the honorable thing here, Olivia. But you're making it so difficult for me.*

"I know," I said in answer the words he didn't say and made myself chill out.

CH. 36 ~ GLORIA

Professor Hennings asked me to help compile data from several focus groups, like the one I had attended, into a report. She said she'd recognized my organizational skills and offered to feed me and her TA dinner at her house as long as we didn't mind working with the interruptions of her kids. She lived in a neighborhood close to campus.

Isabel and I arrived at the same time. "You may end up regretting letting her rope you into this," she said.

"What do you mean?" I asked. What *was* I getting myself into? She knew Professor Hennings better than I did, so I wondered if there was something she was trying warn me about.

She laughed lightly. "Don't look so worried. I'm just giving you a heads up. She scores high on the ADD/ADHD scale."

"Oh, yeah," I agreed. "I've kind of noticed that already." I rang the doorbell and heard happy children squealing all the way to the door.

She muttered, "Kids," right before the door swung open.

Professor Hennings stood there with a little boy attached to one leg and a little girl attached to the other. They looked to be about the same age.

"Ladies! Welcome. Come on in," she said. "Meet my

sugarbabies, Grant and Gracie." Then to the children, she said, "Say hello to Miss Olivia and Miss Isabel." They smiled shyly at us and said hello in adorable little child voices.

"Hello, Grant and Gracie. It's nice to meet you," I said.

"Berry nice ta meet ya," Grant said, and Gracie giggled.

"They're adorable. Are they twins?"

"Yes! They're three years old. And their daddy's *supposed* be home already, but he's running late," she said and swooped Gracie up in her arms. She led us into the house and showed us to her home office. It was in total chaos. I couldn't help but laugh, and Isabel rolled her eyes.

"Yes, it's a mess. But I know where everything is," Professor Hennings said, clearing some space on her desk by sweeping a stack of papers into a box on the floor. She gave me a different stack of papers with instructions for sorting them and had Isabel get started on a computer spreadsheet, all while explaining what we were going to be working on and what the goal was.

She was disorganized, but I discovered she had a brilliant mind, and I liked the way she thought. She processed information very similar to the way I did, and we worked well together. Isabel worked well with her too, but she didn't appreciate her idiosyncrasies the way I did.

Mr. Hennings came home about an hour later, and the children ran squealing to the door to greet him. He came and poked his head into the office to say hello and that he'd get dinner started right away.

As we continued to work, and after I had addressed her as "Professor Hennings" a couple of times, she said, "Olivia, please call me Gloria. And tell me about yourself."

"Oh, okay. I'm from a small town north of Aberdeen called Leeville. Um ..." I chuckled, unable to think of anything else to say.

"That's not telling me anything about *you*," she prodded, but was smiling encouragingly.

"Geez, Gloria, you're embarrassing the poor girl," Isabel

chided because she saw me blush. I loved the easygoing, informal relationship they had. It defied everything I thought I understood about professor-student etiquette.

"Well ..." I cleared my throat. "I have a younger sister who's a freshman in high school. My dad's an engineer. He doesn't like my interest in social sciences, but—" I couldn't help the rebellious feeling that came over "—I'm going to do it anyway."

"Now we're talking," Gloria said. "What else?"

"I drive a maroon sports car that I got over Thanksgiving break."

"Do you like it?"

"Yes!"

"Why?"

"Because I like to go fast, and there's nothing quite like driving a performance vehicle." I stared off into space, thinking about how much I loved my car. "The shifting, steering through curves. How it hugs the road. How you can feel that it's built for speed."

"Oooh, I've got goose bumps," Gloria said and called out the door to her husband, "Honey! I want a sports car!"

"You'll have to settle for dinner. Let's eat!" he replied.

Dinner was fish sticks and macaroni and cheese. "Popular kids' fare," Mr. Hennings said. But they weren't frozen fish sticks or packaged mac and cheese. It was gourmet, and it was delicious.

"This is good, Mr. Hennings," I said.

"Thank you. You can call me Gavin."

"Gavin, Gloria, Grant, and Gracie," I commented on the theme.

"Cheesy, right?" Gloria chuckled.

"No, it's cool. I know a guy named Doug who has seven siblings, all with names that begin with the letter D."

"Now that's excessive," Isabel said.

"Yeah, I'll have to agree with you on that one."

"Miss 'Livia, do you have a boyfriend?" Grant asked me. He and his sister giggled.

"Grant, that's not polite to ask," Gloria gently corrected him and ruffled his hair.

"That's okay. Yes, Grant, I have a boyfriend. His name is Cameron."

"Is he cute?" Gracie asked and giggled some more.

"Oh, yes. He's very cute." I smiled at the way she covered her mouth with her hand and laughed behind it. She was *such* an enchanting little girl.

"Does Cameron go to NHU?" Gloria asked.

"Yes, he's a computer science major."

Her face brightened and she gestured toward Gavin. "Gavin works with computers. Software applications."

"What year is he?" Gavin asked.

"Freshman. Actually, by hours he's a sophomore now."

"It's an exciting time to get into computing. If he ever has questions or is interested in a possible internship, let me know. I don't personally do the hiring for that sort of thing, but the company I work for encourages students to get an early start in the workplace."

"Cool, thank you. I'll be sure to tell him. Where do you work?"

"CompuApp Technologies."

I nodded in acknowledgement that I'd heard of it. They had a big office in New Haven and one in Aberdeen, too. If Gavin was serious, this could be a great "in" for Cameron.

Isabel had to leave after dinner, and Gloria and I worked some more on the report that would be submitted to the committee for approval before being presented to the New Student Development Center.

"Olivia, you seem to have a knack for this type of work," Gloria commented.

"Thank you. Collecting data and processing it into something meaningful is fun."

"You sound like a social scientist already. I appreciate the help, and if you don't mind, I'd like you to give the report a final read-through. Can I bring it to you next time I see you in class?"

"Sure. I'd be honored, but isn't that something a TA would do? I don't want to step on Isabel's toes or anything."

"Oh, I'll have Isabel read it, too. It's good to get multiple eyes on it, though."

"Okay." *How cool!*

The next week, I got a copy of the report. Pouring over it for hours, I felt like a total geek for how much I enjoyed doing it. I had suggestions to make, and there were a few grammar and punctuation errors. But I also found what I was pretty sure was a mistake.

I double checked with the original data, and I had to tell Gloria, "We've made an error."

For some reason I felt cruel for bringing it up, but I couldn't, in good conscience, overlook it. I hoped Isabel, who hadn't picked up on the error, wouldn't think I was trying to make her look bad. She might not have appreciated a freshman showing her up that way. She was a hard person to read, but she didn't treat me any differently afterward, so that was good.

* * * * * *

On Valentine's Day, Cameron came through for me with a bottle of my favorite wine.

"How did you manage it?" I asked.

"You remember my friend, Pete?"

"Oh yeah, the guy who taught you how to play guitar."

"Yes. I called in a favor to him."

"Well, be sure to tell him thank you for me."

"You can thank him yourself. He's our chauffer for the evening. He said that if he's going to aid in the consumption of alcohol by minors, he isn't taking any chances that we'll get pulled over after drinking," he laughed.

"Oh, okay. I guess that's cool. He went to NHU, right?"

"Yeah. Graduated last year."

"What's he doing now?"

"Teaching music at one of the local high schools and playing in a couple of different bands."

We stayed in Cameron's room for dinner, and he had

basically the same food that he'd brought on our first Valentine's date; a couple of different kinds of cheese, some fancy crackers and chocolate covered strawberries. We sat on his bed, eating and drinking, talking, and listening to music until Pete called to tell us he was in the lobby waiting for us.

Pete had a date with him and said, "I promise this isn't a double date, you guys, but we want to see this movie, too. If I've got to babysit the two of you underage drinkers, I'm going to at least have a good time myself."

"That's fine," I said and introduced myself to his date, Lilly. She was a teacher at the same school Pete was working at.

True to his word, once we got into the theater, we didn't see Pete and Lilly again until we met in the parking lot to go back to Bellamy.

Cameron and I had seen some of the *Wayne's World* sketches on *Saturday Night Live*, and we liked Mike Myers and Dana Carvey. The movie was hilarious, and I liked the "Bohemian Rhapsody" song in it.

* * * * * *

Scott, Cameron, and I were hanging out in the Student Haven, and Scott asked me if Monique was going to join us.

"She might. Do you want her to?" I asked and wiggled my eyebrows up and down at him.

"Don't tease him, Olivia. He so smitten with her," Cameron said.

Scott elbowed him in the ribs. "I can't help it. She's a goddess. Help me figure out how to get her to go out with me *once*, and I'll take it from there."

"I don't know, Scott. She's in kind of a non-dating mode right now." Monique had told me she wasn't in a hurry to get involved with anyone.

"That's just my luck," Scott said forlornly.

"Come on, dude," Cameron said and stood up from the couch. "Quit pining away for her."

"Give me a break, Cam. I stuck by your side the whole

time you were pining away for Olivia a few months ago."

"Ohhh? You pined away for me? How sweet," I cooed.

"Ugh, there was nothing sweet about it," Scott complained and shook his head.

Cameron looked embarrassed and said, "All right, Scott, let's go get something to eat and let Olivia get some work done."

"What are you working on, anyway?" Scott asked me.

"I'm proofreading a writing assignment for this girl in one of my classes. She's from Afghanistan, so English isn't her first language, and she asked for my help. She's paying me for it, too."

"Is that ... ethical?"

I sighed heavily. I'd already had this conversation with Cameron. "I'm not *writing* it for her. I'm *proofreading* it. How is that unethical?"

He shrugged. "I guess it's not but be careful nobody thinks you're writing it *for* her."

"That's what I said, too," Cameron interjected. I waved them off and tried to concentrate on the paper I was reading.

What's was the big deal? Tutors who did the same thing I was doing, and nobody questioned them for charging for their services.

* * * * * *

"Guess what," I said to Cameron a couple of weeks later during a laundry date.

"What? Give me a clue."

"It has to do with the major question." It was the last time I planned to ever bring up that dreaded problem.

"I hope it's good news."

"It is." I smiled confidently.

"You've decided? Okay, let me guess. Sociology."

"Yes," I replied. He held out his hand, and I took it in mine for a handshake.

"Congratulations. What was the deciding factor?"

"The classes I'm taking. And Gloria has played a big role

in it, too."

"Good. You seem settled. In fact, you seem very happy."

"Thank you. I am."

Now I've got to figure out how to tell my dad and not let him walk all over me about it.

* * * * * *

During the week before Spring Break, Brandy, the know-it-all, became a problem for me. Since I was on a different floor, I hardly ever saw her anymore, but somehow she got into my business and made it hers.

My Afghani friend, Zorah, had referred a couple of other people to me for proofreading. Through some bizarre six degrees of separation, Brandy ended up knocking on my door.

"I thought it might be you," she smirked.

"What?" I asked.

"The one who's accepting payment for writing papers for the foreign students."

"Whoa! I'm not doing any such thing," I denied indignantly. "Who told you that?"

"Doesn't matter. I just know."

"What you *think* you know isn't true. I've been offering proofreading services. In case you don't know what that is, it means I'm looking over something someone else has written and showing them grammar, spelling, and punctuation errors that they've made."

"I know what it is," she said arrogantly, "but how can anyone be sure that's *all* you're doing? I'm sure the university would find it ... questionable."

"What is your deal? Is your life so boring that you need harass me about something that's none of your business?"

She stuck her nose in the air, crossed her arms, said, "We'll see," and walked away.

Monique suggested I go to the tutoring center and ask someone there about the legitimacy of "freelance" proofreading. I took my chances and went and asked.

"Would a person be breaking any university rules by

accepting payment in exchange for proofreading other students' writing assignments?" I asked the upper-class student who was at the center's information desk.

The guy said, "It is frowned upon in general, because students are encouraged to use our services, but there is nothing stopping an individual from doing their own thing. It's a fine line, though. The person would want to remain above reproach and be prepared to defend themselves if ever accused of providing actual writing services."

"What would a person have to do to defend themselves?"

The guy shrugged and smiled knowingly at me. "I'm guessing this person you are referring to is, in fact, yourself. Am I right?"

"Um ... not necessarily. Look I'm just trying to make sure it's not against the rules."

"How much are you charging?" He was smiling again. I didn't get the feeling he was trying to be a jerk, but I kept my guard up.

"How would I know how much the person is charging?"

"Okay, if that's how you want play it. This *person*," he said, leaning forward and resting his elbows on the desk in front of him, "would want to maybe type up a form for his or her customers to sign, agreeing that they are only receiving proofreading services. That ought to do it."

That was a great idea, and I thanked him and turned to leave. "Hey, wait ..." he said, calling me back over to the desk. "If the *person* on whose behalf you are going to all this trouble to find out information for ever wants to work here, we might not pay as much, but it's always an option."

"Oh, okay ... I'll let them know."

"And, *this* person—" he pointed both of his thumbs at himself, "—wouldn't mind seeing you around here more often."

Uh, oh. I didn't see that coming.

"I'm flattered," I said nicely, "but I've got a boyfriend."

He nodded, not embarrassed at all to be turned down. "Okay, good luck to you."

"You, too."

I went and knocked on Brandy's door. I wanted to tell her off, but Gloria had given me a Leo Buscaglia quote: "Only the weak are cruel. Gentleness can only be expected from the strong." So, I tempered my irritation with her.

"Brandy," I said pleasantly.

"Olivia," she said, a bit warily.

"I wanted to let you know that I checked into it, and what I'm doing is perfectly acceptable. I don't appreciate your interference, and I especially don't appreciate you calling my integrity into question. I don't mean to be rude, but please mind your own business."

With a look of disdain, she said, "Whatever."

"Thank you. Goodbye," I said and walked away.

That was too easy. Somehow I sensed my problems with that girl weren't over, and I was right. You've heard of the Bible story about the thorn in Paul's side, right? Well, let me tell you, Brandy was the thorn in my side.

CH. 37 ~ SPRING BREAK

Spring Break couldn't come soon enough. We all needed some time off. I was looking forward to going home. Emma and I had been writing to each other more often. She'd told me our mom was doing considerably better, and that they'd actually started doing the kickboxing video workouts together. Now that was progress!

Before Cameron and I went home to our own houses, we met up with our friends at Lyla's house because Josh and Kate planned to leave for a ski trip the next day, and we didn't want to miss seeing them. Lyla had invited a guy named Bobby to join us. He was her new manager at Blockbuster Video.

I was trying to get a feel for what their relationship could possibly be, seeing as how fraternizing among employees was frowned upon, particularly between supervisor and subordinate. They were comfortable together, but not too familiar, so maybe they weren't necessarily dating.

Lyla's mom fed us all dinner, and then we went to see the movie *My Cousin Vinny*, which was epic. We had so much fun, none of us wanted the evening to end. We stood around the movie theater parking lot talking for so long, Cameron ended up lowering his truck's tailgate, and we all sat in the truck bed talking.

If Bobby and Lyla were an item, it was hard to tell. He was a year older than us and had never gone to college. He was nice but didn't have much personality. Lyla needed to be with someone more dynamic than this guy.

I had called my parents to let them know I was back in town, but that I would either get home late or would spend the night at Lyla's. I opted for going to Lyla's so we could spend more time catching up.

"So, what's the deal with that guy Bobby?" I asked her.

"Good question. I don't know. I agreed to go out with him last weekend because I was bored, but now I think *he* thinks I'm interested. I invited him tonight to see him in a group setting. My suspicions were confirmed. He's a dud, huh?"

"Yeah, kind of."

"Now I have to worry about him treating me differently at work if I tell him I don't want to go out with him again."

I was so glad I didn't have to worry about that sort of thing.

* * * * * *

Emma and my dad were arguing. Neither of them even took notice of my arrival, but my mom came in from the backyard and gave me a proper greeting.

She looked so much better, even though her clothes were dirty from gardening. Yes, gardening. I couldn't believe it. She'd taken up a hobby. She'd lost more weight and was smiling—at least she was until she heard my dad and Emma arguing.

"John, did you even see that Olivia is home?" she interrupted.

"Oh, hello, Olivia," he said. I waved and headed toward the stairs with my suitcase.

"What's going on between you two?" I heard my mom ask Emma and my dad.

"Mom, I got invited to go with Ashley's family to the beach for a few days, and Dad won't even consider it,"

Emma complained.

"Well, why don't you let your dad and I discuss it, and we'll talk to you about it later?" my mom suggested. I saw my dad shoot her a surprised look, and I think I did the same. Since when did Mom start taking charge?

Then she called up the stairs to me, "Olivia, why don't you invite Cameron over for dinner tonight? Emma and I are making chicken parmesan."

"Oh ... okay," I said. Emma came upstairs and followed me into my room.

"Wow. Who is that woman down there?" I asked.

"I know. I couldn't believe she spoke up for me. It's a first. I hope she doesn't catch hell for it, though."

"Yeah. Let me call Cameron and find out if he can come over for dinner. Then we'll hang out if you want."

"Okay, just get me out of the house for a while, please."

"Mall?"

"Perfect."

* * * * * *

"This is great, Mrs. Miller," Cameron complimented my mom at dinner. He still hadn't gotten comfortable addressing her by her first name.

"Thank you. Emma helped, too. So, what are your plans over Spring Break?"

"My dad's got me working on stuff around the house. Oh, and Olivia," he said and turned to me, "James and Jasmine would like us to go to their place on Thursday. They need me to use my truck to help them move the baby furniture into the apartment. Jasmine said for you to come, too."

At the mention of a baby, I knew things were about to get awkward. My dad finally took part in the conversation and asked, "Who's having a baby?"

Cameron glanced over at me, realizing that I'd never mentioned anything about the unexpected pregnancy to my parents. Why should I have? It was none of their business.

"My brother, James, and his girlfriend, Jasmine. They

go to AU and live in Aberdeen," Cameron answered.

My dad had a look of judgment on his face and eyed Cameron like he was seeing him differently. I could already hear in my mind the things he would probably say to me later.

Following dinner, Cameron and I took a walk to the river near my house. "So, you hadn't told your parents about the baby, huh?" he asked. It didn't sound accusatory though, which I was glad for.

"Yeah. I'm sorry. It never came up."

"I understand. I wish I hadn't said anything about it in front of them. I wasn't thinking." I was glad his feelings weren't hurt. I think he'd come to appreciate why I didn't share much information with my parents.

At the river, we took our shoes and socks off and waded into the shin-deep water. "It's freezing!" I exclaimed and rushed to the big, flat rock that had become a special place for us. We climbed up, and he took his T-shirt off for us to dry our legs, so they'd get warmer faster.

"Thank you, but now you're going to be cold when you put it back on," I said.

"That's okay." He draped it across one side of the rock. Eyeing his naked upper body, I thought I might need the shirt back to wipe the drool off my chin. He looked so great! He caught me ogling him and grinned and flexed his muscles for my added pleasure.

"You've been working out more," I said.

"Thanks for noticing." He reached over and squeezed my bicep. "You have, too. I like it. Let me see the gun show." I pulled my shirt sleeves up and assumed a comical body builder's pose. "Awesome! I like it that you take care of yourself and stay in shape."

"Thank you. Did you say that because you're worried I might let myself go someday like my mom?" That was always a concern for me because of the belief that daughters will grow up to be like their moms.

"No. I wasn't even thinking about that. She does seem

to be taking better care of herself though."

"Yeah. Oh, I guess I never told you about the Thanksgiving break intervention." I told him briefly how that had come about and that the improvements he'd seen in my mom were thanks to medication, counseling, and exercise.

"And thanks to you, too, right?" he said.

"Well, I guess so. All I did was confront her and help Emma confront her."

"And you got a professional involved. Kate's mom."

"That's true. You know, my mom used to be thin. Even thinner than Emma. I've seen their wedding pictures. But I guess years of negativity and being controlled and criticized by my dad caused her to sink further and further into depression. The overeating and sleeping all the time were her coping mechanisms to numb the emotional pain. My dad always gave her a hard time about her weight, but the more he insulted her about it and tried to get her to change, the more she dug in her heels and resisted. I think that subconsciously she was determined to not let him control that part of her life. She only hurt herself though, and I think she's started to understand that."

"I'm glad she's getting help. She seems happier."

"Yeah, I think so, too."

We sat looking at each other for a long time without talking. My eyes kept wandering down to his chest and stomach. I resisted touching him because I didn't want us to get all worked up and not be able to do anything about it. That was getting more than frustrating. For both of us.

So instead, I looked and fantasized. I gotta tell you though, the fine vertical trail of hair that ran down the middle of his abs and got thicker where it disappeared under the waist of his jeans nearly did me in. That visual was my weak point for some reason. I wanted to run my finger down it. Even more, I wanted to run my lips down it.

"You okay?" he asked quietly. He took my hand and kissed the back of it. His lips were warm. I sighed, feeling such intense love for him.

"I'm okay. You just look so ... delicious."

He leaned forward and brushed his lips across mine, soft as a whisper. I sat still and concentrated on his incredible kissing abilities. "Hmmm, you taste like dessert," he said.

I couldn't stand it any longer and slowly ran my fingers down the middle of his chest. He caught my hand in his before it went any lower and intertwined his fingers with mine. We made out for a couple more minutes and then sensed, at the same time, that we should back off.

"It's getting dark," I said.

"Yeah, and we didn't bring a flashlight, so we should probably head back to your house."

The water was even colder getting out than it had been going in. He let me dry my legs again with his shirt and then put it on. "Cold?" I asked.

He grinned. "Yeah, but I needed something to cool me down."

* * * * * *

Emma and I stayed up late watching TV in her room. She had dozed off, happy because my mom had somehow gotten my dad to agree to let her go to the beach with Ashley. In leaving her room, I nearly collided with my dad who was carrying a suitcase he was loaning to Emma. He took it into her room, and I heard him run into something and curse under his breath. Something fell to the floor, and he cursed again, louder. He turned on Emma's bedroom light and started yelling at her.

Suddenly, he was in a rage, and it brought back a flood of bad memories. I stood inside my doorway, temporarily paralyzed. I heard Emma wake up in shock, and I could picture him shaking her by the shoulders, one of his signature moves.

"Get up!" he yelled at her. "Get your ass down to the kitchen and bring back a garbage bag! Right now!"

As Emma came out of her bedroom, I went toward her,

but she fled down the stairs. She came right back with a bag, and I followed her into her room, watching her hand it to him. He started shoving everything that was on top of her desk into it, ranting furiously about what a slob she was and how tired he was of telling her to clean her room. She stood there, with her arms wrapped around herself tightly, and started crying.

"You won't respect the rules about keeping your room clean, so you lose the privilege of having all this crap. It's going in the garbage!" he yelled.

"But Dad, some of that's my school stuff," she protested.

"Too bad!" he shouted and turned toward her as if to strike her but noticed for the first time that I was standing there, too. The look on his face was one of such anger and torment. I couldn't help but think that this whole episode had nothing at all to do with Emma's room being messy. He was haunted by something that made him act this way.

He shoved the bag into Emma's hands and growled, "Take it to the garage and put it by the trash can."

She went downstairs with it, and I glared at my dad. He went back downstairs, and I heard his bedroom door slam. Then I heard him start yelling about Emma to my mom. I waited a minute for Emma to come back up, but she didn't, so I quietly went downstairs to look for her. She wasn't in the living room or kitchen. *Would she have run off?*

I was starting to panic but then remembered she'd gone to the garage with the trash bag. Opening the garage door, I called her name but got no answer. It was dark. I turned the light on and looked frantically around for her.

I saw her. She had positioned herself in the space between the wall and a large freezer. She was staring off into space and wouldn't look at me. I'd never been so scared for her. I wasn't sure what to do.

"Emma?" I said softly and stood right in front of her. I reached out and touched her shoulder, and she finally focused her eyes on me. She moved forward and crumbled into my arms, sobbing almost silently, probably scared to make a sound.

She'd been awakened violently by the man who was supposed to be her father, her protector. He'd verbally abused her and may have even been about to physically abuse her. I couldn't believe what had happened. I thought he'd gotten better control of himself than this since I'd been gone at college.

"Emma, I'm so sorry," I said and started crying, too. "I'm going to put that stuff in my room and fill the bag with some other trash, so he won't know. Then I'm going to help you pack and take you over to Ashley's, okay?" She managed to nod in agreement and showed some signs of relief.

I retrieved the bag, and we went upstairs to find our mom sitting on Emma's bed. Her eyes were red from crying. Emma went to her, and I saw something I'd never seen— they hugged each other.

Am I seeing this right? Is my mom actually comforting Emma?

"Why is he such a monster?" Emma asked.

"I don't know, honey. I don't know," she answered miserably. She looked at me, standing there with the trash bag.

"I'm not going to let him throw this stuff away," I said resolutely. She nodded, and I went to empty the bag into a couple of my empty dresser drawers. Then I went around the house, emptying the little trash cans that were in other rooms. I put the bag in the garage to make it look like it was the one that had been loaded up with Emma's stuff. Going back upstairs, I found my mom helping Emma pack.

"I'm going to take Emma to Ashley's *right* now. She was going to leave in the morning anyway."

"Okay. Your dad will be angry—"

"I don't care!" I harshly interrupted her. Then I remembered that, for the first time I could think of, she was at least trying to take an active role in helping us deal with the aftermath of our dad's rage. I softened my tone.

"He'll get over it."

"Yeah. Okay, thank you, Olivia," my mom said. "Try to have a good time at the beach, Emma. I love you."

* * * * * *

Sunday morning, I got up early and got ready for church. I heard my parents talking in their room, but I left early enough to avoid them. I went to church with Cameron and his dad at Cambridge Bible Church.

"You okay?" Cameron asked me.

"We had an episode at my house last night."

"Uh, oh. You and your dad?"

"No, Emma and my dad."

"I'm sorry. Is she okay?"

"Yeah, at least for now. She's gone to the beach for a few days with a friend."

He knew about some past incidents with my dad. He'd helped me work up the courage to confront him about it one time before I'd left for college. I'd tried to get my dad to promise he'd keep his cool with Emma, but leopards don't change their spots.

Cameron held my hand during almost the whole church service, and it was comforting. I did a lot of praying; asking God why? Why had he let my dad get so angry and treat Emma like that? Why was he such a miserable person?

My parents were napping after church, as they often did, and I was glad to not have to talk with them. I spent several hours outside, enjoying the sunshine, and reading. That was the only day I got to work on my tan though because after that, it rained for a couple of days. Lyla and I caught up on *90210* that she'd been taping for us. We turned into total couch potatoes. Her mom threatened to bring in a bulldozer to clear us out.

* * * * * *

Cameron called me to find out if I'd be able to go with him to Aberdeen the next day. "They'd like us to spend the night. Do you think your parents will give you a hard time about that?"

"Yeah, but I'll handle it," I said with more confidence than I had.

"Are you going to tell them you'll be at Lyla's or something?"

"Um ... I don't know. I'll think about it." In the past, I'd learned it was easier to tell my parents I was spending the night with a friend than to tell the truth and risk their interference.

"I'd rather you not lie. If they have a problem with it, we'll drive back tomorrow night."

"I don't want to be the cause of you changing your plans," I argued.

"I know but talk to them. It's not like you're sixteen and have to hide your personal life from them anymore. I understand how growing up under the influence of a critical tyrant for a dad has caused a mental hang up for you, but it's time for them to let you grow up. And time for you to stop worrying about what they think."

"You're right. I won't lie to them."

"Thank you."

As it turned out, the overnight trip to Aberdeen, which shouldn't have been any big deal, was the catalyst that brought about a much needed—and long overdue—change in my relationship with my dad.

CH. 38 ~ IT'S ABOUT TIME

At dinner that night, it was just me and my parents. Emma was due back the next day. I had helped my mom cook, and the mood was light. Of course, that was about to change.

"So, Cameron wants me to go with him to his brother's tomorrow," I said. "And we're going to stay the night there."

"Why?" my dad asked.

"Why what?"

"Why are you spending the night?"

"Beeecauuse ... those are the plans we've made. I don't know. Why does it matter? I promise Cameron and I won't be sleeping together, if that's what you're worried about."

"Well that's some comfort. I still think it's inappropriate. But I'm sure you're going to do whatever you want, no matter what I think. So, I guess go *stay the night*," he said begrudgingly.

"Gee, thanks," I said with an edge of sarcasm, and because I was feeling petulant, added, "but I wasn't asking for permission. I was only letting you know my plans."

He looked at me in mild surprise and asked, "Why would you want to go spend the night where this guy is shacked up with his girlfriend, anyway?"

I silently counted to ten and then, setting my fork down, I glared at him, saying, "Did you really just ask me that?"

In the next few seconds, my palms got sweaty, my mouth started watering, and I got a fight-or-flight adrenaline rush. I think I even got something like a premonition, though I wasn't sure I believed in that sort of thing. But something was coming. Something big. *Be blameless* flashed through my mind, and I willed myself to not freak out on him. If this was going to get ugly, I wanted it to be his fault, not mine.

"Yes, that's what I said." His face held an expression of arrogant amusement. "What they're doing, living together when they're not married, is wrong. Now they're going to suffer the consequences of it with an illegitimate child."

"No. Stop," I said.

"Excuse me?" The air in the room changed. There was no turning back now. This was it.

"You shouldn't talk that way about people you don't even know. And who are *you* to judge anyone else?"

"I don't need to know them to know that what they're doing is wrong. God will always have an answer to sinful ways, and his answer to their particular sin is an unplanned pregnancy. It's simple cause and effect, Olivia."

"Are you saying that God *made* her get pregnant to *punish* them?"

"Well, yeah, if you want to put it like that."

An argument against his reasoning started to form in my mind, and I asked, "Do you believe God sees all sin as equal?"

His demeanor changed, momentarily softened, as though he might be seeing this as an opportunity to impart his vast knowledge to me in a theological discussion. "Yes, God sees all sin as equal, but—"

"Okay. Stop there, please," I interrupted, holding my hand up. "Do you believe that you have ever sinned? You, personally, John Miller?"

"Of course, I have. We all have. You included, Olivia," he answered defensively.

"Oh, I'm well aware of that. Believe me, I can always

count on *you* to shame me for my sins," I muttered and stood up, slowly pushing my chair under the table.

I looked him in the eyes and took a deep breath. "But help me understand something. If, as you say, God always answers sin with consequences," I said calmly, but couldn't control the seething undertone of what followed, "then what the hell kind of heinous sin did Mom commit to have God answer it with the punishment of a rage-aholic husband who is verbally and physically abusive? And while we're at it, I wonder what God's answer will be to *your* sin of uncontrollable anger." By the time I'd finished, I could no longer claim to have kept my cool. But it felt good. So good.

The shocked look on his face was priceless. He glanced at my mom in disbelief for a second which made me look at her, too. She was like a deer caught in the headlights.

Turning back to me, he said, "You sure got a mouth on you since you went off to college. I guess I can thank the liberal arts department at NHU for my daughter's newfound disrespect. It's exactly as I predicted."

"No!"

"You better quit telling me no, young lady—"

I held up my hand to stop him again, making his anger go up another notch. With what I'm sure came across as an evil grin, I repeated, "No," and mentally prepared myself for what I was about to unleash on him.

"Let me tell you something, Dad. What has happened, is that I went off to college and learned to think for myself. I started figuring out that I don't have to believe everything you say and everything you believe. Just because *John Miller* has an opinion about everything doesn't mean it has to be everyone else's opinion, too. And I'm tired of feeling like I've got to live up to your standards and expectations. You're so sure you know what's right for me and what I should and shouldn't do with my life. But being so smart and having a PhD doesn't mean you know *everything*. You. Don't. Even. Know. Me. Or what's important to me. All you've ever tried to do is tell me what *should* be important instead of letting me be my own person."

I managed to keep from yelling all this, knowing that if I did, it would decrease the chance that he'd truly hear anything I was saying.

"You're being ridiculous," he said through gritted teeth.

"Maybe so, but maybe it's time I get some stuff off my chest, and after years of me having to listen to *you*, you're going to listen to *me*. It took me leaving here, getting away from you and your controlling, tyrannical ways, for me to see that *nobody* should have to put up with the crap that spews out of your mouth. You have no idea how hard I've worked over the last nine months to get you out of my head all the time! You've been tearing me down and tearing people and things down that are important to me for too long. All the criticizing. The judging. The belittling. The degradation. I'm sick of it! And it's not just me. You've done it to Mom for twenty years, and you're doing it to Emma, too. Is this the kind of family you wanted, *Dr. Miller?* A house full of women you can keep under your thumb and bully around?"

"Olivia," my mom pleaded.

"No, Mom. I'm not done," I said, trying to sound kinder to her. I turned back to my dad and continued, "Let's get one thing straight. If you believe in a God who would create problems for people in order to punish them, then you're entitled to that belief. But I reject that. I believe in a loving God who *allows* us to have problems in response to choices we make, but he does *not* cause us pain on purpose. You think you're so high and mighty, but you're going to have to answer for your own sins someday, too."

He opened his mouth to speak, but I interrupted him yet again. "You know what else? God wants us to affirm and encourage and strengthen each other. That's something you have almost never done for me! Or for Mom. Or Emma. I can't even imagine what kind of life we might have had if we'd gotten *just a little bit* of that good stuff from you, the man who is *supposed* to be the head of this household!"

He scoffed bitterly and asked, "Are you done?"

"Yes!" I answered louder than I intended, and then tried to get my anger under control.

He slowly stood up and said, "I'll be damned if I'm going to let you talk to me this way. Get out." Surprisingly, he said it calmly, without yelling. My mom sprang into action. She stood up, too, and started saying something to him that I didn't even hear because I was headed upstairs already.

It was a good thing I'd been practically living out of my suitcase since I'd gotten back home because all it took was throwing a few things together, and I headed downstairs with it. The thoughts going through my head were, *What's going to happen now? He'll probably stop paying for college. And my car insurance. And he'll demand I repay the car loan immediately.* Was it worth paying those prices to have finally told him off?

When I got back downstairs, they were still at the table. I overheard my mom say to him in a sad, defeated voice, "Well, congratulations, John. You've managed to chase off both of your daughters in a week's time."

"But I didn't do anything to her!" he argued.

* * * * * *

As I was driving, my mind was going a hundred miles an hour, playing out all kinds of scenarios, thinking of more things I wished I'd said—years' worth of pent up hurt, anger, fear, and bitterness.

I found myself pulling into Cameron's driveway. Without even thinking about it, and without having a plan, that's where I ended up on autopilot. Should I have gone to Lyla's instead? No, somehow I must have instinctively known I needed to go to Cameron's.

I parked and went to the front door. I put my finger on the doorbell but didn't push it. *What am I doing?* I wasn't sure I was ready to talk about what had happened. Doubting myself, I walked back to my car.

"Olivia?"

I turned around to see Cameron standing in the doorway. He must have seen me drive up.

"Hey," I said self-consciously and waved.

"What's going on? Are you okay?" He stepped out onto the porch. He was barefoot and holding a towel that he was drying his hair with.

"Yeah, um ... I'm fine. I'm good," I stammered. "I'm sorry to show up unannounced like this. I drove here without even thinking about it."

He looked at me quizzically and said, "Come here. I don't have any shoes on." I walked up onto the porch and stood in front of him. "You look like you've seen a ghost or something. Are you sure you're okay?"

"Yes. Um, something ... big ... happened at my house."

"Yeah?"

"And I needed to leave. Like *leave*, leave. I'm not going back."

"Uh, oh." His expression became more concerned. He draped the towel over his shoulder and put his arms around me.

"But I'm okay. I came here without even thinking about it. I need to ... do something." I broke away from him, suddenly full of nervous energy. "I need to go for a run ... or a drive. You want to go for a drive with me?"

"Okaayyy ... sure. Give me a minute to get some shoes on. Are we going in your car?"

"Yes! I'm going to take the T-tops off, and we'll go for a drive? Is that okay? I'm not interrupting any plans for your, am I?" I was talking rapidly, and he looked at me funny.

"No, not at all. Give me a second."

I'd gotten one of the T-tops off, and he came back with shoes on and helped me with the other. He kept looking at me curiously. I was sure his mind was coming up with all kinds of possibilities of what I had been referring to by something "big" happening.

I drove us toward a ranch road where I knew I could go

fast. Sensing that I wasn't ready to talk, Cameron turned the radio on. The song that was playing was "Alive" by Pearl Jam. I wasn't a big fan of the band, but that song fit my mood. I turned it up so I could hear it over the wind.

I got into that zone, like I had in Michael's car, and focused on driving. It was me, the car, and the road. And my fabulous boyfriend next to me who knew me better than anyone in the whole world. I didn't want to make him nervous, so I didn't push the speed limit too much. Well, maybe a little. If you consider eighty in a sixty pushing it.

"I think you missed your calling when you didn't become a race car driver. You're so hot!" He laughed and put his hand on my knee. What was the deal with guys getting turned on by girls driving a stick shift?

"Thank you!" I exclaimed and laughed, too. "You want to drive?"

"No. *You* keep driving. You seem to need it right now. I don't want to get in the way of that."

Letting out a loud whoop, I pulled the scrunchy out of my hair and shook my head. My hair went all over the place and then whooshed behind me as I sped up again.

I eventually slowed down and pulled over next to an old water tower. I got out of the car, and Cameron followed my lead toward the tower. He leaned his back against one of the legs of it and studied my face.

"You feel like talking now?" he asked.

I inhaled deeply, wrapped my arms around myself, and spun in a circle. "Oh! My! Gosh!" I exclaimed and laughed. I looked up into the darkening sky and said, "I told my dad off." I brought my head back down and looked at Cameron. "I mean ... I *really* told him off."

"Wow! Okay. What do you mean? What did you say?"

"I basically told him he was a rage-aholic tyrant, and I was sick of it. I told him he'd bullied me and my mom and sister for too long. I told him I've figured out how to think for myself, and that I'm done with him judging me." I said a lot of other stuff too, and it was all a bit jumbled and nonsensical, but Cameron got the gist of it.

"Wow. You said all of that to him tonight?"

"Yes!" I triumphantly threw my head back and laughed. "And I probably could have been nicer, and I'll probably regret some of it once I have a chance to think it through, but right now, I feel ... free!"

He stood up from his leaning position and came to me. Wrapping his arms around me, he picked me up off the ground a couple of inches and spun me around. We both started whooping like crazy people and collapsed against each other in laughter.

"What are you going to do now?" he asked.

"I have nooo idea," I said, almost giddily.

"How about this. We're leaving in the morning to go to Aberdeen, so stay at my house tonight."

"Yes!" I readily agreed and kissed him emphatically. He laughed at my exuberance and took my hand, leading me back to the car, but he went to the driver's side and said he wanted to try it out.

"Do you know how to drive a stick shift?" I asked.

"Uh, yeah. Does the Pope poop in the woods? Is a bear Catholic?" he asked, making me laugh. He drove well. Not as well as me, but then it was my car, so that was to be expected, right?

"Holy cow! That was a rush!" he said, pulling into his driveway. He'd gotten it up to about ninety, surprising himself *and* me. "I have *never* driven that fast in my entire life."

"Really?"

"No. How fast have you gone?"

"A hundred."

"Are you serious? In this car?"

"No, not in *this* car yet," I said, which might had led him to ask *what* car I'd done it in. I distracted him by pointing at the speedometer. "But this thing is *meant* for speed. Why would they make a car capable of going that fast if they didn't want me to try it out?"

He shook his head at me in amusement, and we put the T-tops back on. Then he carried my suitcase inside. His dad was in the kitchen, eating dinner. Cameron grabbed a plate and asked if I wanted anything. Since dinner at my house had been so unexpectedly interrupted, I was hungry.

Cameron asked his dad if he would object to him pouring me a glass of wine. Mr. McClain asked if I'd be driving. "No, I'm not driving anytime soon," I replied.

"I offered to let Olivia stay here tonight, Dad. She kind of had a falling out with her folks. And since we're heading for Aberdeen in the morning anyway, it makes sense for her to stay here," Cameron explained.

Mr. McClain nodded in understanding but didn't say anything. For the remainder of the dinner conversation, he was quiet and thoughtful. I wondered if he had a problem with me staying. I'd only ever spent the night one time. It had been unplanned, and Cameron and I had slept on the game room floor. Mr. McClain didn't get upset about it because Cameron had assured him nothing inappropriate had happened.

CH. 39 ~ SLEEPOVER

Cameron and I were hanging out in his room, listening to music and talking. I was lying on his bed, on my stomach with my chin propped up in my hands, and he was sitting on the floor, leaning on the bed. It had gotten late, and his dad knocked on the door.

"Yeah, come in," Cameron said.

Mr. McClain stuck his head through the doorway and asked, "Hey, Cam, could you come here for a minute?"

As Cameron got up and left the room, I rolled over onto my back and stared up at the ceiling. I had been postponing thinking about what might be going on at my own house. What had I left in my wake? Was my mom having to deal with the aftermath?

Oh, man! What have I done? The gravity of it started to sink in. Cameron came back with a look of bewilderment on his face that distracted me from my own unsettling thoughts.

"What's going on?" I asked.

"So, um ... my dad's wiggin' out on me," he replied, laying down next to me.

"What do you mean?"

"Well ... he doesn't mind you staying the night, but he wanted to make sure we weren't planning on sleeping together—"

"What?" For some reason I started laughing.

He joined me in laughter, but then he got serious again. "He's been weird since he found out about Jasmine being pregnant."

"Weird like how?"

"Kind of nosy about ... us. He flat out asked me if you and I are having sex," he said quietly. My jaw dropped open in surprise, and our eyes met. "I told him we aren't ... we haven't. But he'll feel better about it if we don't stay in the same room together tonight."

"Well, that makes sense. That's fair ... Should I go to Lyla's?"

"No, no, no," he rushed to say. "You're not going anywhere." In one swift move, he pulled me on top of him and wrapped his arms around me.

"Okay," I whispered. Good, because I didn't want to go. I needed to be with *him* right then and nobody else.

There was a look on his face and a hunger in his eyes that sent a wave of butterflies fluttering through me, making me weak with desire. Something new was happening between us as we laid there looking at each other. I think he felt it, too.

He ran his hands down my back, to my waist and hips, and his lips found the sweet spot on my neck below my jaw. I shuddered, and he put his hand on my face to guide my lips to his.

He was, and would always be, the best kisser. He had this way of building it from slow and sensuous, to deep and intense. I let myself get carried away in his passionate kisses that were so insistent that he *literally* took my breath away.

He rolled us over to where I was on my back, underneath him. "I love you so much, Olivia," he said hoarsely and started kissing my neck, throat, and collarbone, making his way down along the V-neckline of my blouse. He inhaled deeply, pressing his face between my breasts.

"I love you, too."

His fingers began unbuttoning the top of my shirt, pushing it open. I watched in anticipation as his mouth made its way down to my chest. His amazing lips and tongue sensuously teased the bare skin above the top of my bra, and his hand gently caressed me. Slowly pulling one of the straps down off my shoulder, he left me more exposed, but not entirely. Enough to give him a visual that he excitedly gave his full attention to with his hands and mouth.

Wanting to touch him so badly, I slipped my fingers under the waistline of his jeans. His eyes suddenly opened, bore into mine, and he moved my hand away. I whimpered softly in disappointment, about to plead with him, but he crushed his mouth onto mine, kissing me hungrily and rolling me onto my back.

His hands trapped mine on each side of my head, and he deliberately positioned himself between my legs, rocking against me seductively. He was more aroused than I could remember him ever being, and he closed his eyes, lost in the pleasure we were giving each other. I was close to finding release for all this sexual energy and was surprised at how easily he'd gotten me to that point. It was new territory for us, but I was ready to go there.

I pressed my hands on his butt, moving in rhythm with him, letting the feeling build in me, and whispered, "Cameron, I'm about to—"

A low groan came from deep within his throat, and he suddenly moved off me, saying "Ohhh, Olivia, wait, I'm—"

"Please," I begged and threw my leg over his hips. His breathing was hard and fast, and his eyes smoldered as he searched my face and then gave me what I wanted. He pulled me closer so I could feel him against me again.

"Do you have any idea how much I want to make love to you right now?" he whispered.

He was driving me wild, and I was breathing so heavily

that I was practically panting. Burying my face against his neck, my movements increased, but he'd gotten still. Something told me I should stop, too. He let me take my time coming down from the intensity. *I guess it's not fair for me to get satisfaction and leave him frustrated.*

Once our breathing slowed, I hummed softly near his ear. A shudder ran through him, and he raised up to look at me. I was worried he'd be upset and start to apologize or something, but he surprised me. He smiled. Oh, that gorgeous smile! I loved him so much and smiled back at him in adoration.

He lifted onto his elbow and whispered, "Did you almost have an org—"

"Yes. Twice!" I confirmed in a loud whisper.

"Oh, my gosh," he murmured and looked down at me in wonder. We smiled at each other again, like we shared a secret. He kissed me one more time and said, "How about you go get ready for bed and do what you need to do in the bathroom. Then I'm going to take a cold shower." The grin on his face made me giggle.

He eased himself off me and stood up. Rolling over onto my stomach, I looked at him standing there and sighed in appreciation of the awesome bulge in his jeans. He quickly turned around and chuckled self-consciously. "I'll go get your suitcase from downstairs, okay?"

"Okay," I said. While he was gone, I kicked my legs back and forth against the bed in a fit of frustration. He came back through the doorway, and I jumped up from the bed.

Okay, Olivia, playtime is over. I needed to get a grip, but that was easier said than done. Especially because he saw that my shirt was still almost all the way unbuttoned. He wrapped his arms around me and kissed my neck. Things almost got out of control again when one of his hands reached into my shirt. But he let it settle over my heart and whispered, "Mine."

I hugged him and echoed, "Mine."

As I changed into my pajamas and brushed me teeth,

my mind kept replaying what he'd said. *I want to make love to you ...*

Did I want that, too? *Yes, I want it.* Someday. But I wasn't ready, and I knew it. I was proud of us for waiting, and the more we waited, the more I felt like we could—and should—wait. I decided I wasn't going to feel guilty about what had happened, and I hoped he wouldn't either. *We can handle this. We're adults, right? Well, sort of.*

I came out of the bathroom to find him sitting at his desk. "Bathroom's all yours," I said and jumped into his bed and got under the covers. The sexy scent of him greeted me on his pillow. I inhaled deeply through my nose to enjoy it.

He knelt beside the bed, kissed my forehead, and said, "I love you."

"I love you, too." I pulled the covers all the way up, under my chin, and smiled at him.

"Goodnight, Olivia."

"Goodnight, Cameron. Thank you for being here for me tonight."

"Of course. I'll always be here for you. You know that, right?"

"Yes. What did I ever do to deserve you?" I asked dreamily. He smiled, kissed me, turned off the lamp, and left the room.

* * * * * *

I had a dream that I was back at my house, in the kitchen with my mom and dad. I was saying to my dad the same sort of things I'd said that night, but instead he got totally out of control angry at me. He slapped me across the face and pushed me down on the floor. I woke up scared and in a cold sweat. It took me a few seconds to remember where I was and process that what I'd dreamed wasn't the way it had happened.

In a daze, I got up and crept downstairs. I was thirsty, so I got a drink of water in the kitchen as quietly as I could. I'd walked past Cameron on the couch, and he was sound asleep. going back through the living room, I looked at him more closely. My eyes adjusted to the darkness of the room, but I could see that he was lying on his back, shirtless. Oh, he was so good looking.

I sat down on the floor in front of the couch, watching him sleep for a minute, listening to his even breathing. It was all I could do to keep from waking him up. I wanted to run my hands over his chest and kiss his bare skin. My mind played with the idea of waking him up by doing that. I could catch him in semi-wakefulness, and it would be such a rush to see what his reaction would be. But that wouldn't be fair. We'd already tempted each other too much for one night.

I went back to his room and got in bed, thinking about him. Did he fantasize about having sex with me the way I did about him—and as often as I did? Was it wrong for me to be thinking about it? Would we ever, someday, finally give in and do it? Would we feel guilty? Would it make things weird between us after that? So many questions.

Why did God create our bodies and desires to be ready for sex so long before it was "acceptable" to have it? I mean, I guess centuries ago, people got married young—like soon after going through puberty. But what about now? What did God expect people to do when they were trying to go to college and have careers, all before getting married? Well, I knew the answer to that question. God expects people to wait until they're married. That's his perfect plan for blessing a marriage.

Oh geez. What was I doing thinking about all that? Especially about marriage. I fell asleep, letting myself imagine what marrying Cameron would be like. I had a much better dream than the one I'd had earlier.

CH. 40 ~ EAVESDROPPING

I awoke to the sun shining through Cameron's bedroom window and the thrill of him sliding under the covers into his bed with me. I was on my side, and he nestled his front to my back like we were two spoons. It was deliciously affectionate and intimate, and I basked in it. With his arm draped over my midsection, his hand was on my ribs, below my breasts.

If his fingers had moved up one inch, that's all it would have taken for us to get all heated up again. I wanted to, and his lips on my neck made me think he wanted to as well. He pulled the covers away from me, and I repositioned to lie on my back. His eyes made their way down my body, taking in the sight of me in my mismatched pajama ensemble.

"San Francisco and Snoopy," he said appreciatively. The T-shirt was a couple of years old and a bit snug, and the Peanuts shorts showed off a lot of leg. "You're body is so amazing."

"Thank you," I whispered.

Smiling, he hesitantly said, "I'm going to get up now and go make us something to eat."

He didn't get up though, and I asked, "Are you sure?"

"Yes. We need to get going. We're supposed to be there

in about an hour." But he still laid there. "Here I go ... I'm getting up now."

I laughed. "No, you're not."

"I can't. You have this magical hold on me. Let's call the whole day off and stay right here." He intertwined his fingers with mine.

"What would we do?"

"Ohhh, I can think of a few things," he played along.

"No, we have to go. They're expecting us," I said, pushing against him, slowly shoving him off the bed.

"Hey!" He exaggerated his reaction to the push I'd given him and rolled off onto the floor.

"You're being naughty, and you need to go fix me breakfast!" I crawled on my stomach to the edge of the bed and looked down at him.

"Yes, ma'am!" He jumped to his feet and swatted my butt, making me giggle as he ran out the door.

* * * * * *

We arrived at James' and Jasmine's apartment around ten o'clock. Cameron and his brother left in Cameron's truck to go pick up the furniture, and I hung out with Jasmine. It was amazing to see the difference a few months had made in how much she was showing.

"Have you found out if it's a boy or a girl? Or do you even want to know ahead of time?" I asked.

"We tried a couple of weeks ago at a sonogram appointment, but the little booger had its legs crossed and wouldn't uncross them. No matter what the doctor did to try to get it to reposition, all it did was a somersault," she laughed.

"I bet that was cool to see the baby, though, huh?"

"Yeah, it was."

"Are you excited?"

"Excited *and* scared. This wasn't exactly in the plans, as you know."

"Would you be offended if I asked if you and James plan to get married at some point?"

"I don't mind you asking. Actually, James asked me to marry him back in January."

"What did you say?"

"I said no ... for now. I can't get over the feeling that he only asked because of the baby."

"Well, would that be such a *bad* thing?"

"I don't know," she said thoughtfully and sat down in the rocker recliner that was in the room they planned to use as a nursery.

"I'm sorry. We can talk about something else."

"No, it's okay," she assured me. "It's just that ... I've got a hang up about marriage in general. Growing up, I had a bad example set for me of what marriage is like." Her expression changed, making her look like she was scared or sickened by a memory.

"Are you okay?"

"Yeah," she said and snapped out of it. "I guess I'm scared of making that commitment. It means putting *a lot* of trust in someone else. And someone else putting *a lot* of trust in me."

I could sort of understand where she was coming from. I didn't exactly have the greatest example set for me about what marriage should look like, either. But James and Jasmine were about to have a baby together. That was one heck of a commitment already. Wouldn't getting married make it easier?

"Yeah, it is a pretty big commitment," I said generically.

"I never saw myself as being married. Or having kids. But here I am, about to have one." She rubbed both hands over her stomach and said, "Oh, it's moving. Do you want to feel it, Olivia?"

"Okay," I replied, unsure of myself.

I'd never touched a pregnant woman's stomach. She put my hand on her side, and I was surprised at how hard it was. I waited a second, and then something underneath my hand moved. "Oh, my gosh. That's amazing!"

"I know. Watch," she said and lifted her shirt up. She

leaned back in the chair, and we could actually see the movement. "I think that's a knee or an elbow." She giggled, and her whole demeanor changed from a minute ago. I knew she was scared and nervous about the baby, but I could tell it gave her a certain joy too.

I personally got a feeling I'd never had before. The wonder of it all made me long to experience pregnancy myself someday. Someday in the distant future, that is!

* * * * * *

I helped the guys unload the truck. There was a cradle, changing table, and crib that all had to be assembled. The furniture had come from a friend of Jasmine's who had an older toddler and didn't need it anymore. We all set to work putting things together, but it was a challenge because there were no assembly instructions with the hand-me-downs. Without making much progress, we decided to take a break.

By the time we finished lunch, a friend of Jasmine's showed up to help. Her name was Hillary, and she was in nursing school, too. She brought over some baby clothes that her niece had grown out of.

As Jasmine was looking through the bag of clothes, she said, "Everything in here is pink, Hillary! What if it's a boy? "

"I'm telling you, it's going to be a girl. My predictions have never been wrong," Hillary insisted.

"Have you and James decided on any names yet?" I asked.

"No, and even when we do, we're not talking about it to anyone."

"Why not?"

"They don't want any of our opinions," Hillary remarked with an eye roll.

"Because no matter what we come up with, there's bound to be someone that won't like it, and they'll think it's their place to talk us into something different," Jasmine explained.

I chuckled and told them, "My parents were going to name my sister Bartholomew if she'd been a boy." They made gagging sounds, and we laughed. "And if that wasn't bad enough, they wanted to call him Barth for short!"

"Oh, no! Thank God she's a girl then!" Hillary exclaimed.

"What did they end up naming your sister?" Jasmine asked.

"Emma."

"That's a good name. How about that, Jazz?" Hillary asked.

She shrugged and shook her head. Her lips were sealed. I wondered if they'd pick something that started with a J.

* * * * * *

We finally got everything put together and set up the room how Jasmine wanted it. Hillary mentioned to me that she and another friend were planning a baby shower in mid-May. She asked if I'd be able to come.

"Yeah, I'll be back home by then. I think finals will be over on May eighth."

"What's your major?" she asked.

"Sociology."

"Oh, you decided then?" Jasmine asked. "What did your dad say?"

"Um, well, I haven't told him. I was going to over Spring Break, but ... I didn't have a chance to yet, and I don't think I'll be seeing him again before I head back to New Haven. So, it'll have to wait."

The ramifications of what I'd done weighed heavily on me. There'd been some good distractions since the incident with my dad, but soon I'd have to face reality. Cameron and I weren't going back to NHU until Sunday, and it was only Thursday. Where would I stay Friday and Saturday night? I may have been pushing my luck by expecting to stay at Cameron's, but I wasn't about to go home. *Maybe I'll call Lyla or Kate. Or Mrs. K.*

We had dinner and watched a movie, and then Jasmine

and James went to bed. Cameron asked what was wrong because I'd gotten quieter throughout the evening.

"Oh, Cameron, I don't know. What have I gotten myself into? I can't go home tomorrow. Where am I going to go for the rest of Spring Break?"

"Come here," he said and pulled me into a hug. "Let's not try to figure that out tonight. I don't know about you, but I'm tired. Let's go to bed."

"Okay ... What's the plan for that anyway?"

"I think you should get the spare room, and I'll stay out here on the couch."

I smiled at him and asked, "You don't trust me?"

"I trust *you*," he said and kissed me. "I don't trust myself."

"All right. Goodnight. I love you."

"I love you, too. I'll see you in the morning."

* * * * * *

The interior walls of the apartment were thin. I overheard James and Cameron talking the next morning. James was surprised to find Cameron on the couch.

"Hey, little brother. What are you doing out here? Did Olivia kick you out of bed for snoring or something?"

"What? Oh. No, I slept out here," Cameron said sleepily.

"Did y'all have a fight?"

"No. Why?"

My curiosity was piqued about what Cameron would say, and I went to the door of the bedroom so I could hear them better.

"Dude, then what's up with you sleeping out here?"

"Don't give me crap about this, okay?" Cameron sounded annoyed. I wondered if he was getting tired of explaining to his family members about our unusual relationship. "Olivia and I haven't ... We aren't ... Look, how about you mind your own business."

I heard what sounded like one of them throwing a pillow at the other.

"Oh, man," James said in surprise. "I'm sorry. I didn't

know. I figured—"

"Yeah, don't worry about it. It's just that, we've decided *not* to ... have sex."

"Not ever?"

"What? No. I don't know. Look, this is between me and her."

"Okay, sorry. Didn't mean to ruffle your feathers. You've been together for a long time though, haven't you?"

"January was a year. What does that have to do with anything?"

"A year?" James made a whistling noise. "*What* are you waiting for?"

I strained to hear Cameron's reply. For some reason he chose right then to speak more quietly. All I could make out was the tail end of a sentence that sounded like "graduate". Or maybe it was "wait."

What is he saying?! And why won't he speak up so I can hear?!

James' reaction to whatever Cameron had said *was* loud enough for me to hear. "Wow. That's kind of cool, Cam," he said, almost reverently. "I'm impressed!"

"Gee, thanks," Cameron said sarcastically and chuckled. "Now, if you'll excuse me, I'm going in there with her to *sleep* a little longer."

Uh, oh, he's coming. Running back to the bed, I heard James call out to him, "Good luck with that."

Then Cameron tapped on the door and said, "Olivia?"

"Yeah?"

"Can I come in?"

"Yes."

He came in and closed the door behind him. Sliding under the covers, he spooned me like he had the morning before. *I could get real used to this.*

I was wide awake but wanted to let him sleep, so I laid still until I could tell by his breathing that he was out. Then I carefully lifted his arm that was around me and rolled over to face him. He was so cute, sleeping soundly.

I was overcome with love and admiration for this man. What did I ever do to deserve him? I couldn't possibly know, but God did. I prayed, thanking God for putting Cameron in my life, and for making him such a man of integrity.

I also thanked God for making Cameron the complete opposite of my dad. God knew that I needed someone like Cameron to show me that it was possible for a guy to be compassionate, affirming, and encouraging for me. To love me for who I was and not who he *thought* I should be or tried to make me be.

Later, I wanted to ask him what he'd told James that morning, but then I'd have to admit I'd been eavesdropping. Maybe it was better if I didn't know. That was between him and his brother.

CH. 41 ~ JOB OFFER

Cameron and I went to a movie at the Province Mall in Aberdeen, and then we did some shopping and hung out at a music store, killing time before heading to Leeville.

Going up his driveway, he said, "Stay with me tonight," like he must have been thinking about for a while.

"Okay, but do you think your dad will mind?"

"I don't know. I'll talk to him about it. Maybe you can go to Lyla's tomorrow, but I'm not ready to be without you yet."

"Thank you." I wasn't ready to be away from him either and was grateful for his invitation for another night.

His dad had gotten home from work about the same time that we arrived and suggested we go out to eat somewhere. We decided to try a new cafe in Cambridge.

"So, Olivia, if you're interested, I have a job offer for you this summer," Mr. McClain said.

"At Snyder?" I asked doubtfully. What could I possibly do at an architecture firm?

"Yes. There's a lady, Crystal, who works in the office and needs some time off for foot surgery. If I can talk her into waiting until May, would you be interested in some temporary work? Cameron mentioned you have bookkeeping experience."

"Oh, yes, I do. I'd be honored. Are you sure, though? I've never worked in that kind of office."

"If you're as good as Cameron says, you'll be fine. We could arrange for Crystal to train you for about a week before her surgery."

"Okay, that would be great. Do I need to come in for an interview or anything?"

"Nah, I'm the boss. You're hired," he said and smiled at me.

"Thank you!"

Wow! I couldn't believe how great that was. I'd been worrying about what I'd do for money over the summer. Mrs. K would have some work for me, but since Diana had replaced me at the CCC, it wasn't in the budget for me to work there again.

* * * * * *

"I'll take the couch tonight, Cameron. You've spent the last two nights on couches." I made sure to say that in the car on the way back to their house to ease Mr. McClain's mind about the sleeping arrangements.

"You're welcome to use the spare bedroom." Mr. McClain said.

Cameron laughed and said, "Duh! I don't know why I didn't think of that. I forget about that room." I had forgotten about it too. It was downstairs next to the game room. I'd only ever seen it the first time I'd been to his house when he'd given me a tour.

* * * * * *

Cameron came to the spare room to tell me goodnight and make sure I had everything I needed. He got in bed with me, and we talked for a few minutes but behaved ourselves.

"Did you know your dad was going to ask me to work at Snyder this summer?" I asked.

"Yeah. He told me he wanted to ask you himself though, so I didn't say anything."

"I hope I don't disappoint him. What if I don't know

what I'm doing?"

"You're brilliant, and you'll be fine. Have some confidence in yourself."

"Okay, thank you. What are you going to do this summer? Are you going to work at Snyder?"

"Actually, I've turned in an application at the CompuApp branch in Aberdeen. Your professor Gloria's husband put in a good word for me, so we'll see. It'll be so awesome if I could work there. It's not too far from Snyder. We could go to lunch together sometimes."

"Sounds like fun."

"Did you have a good time at James' and Jasmine's?"

"I had a great time. I got to feel the baby move. It was incredible. I can't even imagine what that must feel like to have that inside of you," I said in wonder.

"I still can't get my mind around the fact that there's going to be a baby in the family soon. James is sooo excited."

"Did you know that he asked her to marry him?"

Cameron looked at me in surprise. "No. What did she say?"

"She said no."

"Did she tell you why?"

I relayed the conversation but felt like I might be betraying Jasmine's trust. "If James didn't tell you about it, maybe don't let on that you know. I don't want her to think I went and blabbed their business to you and your dad."

"I won't say anything. You know, James told me once that Jasmine came from a really messed up family situation. She's from Florida originally, I think. Her mom died when she was about sixteen, and her stepdad was a real jerk. He was abusive, and she ran away."

"Huh, she didn't tell me about any of that. I guess that sort of explains her difficulties with the idea of marriage."

Then I remembered Cameron's conversation with James that I'd overheard that morning. I wanted to ask him about it, but something made me hold back. If that snippet I'd heard was "wait", that made sense. Maybe he'd told James that we were wanting to wait to lose our virginity.

But, if he'd said "graduate" instead, what could that have possibly meant? Was he telling James about graduation night? That night was the first time we'd talked about wanting to wait. But he hadn't said "graduation". He'd said "graduate". Graduate. *Graduate. Graduate.* What could it mean?

"What are you thinking about?" he asked me.

Refocusing because I'd zoned out, I asked, "What? Oh, I don't know. I guess I'm tired."

"Me, too. I'll see you in the morning," he said and kissed me goodnight.

* * * * * *

The next day at Lyla's, I told her all about telling my dad off.

She gave me a high five and asked, "How does it feel?"

"It feels good. I always imagined if I confronted him on all his crap, I'd break down and cry and become an emotional wreck, but I didn't. I mean, I might still do that at some point, but I feel ... stronger. My only regret is that I left my mom and Emma to have to deal with how angry I probably made him."

"They'll be okay. Emma's strong, too."

Yes, she was, but her reaction that night my dad had awakened her so abruptly about her messy room still haunted me. I hoped she was doing okay.

Before I headed back to NHU the next day, I took my chances and called my house. Fortunately, Emma answered.

"Did you have fun at the beach?" I asked.

"Yes, it was great. Where have you been?"

"I've been staying with friends the last few nights. I couldn't go back home."

"Why?"

"They didn't tell you?"

"Who? What are you talking about?"

"Mom and Dad. They didn't tell you that I totally lost it on Dad Wednesday night and packed up and left?"

"No! What happened?"

I gave her a basic rundown and was surprised that my parents hadn't mentioned it to her. "They haven't said anything to you about it?" I asked.

"No, but it's not like I've spent much time around Dad. Mom's doing okay. She's been outside a lot, gardening."

"Okay, well, I guess that's good. Did Dad ever apologize?"

"For what? Being such an ass that night and trying to make me throw my stuff away? No. He sure as hell didn't. He thinks it's okay to act like it never happened."

"Figures. You sound okay, though. I was worried about you that night."

"I'm fine. Thanks for saving my stuff. And thanks again for taking me to Ashley's." Emma was amazingly resilient, and I envied her in that regard.

"You're welcome. I love ya, sis."

"You too, bye."

CH. 42 ~ BEGRUDGING BRANDY

Having been a bit homeless over Spring Break, it was good to get back to school. Monique was already there. She'd gone home to Louisiana for the break and told me about her week while I unpacked.

"There's something different about you," she said, eyeing me curiously.

"What do you mean?"

"I don't know." She studied me closely. "I can't put my finger on it." She sucked in her breath and her eyes got wide. "You did it! Is that it? You and Cameron?"

"What?" I laughed. "Nope, still a virgin." I flopped down onto my bed dramatically.

"Ohhh. What is it then? *Something* happened."

"I told my dad off."

"Your dad?"

"Yeah. I finally had all I could take of his crap and flipped out on him."

"How did he take it?"

"Strangely enough, he took it sitting down. And quietly. But then he told me to get out."

"Where did you go?"

"Cameron's."

"And you spent the night with him?"

"*Three* nights."

"And you're still a virgin? Mon Dieu!"

"Geez! Is that all you think about, Monique?" I threw my pillow at her.

"No, but I can't believe it. You've got more restraint than I do, that's for sure."

"Yeah, well, so does he. It's mutual. It's good, though. I'm happy with it."

"I've gone about five months without, and it's starting to make me crazy. I don't know how you do it."

"Well, I guess it helps that I've never done it. I don't know what I'm missing." I held back from telling her I'd gotten a glimpse of what I was missing a few nights ago.

"That's true."

Ready for a change of subject, I said, "Scott's got the hots for you. You know that, right?"

"Yeah. I might finally tell him yes if he asks me out again."

"Oh, yeah?"

"I've been holding out because I didn't want it to be like a rebound thing for me. He's a good guy, and I don't want to play with his feelings. But Spring Break was good for me. I'm completely over the ex and can move on now."

"I'm sure Scott will be delighted to hear this."

"Don't you go telling him. Or Cameron. Let's just let it happen. If it doesn't, so be it. Maybe he met someone over Spring Break and has lost interest in me anyway."

"I doubt that. He said you're a goddess."

"He what?" she exclaimed, and we laughed.

"I'm starving. Do you think the dining hall is open yet?"

"No, it's not. Let's go see if Scott and Cameron want to go out for dinner," she suggested. I smiled knowingly at her and agreed.

We went to Cameron's room. He and Scott were playing Nintendo with Gary. We invited him to come with us too. Scott drove a Nissan Pathfinder that accommodated all of us, so he drove. I orchestrated it to where Monique would be sitting in the front seat with Scott.

After dinner, we all went back to Cameron's and Gary's room and shared a bottle of wine that Cameron had brought with him. I wished Gary wasn't the odd one out, but I didn't know who to fix him up with. He was so shy and quiet, and antisocial, but not in a bad way.

"Ahhh, sweet nectar," I said, sipping from a bathroom cup. Nothing like drinking wine from a plastic shot glass-sized cup.

"Come here, woman," Cameron said in a hilarious caveman voice and pulled me out into the hallway.

"What are we doing out here?" I asked with a giggle.

Without saying anything, he playfully pushed me against the wall and started kissing me. A couple of guys walked by and made inappropriate noises which made Cameron back off a little. It was so cute that his face turned red.

"More," I said, pulling him back to me.

"Yes, but that's not why I brought you out here. I wanted to ask what's going on with Monique?"

"What do you mean?"

"Scott's been trying to get with her for a few months, but she was never interested. Until tonight."

I shrugged, wanting to keep my mouth shut and honor Monique's request. "I don't know. Maybe something has changed ..."

"Uh, huh? Okay. That's all you're going to tell me?"

"Yes." I grabbed his shirt to pull him closer, kissed him, and said, "Hey, there's nobody in my room right now. We could be alone."

He smiled but extricated himself from my grip. "You're trouble," he said and pointed at me as he reached for his door handle for us to go back in with everyone else.

We spent the rest of the evening hanging out and playing Nintendo. They talked me into playing, but it was laughable. I had no eye-hand coordination and sucked at video games.

* * * * * *

Paula called and said they were getting the soup kitchen ready in earnest, and if I was willing, my help would be greatly appreciated. It became my main community service focus. I got Jenny and some of her other volunteers from NHU to help sometimes, too. To my utter disappointment, Brandy was also involved. Apparently, she'd recently become a member of that church and decided she wanted to help with the project.

She didn't necessarily make my life miserable, but she was always *there*, sort of throwing an undercurrent of doubt at me and my participation. The more I got involved, the more she did and practically mirrored my every move. It made me irritable and robbed me of the joy I should have been able to experience from the whole thing.

"What exactly has she done to you?" Cameron asked one night because I'd been complaining about her.

"Well, you know about her implying that I was writing papers for students when all I was doing was proofreading, right?"

"Right, but didn't you kind of put her in her place about that?"

"Yes, but ..." I struggled to articulate what it was that bothered me so much about Brandy.

Cameron put his hands on my shoulders and pressed his forehead against mine. "Take a deep breath. I'm sorry she's always around, but maybe she's not as out to get you as you think."

"Whatever." I rolled my eyes at him.

He didn't get it. He didn't understand why this girl got under my skin the way she did. I didn't really understand it either. Was it that she was a know-it-all? Always with the "right" answer? The "Sunday school" answer. She was always trying to show me up and be better than me, or at least appear to be. Why did I feel like I had to compete with her? Well, because community service was *my* thing. And somehow she'd became the fly in the ointment of it.

* * * * * *

It was time to think about housing for the next school year. Monique and I agreed that we wanted to keep being roommates, but we couldn't stay in Bellamy because it was a freshman-only dorm.

"Let's find out if we can get into Spalding," I suggested.

"What's that?" she asked.

"It's a suite-style residence hall. A living room sits between two-bedroom units that each have a bathroom."

"Oh, that sounds awesome. Do you think it's a lot more expensive than Bellamy?"

"I don't know. I mean, yes, it'll be more expensive, but we could compare it to off campus apartment prices. It's probably still less than that."

"Let's find out. I'd prefer to stay on campus, since apartments will require a co-signer, and I'm not sure I'll be able to swing that," Monique said. She had a good point, and I wasn't sure I could swing that either. I hadn't had any communication with my family since that fateful night.

Where price and location were concerned, Spalding turned out to be the best option. Monique and I asked Elaine and Lisa if they wanted to be the other two in our four-person suite. They were interested, so we put in our housing requests.

Cameron, Scott, and Gary decided they would try for Spalding too, but needed a fourth guy and left that up to chance. It would be interesting to see how that turned out for them. I was glad to know well ahead of time who I'd be sharing space with come August.

It was also time to start thinking about what classes to take for the fall 1992 semester. Cameron and I got to register early since we were considered sophomores already. That was cool, because one of the classes he needed filled up fast, and he might not have been able to get it otherwise.

All the classes I was going to sign up for were sociology, plus Intro to Anthropology for my minor. I was done with almost all other general requirements except for a couple of things I'd take at Cambridge Junior College over the summer.

Gloria called on me more and more often to help with various things. Isabel took a backseat as her TA and didn't mind me stepping in. I found myself spending a lot of time at Gloria's house, and she and Gavin invited Cameron to join me whenever he could.

The guys talked computer stuff, and Gloria and I talked sociology. The twins ran around being cute little attention-hogs, and I got to see Cameron interact with children for the first time. He was going to make a great uncle to James' and Jasmine's baby! There's something so endearing about a guy who's comfortable being around children.

Gloria and I were working on stuff for the upcoming school year's Freshman Seminar course material, and she paid me a compliment. We were in her office, and the guys were out back playing with the kids. She said, "You seem different, Olivia, more settled, more content."

"Thank you."

"What happened to you over Spring Break? Ever since we came back, you seem ... more confident."

I was surprised at her observation. "Well, as a matter of fact, I had an incident with my dad that has kind of freed me from a lot of baggage."

She set aside the notebook she'd been looking at and leaned toward me, exhibiting great interest. "That's great! That makes sense to me now. I see it. I see that you have freedom from something that was holding you back."

"Is it that obvious?"

"Yes! You're like ... your own person now or something."

"Hmmm. Thank you. The problem is, I probably could have gone about it in a more ... Christian way."

Gloria had miraculously been able to balance being both a Christian and a college professor at a public institution. It wasn't an easy thing to do in an environment where other intellectuals frowned upon, and even belittled, the

Christian faith. She found unique opportunities to intermingle her beliefs in a "safe" way that wouldn't get her in trouble with the "powers that be". It was cool how God put a Christian professor in my life at the time he did.

"Well, that's true of most confrontations. Did you come to any agreement with him?"

"No, he told me to get out. And I did. We haven't spoken since."

She nodded thoughtfully and told me she'd be praying for me about it.

CH. 43 ~ GOT ANY BREAD?

The grand opening of the soup kitchen was scheduled for the Saturday before Easter. The week leading up to it was hectic with preparation. My schoolwork suffered, but I would have time to catch up for finals. Mr. Barnes, the guy in charge of the project called me one evening. He was in a bind.

"Olivia, I hope you don't mind me calling. Paula gave be your number," he said.

"I don't mind. What's up?"

"We've got a hiccup with one of the food suppliers that was going to make a delivery tomorrow. There was a misunderstanding about the day they were supposed to bring the stuff in. They had it on their calendar for next weekend."

"Uh, oh."

"Yeah. So, we either postpone the opening and risk other supplies spoiling, or we find another way to get what we need."

"Have you tried calling any other suppliers?"

"Paula's been making calls all day, but we're finding out it's too short notice."

"What can I do to help?" I was instantly jazzed. I worked well under that kind of pressure. I just needed to be told what to do, and I would get to work.

"The best plan I can come up with is to get a team of volunteers to start making the rounds to all the local grocers and bakeries and see if we can get what we need. Maybe branch out to Stonehollow and Clearvale if we have to."

"That's a great idea. I get out of class tomorrow at two o'clock, and then I'll be available to help for the rest of the day. I'll see if Cameron can help too."

"Thank you. Anyone else you can round up would be a great help."

"You bet."

By the next afternoon, I'd recruited Elaine and Jenny, who each had cars to take a couple of other volunteers from the church along with them. Cameron went too, and somehow, Emily, who didn't have a car, got paired up with him. I tried not to let it bother me. I got paired up with none other than Brandy. *What are the chances of that?*

Mr. Barnes gave us lists and instructions, and we all headed out in different directions. Between having to be civil to Brandy and thinking about Emily and my boyfriend driving all over town together, my mood suffered. But I tried to remain positive. I was on a mission to help the soup kitchen, and I could rise above the circumstances.

Mine and Brandy's task was to visit several bakeries and get as much bread and baked goods as we could fit in my car. The first bakery we went to said to come back after five o'clock the next day, and they'd donate whatever was left in their display cases.

I let Brandy carry on most of our conversations in the car. She loved to hear herself talk. I got to hear all about the important things she did and was involved in. I wasn't sure why she had such a burning need to brag about all her accomplishments. Was she trying to impress me? Why did she think I cared?

At another bakery, I took the lead and asked to speak to the manager who was happy to help. In fact, he had a freezer full of bread that was left over from an order that a customer had cancelled.

He said, "I wasn't sure what I was going to do with it, so it's awesome that you came along to take it off our hands for a good cause." He also mentioned that a friend of his who ran a cafe across the street may be able to help us out.

We loaded the bread and got back in the car, and Brandy said, "That cafe isn't on our list. I don't think we should do it."

"Why not? It's not like the list is sacred."

"I don't think we should do something we weren't asked to."

"It's worth a try. That's how these things work. When you're looking for donations, there's nothing wrong with being resourceful."

"Fine, you do it then, but leave me out of it."

I drove across the street, and she stayed in the car while I went in and asked for Mr. Caruthers, the person the baker had referred me to. He was an older gentleman and was interested in helping.

"I don't have any bread, but I'll tell you what I do have. Crackers," he said with a smile.

"Crackers?"

"Crackers. Hundreds and hundreds of them. We had an ordering error and ended up with more than we'll ever need. The supplier wouldn't let us return them, but they'll expire before we can use them up. Would crackers be something a soup kitchen could use?" he asked with a twinkle in his eye.

"Mr. Caruthers, they certainly are. And that is an amazing offer. Thank you so much."

"Come with me, young lady."

We went to a storage room, and he showed me more boxes than would fit in my car. I explained I'd have to find someone to come back later to pick them up, but he offered to have his son deliver them to the soup kitchen that evening. He walked me out to my car, and I thanked him again. Brandy saw us and got out. I told her what Mr. Caruthers had offered to do.

"That's so generous of you," she said to him, suddenly oozing with charm. "Aren't you glad we came over here and asked, Olivia?"

What game is she playing?

"Uh, yes, I'm very glad. Thank you again. I'll be sure someone is at the soup kitchen around seven for your son to drop those boxes off," I said and shook Mr. Caruthers' hand.

In the car, I held my tongue, knowing I'd be snarky to Brandy if I tried to speak. We stopped at a couple of other places, one of which had nothing for us, and the manager was sort of rude. The other had some items that took up the remaining space in my car, so we headed back to the soup kitchen.

I saw Cameron's truck backed up to the side door. He and Emily and Mr. Barnes were unloading boxes.

"Your boyfriend went out with that girl Emily last year, didn't he?" Brandy asked me.

I was *not* too crazy about her brining that up. We didn't know each other well enough to be chatting about such things. My defenses went on alert. Why was she always looking for a way to get at me?

"Yeah, but they're just friends now."

"Oh?" she said in a vague way, making it seem like she knew something I didn't. Was she trying to bait me? Why?

I parked next to Cameron's truck and started unloading my car. Brandy went inside and didn't help unload.

"That's great news, Brandy," I heard Mr. Barnes say to her as they walked out of the building together.

"Thank you. I'm so glad we decided to follow the lead from the baker and visit the cafe. I was sure you wouldn't mind," Brandy said.

My jaw dropped. It was all I could do to not cause a scene. She had gone in and given herself credit for scoring all those crackers.

"Hey, guys. Did you hear that? Brandy says there's a guy delivering a bunch of crackers later. How many boxes did you say it was?" Mr. Barnes asked her.

"Oh, um, I don't know exactly," she stammered. *Ah, ha!* She wouldn't be able to answer since she hadn't even gone in with me. "Do you remember how many, Olivia?"

"Yes, I do, because I saw them in the back storage room when Mr. Caruthers showed them to *me.* Mr. Barnes, there's about four boxes with probably four or five hundred single-serve packets per box."

"That's Great! Good job ladies," he said.

Brandy gave me a smug smile. I thought about confronting her but decided to be the bigger person. This whole operation wasn't about me, so I didn't need to get credit for anything. Whatever Brandy was trying to do, I wouldn't let her get the best of me.

CH. 44 ~ GRAND OPENING

Mr. Barnes had made assignment lists for what each of us needed to be responsible for on the soup kitchen grand opening day. My name was down for the serving line. I was excited that Paula would oversee it but disappointed to see Brandy's name alongside mine. Would I ever get a break from her?

Cameron was put to work with some of the other guys getting tables and chairs arranged and would then be part of a team that would circulate in the dining room once the food started being served.

I had no idea what to expect. How many people would we be serving? How crowded would it get? How needy would the people be? My experience with that type of thing had been limited to handing out bags of groceries from the food pantry at the CCC. But this would involve filling plates and bowls for people who were going to go sit down and eat right then. And they would be lined up, looking at me as I served them. I got nervous and said a prayer.

Brandy arrived last minute, and even though I'd been already there helping all morning, she stepped right in and started bossing me around. Or at least it felt like she was bossing me around. I don't know since I was overly sensitive when it came to her. At any rate, I decided I'd answer to Paula—not Brandy.

The church had done a good job of getting the word out. There was a long line of people already there when we opened the doors. Brandy positioned herself at the beginning of the serving line where she put bowls, plates, napkins and silverware on trays and passed them to Paula who ladled soup into the bowls. Next was me, placing sandwiches on the plates, and passing the trays to the people. Emily and Cameron were floaters, ready to assist wherever they were needed, especially with carrying trays for people who needed the extra help.

The whole atmosphere was pleasant and even a bit festive. There was soft music playing in the background to break up the awkward silence at first. By the time people started congregating at tables to eat, their chattering voices created a cafeteria-like feel to the room.

Besides some younger people, and even a few children, we saw lots of elderly and handicapped people. It was disheartening to see the struggles these people had. Most of them were openly gracious and unashamed of their neediness, but there were some who were downright unfriendly. I saw it for what it was—a reaction to how they felt about their situation—and didn't take it personally.

The serving line got a break after the first wave of people had come through. Paula asked if I minded manning the station and then motioned for Brandy to follow her. A few minutes later, Paula came back out and asked me if I would assume Brandy's role at the front of the line.

"Sure. Did she need to leave?" I asked.

"No ... I asked her to," Paula said hesitantly.

"Oh?"

"She's still going to help, but I found something for her to do in the kitchen. I think she'll be more comfortable *behind* the scenes."

"Oh ... okay." The rest of us had been friendly to the people, making small talk and conversation, but Brandy had been quiet. "Was she bothered by being out here?"

"Yes, and she wasn't doing a good job of hiding it. I worried she was making some people feel uncomfortable with her inability to smile and overlook the conditions. We need volunteers out here that are willing to help these people feel welcome, you know?"

"Yes, I agree. Not everyone is cut out for this kind of volunteering."

By the time we closed the doors several hours later, Mr. Barnes estimated we'd served about one hundred thirty people. "Not bad for the first day!" he said.

* * * * * *

Cameron and I went back to the dorm. He said he had a surprise for me.

"What's the occasion?" I asked. We were standing in the lobby, and all I could think about was going to take a shower, getting something for dinner, and relaxing for the rest of the evening.

"No special occasion. Just special *timing*." He smiled like the cat that ate the canary. "My mom and Jerry went out of town for the night, and I want to take you over there. You can soak in her Jacuzzi tub for as long as you'd like. I'll make us dinner, and we can stay there and have the place to ourselves." My look of surprise and excitement made him laugh.

"Well, this is an offer I can hardly refuse. Are you sure your mom won't mind?"

"She already gave her blessing. Can you go pack an overnight bag and meet me back down here in about fifteen minutes?"

"Yes!" I exclaimed and kissed him. Heading for the elevator, a giddy giggle escaped me, and I heard him laugh.

The dorm was fairly deserted because of the holiday weekend, but Monique hadn't left town and was in our room.

"I'm spending the night with Cameron at his mom's house," I told her.

"Have fun, but behave yourself, young lady," she

playfully admonished, watching me pack some clothes and things into a bag, including a book Gloria had loaned me called *Vienna Prelude.*

"Oh, I will. I'm thinking of that Jacuzzi tub!"

"Yeah, but I bet that's not all *Cameron's* thinking about!"

"Goodbye, Monique," I said in a sing-song voice. "Happy Easter."

"You, too."

* * * * * *

Cameron showed me to the master bathroom where I found a note from his mom. It said, "Dear Olivia, When Cameron asked if I would mind you using my tub, I learned another reason I like you so much. My favorite way to relax is a good long soak by candlelight too. Enjoy!"

Anita had left a few candles on the edge of the tub, and on a small table next to it were fresh towels and some bath salts.

Oh, heaven!

"Do you have everything you need," Cameron asked. He set a glass of wine on the counter and came up behind me, putting his arms around my waist.

"Yes. Your mom is amazing. *You* are amazing! Thank you so much." I turned and hugged him. "You do understand this could take several hours though, right?"

He chuckled at me and said, "Yes, I do. I'm going to bring you something to snack on, and then I'm going to take a shower downstairs. I'll have to make a run to the store for a few things for dinner. You take all the time you need."

"God bless you," I said and did a happy dance as soon as the door was closed. Funny how something as simple as a bathtub could make my heart sing.

I got the water running and was pouring in some bath salts when he returned with some fruit and cheese. Then I stripped down and slid into the hot water. It was so relaxing. I couldn't remember being so content in a long time.

The book I was reading, *Vienna Prelude*, by husband and wife writers Brock and Bodie Thoene, was historical fiction set in Germany during World War II. The writing style was so excellent, the characters so dynamic, and the story so captivating, that I had no idea how much time had passed when Cameron knocked lightly on the door.

"Honey," he called.

"Yes, darling," I said sweetly, enjoying playing house with him perhaps a little too much.

"Can I come in?"

"Um ..." I said in surprise. I put the book down on the table and sunk further into the water. With nothing but candlelight and the way the tub was positioned, he could conceivably come in and still not see me. "I guess so."

"Okay, I promise I'm not looking ... much," he said playfully and opened the door. "Have you heard the rain? The news is saying we're in for some major thunderstorms."

"Oh, yeah, I heard something and wondered if it was raining. How long have I been in here?"

"About three hours, which I don't mind, but dinner's ready."

"Okay, I'll be down in a few minutes."

I heard the door close and pulled the plug. I smoothed on some vanilla scented moisturizer I'd brought with me and left my hair up in the messy bun I'd put it in to keep it from getting wet.

Walking into the kitchen barefooted and wearing a pink T-shirt and shorts pajama set, I was completely relaxed. He had set the table with candles and was taking a pan of roasted vegetables out of the oven.

"Thank you so much for setting this up. The bath was wonderful. And this food smells great. I'm starving!"

He'd made some roasted chicken, and the veggies were sprinkled with parmesan cheese. Delicious! Around the time we'd finished eating and were clearing the table, the electricity went out.

"Uh, oh," I said. "Do you have some more candles, or a flashlight?"

"Yeah, there's a flashlight in that drawer over there." He pointed to a drawer where I found a flashlight and clicked it on.

"I love thunderstorms," I said. "Not crazy about power outages, but I love watching the lightening and hearing the thunder."

"I do too. Let's go sit on the porch."

We snuggled on the porch swing in the front of the house and watched the rain falling and the light show in the night sky. When it died down, we went inside to find that the electricity had come back on.

He turned some music on, and we settled on the couch. I was sitting on one end with my legs over his lap and was glad I'd shaved them that morning because he was running his fingers up and down my shins.

"You were amazing today," I said.

"Thank you. You were, too."

"You were so nice to those people, and I could tell they appreciated it."

"I have to admit I was a little out of my comfort zone at first. But when I saw how grateful most of them were, it felt really good. I see why you like doing that sort of thing so much."

"Good. I like the feeling of being able to help other people, you know?"

"Yeah. That's something I love about you."

I was getting sleepy, and he stood up and reached for my hand. Pulling me into a hug, he quietly asked, "Sleep with me tonight?"

My eyes widened in surprise. "Sleep?"

"Yes. Sleep. I want to stay with you ... hold you all night long. Wake up with you in the morning."

"Sounds perfect," I sighed and melted into his arms. He kissed me and then went to turn the stereo off and made sure we'd blown out all of the candles. We went upstairs and stood in the bathroom brushing our teeth together.

Taking my hand, he led me to his old bedroom. He took his shirt off, making my heart beat faster, and sat down on the bed. I was willing myself to behave.

He asked, "Are you going to be okay with this?"

I smiled and took a running jump into the bed which made him laugh. He turned off the lamp, and we laid down together. I snuggled against him, enjoying his bare chest.

"Goodnight. I love you," I said.

His arm around me pulled me closer. "I love you too. Goodnight."

* * * * * *

Following the Easter service at church the next morning, Cameron and I were invited to go to lunch at Paula's house. A few other people were invited too. Emily was her niece, so obviously she was there. I was starting to feel about Emily like I did about Brandy—I couldn't get away from her. But at least Emily was nice.

The other guests were the pastor, Simon Mueller, and his wife, and Mr. and Mrs. Barnes. During lunch, Paula mentioned that I had experience working with a food pantry in Cambridge.

"Is that right?" Pastor Mueller asked. "Tell us about that, Olivia. We've been considering adding one to the soup kitchen at some point in the future."

I gave them a little history of my role at the CCC, and Cameron chimed in with a compliment about seeing me "in action". I blushed, and he lovingly put his hand on my cheek and kissed my forehead. Emily was watching us. The expression on her face was hard to read. I didn't think it was jealousy though.

"Simon, it sounds like when we're ready to get started with our own food pantry, we have someone who can show us the ropes," Mr. Barnes said.

"It sure does. Would you be willing to work with us on that, Olivia?" Pastor Mueller asked.

"I'd love to. I'll be gone for the summer though."

"No worries. We won't be in a position to get something like that under way until the fall. You'll be back, right?"

"Yes, I'll be back for the fall semester in August. Give me a call. I'd be honored and excited to help." I tried to refrain from jumping up and doing a happy dance. What a great and wonderful thing God had done leading me to this opportunity!

Emily followed me into a spare room where I'd left my purse and said, "Olivia—"

"Yes?"

"Can I just say that ... you're really lucky. Cameron is such a great guy. I hope someday there's a guy who loves and adores me the way he does you."

"Oh, Emily, that's so sweet. Thank you."

"And if you've ever worried that I've got designs on him, I want to put your mind at ease. You're the only one he wants, and I can respect that."

"Wow. I appreciate your honesty. I love him, too. I hope there's no hard feelings between us."

"None at all."

Cameron came in asking, "Olivia, are you about ready to go? ... Oh, sorry." He backed out, embarrassed that he'd intruded.

"It's okay, Cameron. Yeah, I'm ready. Thanks again, Emily."

"Happy Easter, you guys," she said as we left.

In the truck, he asked, "What was that about?"

"Nothing. Don't worry about it," I said and smiled at him. "Emily's a sweet person."

"Yeah. She is. I think it would be cool if the two of you could be friends, but I didn't know if that would be weird for *you*."

"It might be. But we'll see."

CH. 45 ~ WELCOME HOME ...?

The rest of the semester went by in a whirlwind. Finals went well, and I added five As and a B to my transcript. I'd learned so much that semester, inside and outside of the classroom. The self-defense class had given me confidence and awareness, as well as physical strength. My "major question" had been answered, thanks to what a great sociology professor and mentor Gloria turned out to be.

There was a great network of friends to return to in the fall and community service plans with the soup kitchen and upcoming food pantry. My relationship with Cameron had survived the first year of college despite our seven-week separation, which had actually made us stronger.

I had a well-paid summer job lined up, and with a couple of summer classes at CJC, I was on track to graduate in three years instead of four. Things were falling into place for me.

I still had something hanging over my head, though. There had been no communication between me and my parents since Spring Break. Once finals were over, I allowed myself to start thinking about what I might be going home to. If I wasn't welcome at home, I was prepared to ask Lyla and her mom if I could live with them over the summer.

The other thing I was worried about was money. If my dad demanded repayment of the car loan on the spot, I doubted I could go to a bank and get a loan without a co-signer. And it was time to tell him what I'd decided on for a major. There was a good chance he'd disapprove and stop paying. I checked into applying for school loans in case it came to that, but I hoped and prayed it wouldn't. I truly believed that God had allowed me to finally stand up to my dad for a reason—to get free from the hold he had on me.

* * * * * *

Move-out day arrived, and Cameron let me put some stuff in his truck because my Nissan couldn't hold everything the way the Mustang had. I asked him to take it to his house though because I wasn't sure how things would go at mine.

"You've been worrying about that, huh?" Cameron asked.

"Yeah. Trying not to, but I don't know what to expect."

"Come here," he said and pulled me close to him. We were standing by his truck, all loaded up, ready to hit the road. "Can I pray for you?" he asked.

"Sure," I replied. He held my hands and said a sweet, heartfelt prayer. He asked God to help me smooth things over with my dad but still hold my ground and not let him break down the boundaries I'd managed to put up.

It was almost magical how he spoke to God on my behalf and reminded me of Mrs. K and the times she'd done the same thing. It helped me feel stronger, and I faced the drive home with a little less dread.

* * * * * *

Relieved that only my mom's car was in the driveway, I went inside and called for her.

"I'm in here," she yelled from the kitchen. She had mounds and mounds of vegetables laid out on the counter. What a sight! "Olivia!" she exclaimed, and her smile was so big and welcoming. Well, at least *she* was glad to see me.

"Hi, Mom. How's it going? Where did all this come from?"

"My garden! Can you believe it? I don't know what I'm going to do with all of it."

"Open a vegetable stand?" I joked.

"That's an idea," she said thoughtfully.

"Mom, can we talk?"

"Yes. I knew this was coming. I thought you'd be home tomorrow, though."

"I took my last final this morning and figured it was time to come home. Am I allowed to come home?" I felt emotional tears coming on.

"Of course, you are." She rubbed my shoulder comfortingly.

"I think I could have handled things differently with Dad."

"I know. But don't go beating yourself up about that. Let me tell you what all has happened since then, okay? Can I get you something to drink?"

"No, I'm fine. Is he still mad at me?"

"Well, let's start back at that night. After you left, he went on the war path. I listened to him rant and rave for about ten minutes, and then I went into our room and packed a bag. I said 'John, I love you, but for the sake of my own sanity, I can't be around you right now. You take a day to get the verbal diarrhea out of your system, and if you want to talk tomorrow, I'll listen. But I'm done watching you act like a two-year-old child. I'll be at a hotel for the night.' And he let me leave."

"Verbal diarrhea?" I couldn't help laughing.

"That's what Mrs. Davis calls it," she said, laughing with me.

"Mom, I can't believe this. What did he say when you came back?"

"He apologized. I told him he should call *you* and apologize, but he said he wasn't ready to do that. I decided to let it go and wait to see what happened. I was so proud of you, for the way you stood up to him. It helped me do it too."

"Thank you. You look good. How are you doing?"

"I'm doing well. I still have bad days, but they're getting fewer and easier to handle. I've lost about thirty pounds."

"I can tell. Great job."

When I was younger, I'd had a dream that one day, out of

the blue, my mom had decided to take better care of herself. I remembered that in the dream I'd been so excited for her and relieved that she was interested in being healthier. That was many years ago, but I felt just as excited and relieved right then as I had in the dream.

She beamed with pride and said, "Thank you. The doctor has figured out the best dosage for my meds, and I've got so much more energy and feel more alert."

"Has Dad even noticed?"

"Yes. In fact, a few weeks ago, he said something about the weight loss. He tried to take credit for it."

"What? How?"

"He said, 'I'm glad you finally took my advice and started eating better and exercising. You feel better now, don't you?' and I thought I'd just agree and let it pass. But it made me angry. I decided to take a chapter out of your book and stand up for myself. I said, 'Actually, *you* didn't have anything to do with it, and I'm not going to let you think you did.' Then I took the plunge and told him I've been taking medication and going to counseling."

"Oh, my gosh! What did he say?" I was in shock.

"He started to splutter and fuss, but I told him to hush. I said, 'It's been helping me feel like a real person again, and you can keep your opinion to yourself.' Well, he didn't like that and accused me of being like you."

"He did? I'm so sorry."

"No, no. You see, that was one of the best compliments he'd given me in a long, long time. If comparing me to you means I'm putting my foot down and demanding he treat me nicer, then so be it."

I was speechless. Tears started rolling down my cheeks. I never would have guessed that taking a stand against my dad would have that particular side effect. It made what I'd done all the more worth it.

"How is he now? Has he given you a hard time about it?"

"Not necessarily. I know what he's thinking most of the time, and it's not nice, but he's keeping his mouth shut. I tell you what though, he's less critical. He manages to hold his tongue in situations where he normally would have spouted off rude things. I've been sure to tell him thank you when I notice. The more I compliment him on behaving better, the more he improves."

I chuckled. "Positive reinforcement. Like a little kid."

"Yes, in fact, exactly like that. You may not know this, but his dad treated his mom a lot like he treats me. Mrs. Davis has helped me see that pattern. I'd never made the connection before. It was the example that was set for him, and as far as I know, his mom never stood up to his dad about it. Well, we're breaking that pattern in this family. I'm glad that you had the guts to bring it into the light and call him out on the carpet."

"Mom, thank you. But you give me too much credit. You've been working hard at this. I'm glad to hear that things have improved."

"Well, they've improved, but there's still lots of work to be done. It's not an overnight kind of thing. He is still who he is. And I'm still who I am. We're all far from perfect."

"I know. Do you think he'll be willing to talk to me when he gets home?"

"I think so. All you can do is try."

* * * * * *

My dad came home later, and we greeted each other a little formally, which was more typical than not. It wasn't like we'd ever had the kind of warm, close relationship where the daughter goes running into her dad's arms, and he acts elated to see her.

"Can we talk?" I asked him.

"Sure, what's up?"

"I want to apologize for the way I spoke to you last time I was home."

"Okay. Thank you."

"To be clear though, I'm not sorry for *what* I said, but I know I could have said it nicer."

"Oh, so you're not *really* apologizing?"

"Yes, I am, but I needed you to know those things. My only regret is that I didn't do it more calmly."

"That's fair." He nodded. He looked at the floor for a moment and actually reiterated and affirmed what I'd said. "I understand that you feel those things needed to be said."

"Thank you." I'd about decided I wasn't going to hear an apology, but he surprised me.

"I'm sorry you feel like I've been so terrible to you and your mom and sister. For the record, I'm working on that."

I guess that *sort of* qualified as an apology. I chose to take it as one anyway. I resolved to wait and watch to see if he was, in fact, working on being less terrible.

* * * * * *

I called Cameron and told him he could drop my stuff off whenever he wanted to.

"I think everything is going to be okay," I said.

"That's good. I'm relieved."

"Thank you. I am too."

We got together with our friends and that weekend went to Jasmine's graduation. She was beautiful! I was excited for that baby to come and to see what kind of mother she'd be.

I called Mrs. K to tell her I wasn't going to have a lot of time but asked if I could help with the annual food drive. Billy took the phone from her and told me I was always welcome to help out.

"You've been sorely missed. Welcome home," he said and handed the phone back to Mrs. K.

"You doing okay, sweetie?" she asked.

"I am. Things are good." I told her about the job at Snyder and improvements at home.

"I'm so glad. I wish we could have you come back to work at the CCC, but this will be a good opportunity for you to branch out and do something different. I'm interested to see what God's got in store for you."

I was interested in seeing what that was, too!

ABOUT THE AUTHOR

Tessa Palmeri lives in Texas with her family. She has a special interest in how the family, as a social institution, shapes the attitudes, motivations, and goals of young people. She enjoys portraying complicated family dynamics and the catalysts that launch teenagers into adulthood. Her hope is that readers, of all ages, will be entertained and encouraged by the main characters in her novels as they learn to define themselves, their relationships, set personal boundaries, and triumph over obstacles and limitations.

Tessa Palmeri invites you to share your thoughts and reactions to *Olivia, Finding Her Way* by leaving a review on Amazon, Goodreads, and anywhere else you'd like. Contact her via her website at www.tessapalmeri.com or Twitter @tessapalmeri.

OTHER BOOKS BY THIS AUTHOR

Olivia, On the Brink - Olivia Series Book One

Olivia Miller is pretty sure she'd win the high school senior award "Most Likely to Never Figure Out What They Want To Do With Their Life". Her critical father and neglectful mother contribute to her anxiety and lack of direction about her future. She's a model student with a big heart for community service, but her dad belittles any ambition she's ever had in pursuing something she's interested in.

A new guy at school named Cameron McClain becomes a fabulous distraction from Olivia's college worries. He's swoon-worthy, and not just because he's a gorgeous romantic who plays guitar. He's thoughtful, respectful, and offers acceptance and encouragement to Olivia. He fits right in with her circle of friends: future fashion designer Lyla, photographer Kate, and all-around popular Josh.

This story is about Olivia's journey in learning to think for herself, set personal boundaries, and overcome limitations imposed by her overbearing parents, all while trying to set a good example for her younger sister, Emma. Thankfully, Olivia's boss and mentor, Mrs. K, is looking out for her, offering guidance in life and Christian faith.

Will she ever be able to get her dad's judgmental comments out of her head? Most of all, she can't wait to get away from home!

Olivia, All In - Olivia Series Book Three

Olivia Miller is back home in Leeville, TX for the summer of 1992. Her freshman year of college didn't go as she expected, but she's a better and stronger person for it. Confident about her decision to major in sociology, she still needs to tell her dad about it and hopes that he'll respect the boundaries she recently set in their relationship.

A temporary bookkeeping job at Snyder Architecture gives her a taste of working "in the real world." Certain aspects of the job weren't being done right by the person she's filling in for, and she tries to find a way to address the problems without making enemies.

Though her relationship with her boyfriend Cameron McClain is stronger than ever, their summer takes an unexpected turn, testing their faith and future—individually and as a couple.